# EYE FOR

# By Kim Hunter

# INDEX

Copyright
Authors other works
Quotes
Index of characters
Chapter one
Chapter two
Chapter three
Chapter four
Chapter five
Chapter six
Chapter seven
Chapter eight
Chapter nine
Chapter ten
Chapter eleven
Chapter twelve
Chapter thirteen
Chapter fourteen
Chapter fifteen
Chapter sixteen
Chapter seventeen
Chapter eighteen
Chapter nineteen
Chapter twenty
Chapter twenty-one
Chapter twenty-two
Chapter twenty-three
Chapter twenty-four
Chapter twenty-five
Chapter twenty-six
Chapter twenty-seven

Chapter twenty-eight
Chapter twenty-nine
Chapter thirty
Chapter thirty-one
Chapter thirty-two
Chapter thirty-three

Kim Hunter

Copyright © 2023 By Kim Hunter

The right of Kim Hunter to be identified as author of this work has been asserted in accordance with sections 77 and 78 of the Copyright, Designs and Patents Act 1988.

**All rights Reserved**

No reproduction, copy or transmission of this publication
may be made without written permission.
No paragraph of this publication may be reproduced,
Copied or transmitted save with the written permission of the author, or in
accordance with the provisions of the Copyright Act 1956 (as amended)

This is a work of fiction.
Names, places, characters and incidents originate from the writers imagination.
Any resemblance to actual persons, living or dead is purely coincidental.

# AUTHORS OTHER WORKS

WHATEVER IT TAKES
EAST END HONOUR
TRAFFICKED
BELL LANE LONDON E1
EAST END LEGACY
EAST END A FAMILY OF STEEL
PHILLIMORE PLACE LONDON
EAST END LOTTERY
FAMILY BUSINESS
A DANGEROUS MIND
FAMILY FIRST
A SCORE TO SETTLE (BOOK ONE)
A SCORE SETTLED
A DANGEROUS MIND 2
BODILY HARM
SINS OF THE FATHER
GREED

Web site  www.kimhunterauthor.com

# QUOTES

'An eye for an eye only ends up making the whole world blind'

Mahatma Gandhi

'Before you embark on a journey of revenge, dig two graves.'

Attributed to Confucius

# Index of main characters

Eli Carter had been born into a traditional Romany family but eventually leaves all that he knows behind when he marries Angela Coe. As a non-traveller and referred to as a gorger, his relationship with Angela was frowned upon by Eli's family. Life as a newlywed was difficult and money was short, even more so as Eli struggled to find work but a chance encounter soon sees him enter a life of villainy and eventually he goes on to run his own successful firm of men.

Morris Carter is the eldest son of Eli and Angela. He's a vicious, hard-nosed villain who longs to take over the family firm but Morris has a dark secret, a secret that will be his downfall.

Marcus Carter is the youngest son of the Eli and Angela. He is caring and hates violence and is nothing, much to his father's disappointment, like his elder brother but the one thing he has that Morris doesn't, is the fact that he adores his family and would do anything to keep them safe.

Rena Gallagher is a traveller. In her late twenties, beautiful with long blonde curly hair, Rena is stunning. Never having accepted being a traveller, she longs to start out on her own and relinquish the invisible chains that are placed upon gypsy children, especially the females. Taken as the norm within the Romany community, a girls job is to marry and have children and her father Manfri, is desperate to marry her off but Rena is stubborn to the core and to date has flatly refused any of her father's suggestions regarding a possible suitor.

Del Foster is a true cockney. Born in the East End, Del models himself on Ronnie Kray but the similarity only goes as far as business and his dress sense. Del is married to Jean, lives in Edmonton and has two daughters and a son. Keeping his family and work life separate, the Foster firm work out of a small end of terrace house in Bow. Dealing mainly in the class A drug market, the revenue earned is highly profitable, bringing in hundreds of thousands each year. The business never crosses the threshold of his home and what happens in Bow remains in Bow, or at least that's how it was!

Jean Foster. Slim and even in her late forties is strikingly attractive. Not totally aware of her husband's business, Jean does know and regretfully accepts that whatever it is, it's illegal. That said, as long as her family are happy then Jean is content to turn a blind eye to how Del earns a living.

Kenan Foster is the youngest son of Del and Jean. At twenty years old Kenan's life seems to have stalled and he doesn't know what path he wants to follow career wise. The one thing he is one hundred percent sure about is that fact that it doesn't include joining his father's business.

Dawn Foster is the middle child of Del and Jean. Sweet and gentle, she holds down a job at the local bank, has no interest regarding getting a place of her own and just enjoys spending time with her family.

Allison Foster, known as Ally to her family and the eldest child, is more like her father than any of her siblings. Constantly complaining and always causing arguments within the home, everyone, including her parents, were relieved when she finally moved out and gets a flat of her own. That doesn't stop Ally calling at the house weekly for the family meal and it always results in an argument.

Levi Puck is Del's right hand man and confidant. Of Caribbean descent and standing over six feet tall with a full head of dreadlocks, he is a force to be reckoned with. Levi adores his boss and is eternally grateful that Del took a chance on him years earlier. After swearing his allegiance, he would go to any lengths to protect the man.

# CHAPTER ONE

Eli Carter had been born into the Romany community in the winter of 1952. Two months later England's news contained the following facts, King George Vll dies, Elizabeth II is proclaimed Queen, Prime Minister Winston Churchill announces that the United Kingdom has an atomic bomb and compulsory Identity Cards issued during World War ll are abolished. None of those facts affected the Carter Clan and as Eli was born on the side of the road in a traditional Romany wagon, even his birth wasn't registered. Patrick Carter senior and Bonnie Hearn, had, with their respective families, come over to England from Ireland in the nineteen thirties. Married when Patrick was thirty five and Bonnie just sixteen, their family brood quickly expanded. Young Eli's parents spoke with a strong Irish brogue, it was an accent Eli would come to loathe as he grew up. It hadn't taken him long to realise that people shied away whenever they heard it. The youngest of seven children, he soon began to notice that his parents, his father in particular, were far older than the parents of the other kids he would play with at traveller gatherings. He had been conceived when his mother was on the menopause in her early-forties. His four brothers and two sisters had long since married and moved into their own wagons, so as the newest addition, he was spoilt rotten.

Life was hard and by nineteen seventy the family were continually travelling from one county to another. There had been little chance of an education for Eli but a bright child, he had always yearned to read and write. Although you couldn't rob him or any of his family of a single penny, that was the sum total as far as his education went. Tall and thin, though not unattractive, he had been working full time since the age of fourteen and that work consisted of conning respectable homeowners out of their hard earned cash. Eli shovelled tarmac for most of his days. With the promise of a professional job at half the price of local companies, driveways were sprayed with a special long lasting weed killer. It was actually no more than a cheap detergent mixed with water. Hot tarmac was then poured, raked and rolled and the Carters were long gone by the time the holes and weeds began to reappear. It was hard work but profitable and Eli's mother received her first new trailer complete with all mod cons by the time her youngest son reached the age of twenty six. Bonnie had always been house proud but with the arrival of the new wagon, it reached ridiculous levels. No one was allowed to touch anything for fear of leaving finger prints and the original plastic that had covered the sofas on delivery, were still in situ two years later. It saved the furniture but was unbearable against your skin during the long hot summers of the nineteen seventies.

In the winter of nineteen eighty and while parked up in McCready's scrapyard on Billet Road Romford, Elli fell hook line and sinker for a local girl. Like a beautiful little doll, Angela Coe was petite with a fabulous mane of thick blonde hair and her boyfriend towered above her. It was frowned upon by his community and when he'd taken Angie to the wagon to meet his parents, the reception had been little more than lukewarm at best. Bonnie eyed the girl suspiciously and Patrick was convinced she was a harlot and a bad influence on his youngest son. The Carter's had wintered at McCready's for many years but with modernisation and expansion, the council had been trying to shut down or at the very least relocate the yard. So, knowing this could possibly be the last year, Eli didn't waste any time and proposed to Angie before the month was out. Meeting her parents had been a totally different experience and a real eye opener. For the first time in his

life he was spending time in a gorger's home and every room seemed so large, with opulent furnishings and deep pile carpets. To Eli the three bed semi on Hamilton Road felt more like he imagined a stately home to be, albeit on a smaller scale. Whereas his own family had been cold and somewhat rude towards Angela, Mr and Mrs Coe couldn't have been more welcoming, even when they were informed of his background.
"So ya don't have a problem with ya daughter courting a traveller then Mr Coe?"
"Why on earth would you ask that Eli?"
"With respect Mr Coe, most Gorger's hate us."
"Gorger's?"
"That what we call settled folk."
George Coe softly laughed as he placed his hand onto Eli's shoulder and led him outside to the back garden for a smoke.
"Eli I have always judged a person on his or her own merits, treat my daughter well and you will always be a welcome visitor in our home."
For a moment the young man was lost for words. His own family had always instilled how much gorger's hated travellers but from where he was now standing, it felt like it was the other way around. There and then Eli Carter knew where his future lay, he wanted this life, wanted to be settled but more than anything he

wanted Angie always by his side.

The wedding, unlike a traditional travellers wedding, was low key. For one thing Angela's parents couldn't be expected to foot the bill for a couple of hundred people, which would have been low numbers compared to other traveller weddings but also Eli didn't want Angela and her family to see how badly behaved his community could be once they had the drink inside of them. It wasn't that he was ashamed but just sometimes he wished they could all act like normal people, like gorger's. It hadn't gone down well when Eli had informed his parents that it would be close family only. All in all there were just eighteen adults and fifteen, somewhat badly behaved children. That Eli wasn't able to do anything about and he couldn't help but smile when he saw the look of horror on the face of Angie's mum as the youngsters caused havoc inside the Hotels elaborate function room. The couples wedding night was spent in another local hotel but when Eli returned to McCreadys the following morning to collect his belongings, he found his mother in tears.
"Mammie, whatever's wrong?"
"Why? Why are you leaving boy? This is your community and we ain't like them gorger's, you

won't survive Eli they will make your life hell. Please son, please stay where you're loved and wanted."

Taking a seat Eli took his mother's hands in his own and stared deeply into the most amazing hazel eyes, eyes he'd adored since the day he was born.

"Mammie, you have the Gorger's wrong. Angie's parents have welcomed me since day one and I belong with my wife. Please be happy for me."

Bonnie Carter sniffed loudly and wiped her nose on the hem of her apron. Of all of her children, Eli had the strongest nature and once is mind was made up about something there was no changing it and no real point in even trying. Standing up she bent down and taking her son's face in her hands she tenderly kissed both of his cheeks.

"If things don't work out then you know the route, know where we will roughly be. Promise you'll come straight home if you're not happy Son."

"I promise Mammie, cross me heart."

Initially Graham Coe had gotten Eli a job in the office where he worked as a head Accounts Manager but it didn't last much beyond a couple of weeks. Eli found the set time keeping hard to

abide by and the office environment stifling. Angela continued with her job at Woolworths but she could see her husband was unhappy and living with her parents didn't help. One night, as they cuddled in bed she began to softly cry.
"Whatever's the matter my darlin'."
"You're unhappy and you're going to leave me!"
He couldn't bear to see her tears and as she cried, he held her tightly rubbing the small of her back in an attempt to sooth her.
"Never, never in a million years sweetheart, you're my life now."
"Then we have to get out of here and find our own way. I don't care what you do Eli as long as you are happy and we are together."

Eli had money, money he'd saved over several years from the tarmacking and within two months the newlyweds had moved out of Angela's family home and into a small two bed terraced house on Crow Lane overlooking Romford cemetery. In search of work, Eli trawled the streets but his accent saw every door slam shut in his face. Taking a break he stopped off at the Golden Lion situated at the West end of Romford Market. It was his first time in the pub and as such, all eyes were on him as he entered. Ordering a pint at the bar he was about to look for a seat when two men entered and walked up to the man standing to Eli's right. Suddenly and without warning the two heavies started to throw punches at the man, not even giving him time to turn let alone defend himself. Now Eli Carter wasn't one to poke his nose into anyone's business but he had also always been a champion for the underdog and in his mind, two against one was in no way fair. Placing his pint down onto the bar he launched his own assault and a few seconds later the heavies were sprawled out on the floor and Eli was helping this new acquaintance to his feet. Wiping blood from his nose with the arm of his jacket, Tommy Day held out his hand and thanked the stranger wholeheartedly.

"Tommy, Tommy Day. Pleased to meet you pal."

"Eli Carter and likewise."

"You a traveller?"

"Ex traveller though I'm startin' to wonder if I'd be safer back at the camp as I don't think I'll ever shake off the stigma."

The two men laughed but suddenly Tommy stopped and became deadly serious.

"You probably saved my life there pal. Those two are from the Handley firm over in Dagenham and have been trying to muscle in over here for a while now. Usually I have my second, a fella called Binto with me but strangely he asked to take a day off. I think the cunt has set me up but no worries, he'll get his in good time."

Eli smiled. He knew all about warring Romany camps and feuding families so fighting within organizations was really nothing new to him. Tommy drained his glass and then offered to take Eli for a drink somewhere a little less explosive. It was a short journey to the other end of the Market Place and climbing into Tommy's Jag felt good. Eli's hands caressed the soft calf leather of the seats and then glided across the highly polished walnut on the dashboard.

"Nice motor Tommy."

Tommy Day grinned, he guessed that his newest friend was probably more used to a flatbed truck than a luxury car. He liked this man but how his firm were going to react was another matter altogether. All eyes were on them as they stepped into the Bull but this time it was for entirely different reasons. Eli would quickly learn that the man whose life he had supposedly just saved was in fact a vicious and revered gangster and head of one of the most violent Firms in the area. Taking a seat the two talked effortlessly and both enjoyed the conversation which was actually about nothing in particular. Not wanting to outstay his welcome, Eli decided

that it was time to leave and set out once more on the trail of trying to find employment. Bidding Tommy farewell, he was about to head for the door when his host spoke.
"If there's ever anyway that I can repay my debt Eli, you can always find me in here or at least leave word that you're looking for me."
Taking a moment to think, Eli turned back.
"Actually there is, I'm in dire need of work but as soon as I open my mouth all doors close. Guess I have traveller written all over me face."
Now it was Tommy's time to take a moment and he studied Eli for several second longer than was comfortable. His life had just been saved by this stranger and if that wasn't reason enough to employ him, nothing was.
"Take a seat my friend. Now you obviously realise that we don't exactly work within the law?"
The question was rhetorical but all the same Eli nodded his head.
"It's cutthroat and dangerous, not to mention extremely fuckin' violent. The Old Bill are constantly on our backs and then there's the ongoing threat from other firms on the lookout to muscle in, just like what happened today. Is that really the kind of work you're after?"
Eli inhaled deeply, took a swig of Tommy's pint and then smiled.

"A couple of years back I had a long stint as a bareknuckle fighter and you obviously know that coming from my background it's a tough game."

"Were you any good?"

"I was better than good and only hung up my gloves, metaphorically speaking, after I got married. Angie's a Gorger and never knew what I did as a side line and I want it to stay that way."

"Gorger?"

Eli wanted to laugh, if he had a pound for every time he had to explain the word he wouldn't need to worry about finding a job."

"One of you lot, a non-traveller."

"Fair enough. Be here at ten tomorrow morning. I will warn you, the fuckin' hours are long but the pay reflects that and it will keep the little woman more than happy and off of your back."

Eli left the pub on cloud nine, he didn't plan on elaborating to Angie exactly what the work entailed as he knew she wouldn't be happy but at least there would be regular money coming in. Back in the Bull, Tommy gathered his men around him to make an announcement.

"The geezer who just left is called Eli Carter and he will be joining us as from tomorrow. I'll set the record straight from the off! He's a fuckin' gypsy but he has also just saved my life.

A couple of the fuckin' Handley firm tried to take me out today. It was my own fault, I shouldn't have been out on my own but I won't make the same fuckin' mistake again. If any of you have a problem with that, close the fuckin' door on your way out! By the way, anyone know why Binto wanted the day off?"
There was general muttering amongst the men but no one actually knew anything.
"No prob's, I'll sort that fuckin' little irritation out later. Jojo, bring me a scotch, I've got some thinkin' to do."
Jojo, full name Joanna Murrow, was the barmaid and part time girlfriend of Tommy Day or at least that's how she saw herself but to Tommy she was just a casual lay. As she placed the drink down onto the table she stared lovingly into his eyes and when Tommy winked, her heart fluttered.
"Thanks babe. As for you lot, get some rest, tomorrow we pay back the Handley's for their fuckin' skulduggery."

Arriving back at Crow Lane, Eli was all smiles as he placed his key into the lock and as he opened up, his eyes instantly saw his wife standing in the doorway to the kitchen. Angela was stunning and with a tight little figure, was ever man's dream.

"Hello sweetheart, had a good day?"

"More than good Ange, I've landed a job and it's goin' to be good pay. From now on there's no looking back for the Carter's so why don't you glide over her and give you're old man a kiss?"

Doing as she was asked, Angela was standing in front of her husbands in an instant and kissing him, a kiss so passionate and fervent, it saw the couple naked in a matter of seconds. The sex between them was fiery and when it came down to lovemaking, his beautiful gentle wife, turned into a tigress.

# CHAPTER TWO

Arriving at the Bull as instructed, Eli was welcomed by all in a very friendly way and to say he was surprised was an understatement. Only used to being abused when people found out he was a traveller, surprisingly, this new way of being received had Eli stumped for a few seconds. The men seemed nice, well that wasn't exactly true, he was welcomed by all except a short stocky man who stood at the end of the bar eyeing him suspiciously. The man, as he would soon come to learn, was Binto Davenport and even though all in the pub were aware of what had occurred yesterday, no one had said a word. Dealing with the backstabbing cunt would be down to Tommy Day and him alone.

The back room was permanently rented out to the Day firm and all daily business was conducted there. No one entered unless they were invited and if on the odd occasion a stranger should wander through, it was something they would never do again after a good talking to by the lads, which mostly ended up with the culprit exiting the back room with a black eye or fat lip. Tommy had been the boss since his father retired and he had plans that when it was his time to step down, his own son would replace him. Little Tommy junior was only three years old so that would be in the distant future but Tommy was happy with his lot and he was a respected boss. The six men who permanently worked for him all held him in high esteem, well as high as any villain could be held. Eli scanned the room, a couple of the blokes, Basha and Gus, were playing pool, tall Dave was reading a newspaper, Mike was coming out of the lav and Andy was throwing darts into a dilapidated board on the wall and then there was Binto, who just stood staring at Eli. Standing around was the normal day to day practice until Tommy arrived and gave them their orders for the day. Eli continually studied the men, it was bred in him to be on his guard at all times and something about Binto didn't sit right and it had nothing to do with the events of the previous day. Deciding to take the bull by the horns and break the ice, he walked up to the bar, smiled and offered his hand.

"Hi, I'm Eli."

"I know who you fuckin' are and I fuckin' hate pikey's!"

"I'm not a pikey."

"Not what I've fuckin' heard sunshine."

"I don't know if you're just being fuckin' rude or if you're not aware of the fact but the word Pikey is offensive."

Binto sneered in Eli's direction and then ignoring him, turned to face the others.
"Here lads, wanna hear a joke? I was approached by a gypsy this morning. She was dirty, smelly, ugly and wart-ridden. Told me she lives in a flea-infested caravan and gets raped by her dad and brothers, and then she tries to sell me heather to bring me good luck!"
There was no laughter only the sound of imaginary tumble weed running through each of their heads. Aware that Tommy liked the newest recruit and all that he had done for their boss, they felt bad for Eli but none of them expected what happened next. Before he knew what had hit him, Binto was sprawled out on the floor unconscious. Eli didn't take kindly to rudeness from anyone, especially when it was directed at him personally. Just at that moment the door opened and Tommy walked in.
"Mornin' all."
Strolling over to the bar to greet Eli, he stopped dead in his tracks when his eyes fell upon Binto's massive frame sprawled out on the floor.
"I see you two have met then?"
The whole room burst into laughter and even Eli had to chuckle.
"Basha! Get a jug of water and wake the prick up."
With Binto revived, Tommy took a seat at the

table and was quickly joined by his men. The atmosphere was tense as Binto continued to glare nonstop at Eli and Eli knew that what had occurred a few minutes earlier, was far from over.

"Right, I've got a delivery that needs picking up today and I want Gus to go, actually, take tall Dave with you. It's at one of the warehouses at the back of the greyhound track. Be there by two and keep an eye out as its valuable and we don't want any fucking shenanigans like I had yesterday."

Unbeknown to Binto and Eli, Tommy had spoken to the men late the previous evening and they all knew the plan and what was actually going to happen. Handing Eli a piece of paper Tommy instructed his newest employee to go on an errand for him. Nodding his head Eli left the Bull but didn't look at the note until he got outside. Fortunately he had now learned to read but it didn't flow easily and Angela had been coaching him for the last few months.

'Go to the florists on Western Road and order a funeral wreath. I want it sent over to Micky Handley at three thirty this afternoon, not a minute before or a minute later, pay extra if you have to. Write on the card 'YOU'RE NEXT!' and don't say a word to anyone.'

Eli now had an inkling of what was going to go

down and he smile to himself at the cunningness of his boss. Back in the Bull Binto was given an errand that would take him away from base for a few minutes and if Tommy's suspicions were correct, his man would then contact the Handley's.

By one o'clock, Gus and Tall Dave were in position, with Basha, Mike and Andy well-hidden but ready and waiting to intervene at a seconds notice. As expected, a car pulled up at just before two. Inside were seated two of Micky Handley's heaviest men, Joey Sinclair and Jock the Scot. As soon as they stepped from the vehicle no more than a few seconds passed before all hell broke loose but even though they were hardened gangsters, the two enemies were overpowered due to simply being outnumbered. The Handley firm was far larger than the Days, both in muscle and bodies on the street so this wasn't going to be just a beating, a message had to be sent out letting them know in no uncertain terms that any attempt at a takeover should cease immediately or the consequences would be grave. Jock's throat was slit from ear to ear and the look on his face as his blood flowed freely around him was one of pure terror. Witnessing the event, Joey Sinclair began to fight for his life, he lashed out catching Tall Dave with a powerful kick directly to the shin but it was futile and a couple of seconds later he received the same fate as Jock. The bodies were swiftly wrapped in polythene and loaded into the boot of one of the cars, a car that had been stolen the night before and now with fake registration plates, it was driven over to wasteland on Rainham Road, where later that night it would be torched, leaving no forensic evidence.

The men had all arrived back at the Bull by two thirty and when they came in en massee, Binto had a quizzical look on his face as he thought Tommy had told only Gus and Dave to go. Tommy quickly came at him from behind and as the knife was driven into his ribcage, Binto gasped in shock and pain.
"That you cunt, is for selling me and these guys out! Think I wouldn't find out Binto? Well I hope it was fuckin' worth it Pal 'cause you won't have the fuckin' opportunity to do it again." Tommy thrust the knife in several more times before he nodded in Gus's direction and he and Andy stepped forward in readiness to dispose of the second body of the day. Again using polythene wrap, they would wait until dark and then Binto would be joining Micky Handley's men. Tommy stared at Eli trying to gauge his reaction but there was nothing, no expression of

disgust or fear. His instincts had been correct and Eli Carter would make a good edition to the firm.

The next two years were fruitful, money was plentiful, there hadn't been any pulls from the Old Bill and everyone in the firm had come to love Eli, all except Andy Marshal but he never let on in any way to his colleagues. Unlike Binto, this dislike wasn't anything to do with Eli's heritage but purely the fact that he was too close to Tommy, something Andy had been before the newcomer had arrived. When thing are going good something always happens to knock you off your feet and it happened to all of them on the first Monday in April 1982. As usual, Eli had been the first one in and had opened up around ten thirty using the back door key which they had all been issued with as Jojo didn't come in until eleven. About to put the kettle onto boil Eli spun around when he heard the door open. It was someone Eli didn't recognise and he was instantly on his guard until Suzy Day slowly walked across the carpet and introduced herself.
"Hi, I'm Suzy, Tommy's wife."
Eli was surprised. Suzy was petite and a bit mousy and if he was honest, nothing like blonde busty Jojo, who hung on Tommy's every word.

"Eli, Eli Carter. Pleased to meet you Mrs Day."
To say Eli was concerned was an understatement. Tommy had always kept his home life totally separate from his business and it wasn't just for safety's sake. As far as he was aware, Suzy didn't have any idea about Jojo and that was the way Tommy wanted it to remain. Eli held out his hand but all the time his eyes were darting in all directions in case Jojo came in.
"If you're worried about Joanna Murrow, don't be. I've known about Tom's relationship with her for years and to be honest I really didn't mind so long as he always came home to me and the kids. I'm here Eli with some very sad news."
Suddenly Suzy Day's voice began to quaver and her eyes filled with tears.
"My Tommy died last night."
Eli was devastated and took a step back in shock but straight away he was on his guard.
"Who was it? The Handley's, the Clapham Common firm?"
"No, no it wasn't anything to do with work. My Tommy suffered a massive heart attack at the dinner table or at least that what they think it was but we won't know for sure until the autopsy's been done."
At her own words Suzy Day then broke down and wracking sobs filled the room. Eli took the

woman into his arms and consoled her in the only way he knew how but in all honesty he'd never been very good with emotions, it just wasn't how he'd been raised. Suzy finally composed herself, told Eli she would be in touch regarding the funeral arrangements and then with her head hung low, slowly walked away from her husband's place of work, knowing that she would never return. When the rest of the lads finally came in, it was down to Eli to break the sad news. Instantly they were all in a state of shock and it was again down to him to tell Jojo when she arrived for her shift a few minutes later. If Suzy's show of emotion was sad, it was ten times worse with Jojo. The woman dropped to her knees and wailed in a way that sent shivers down everyone's spines. It seemed to go on for what felt like an eternity though it was actually only a few minutes but no matter how hard they each tried, no one was able to comfort her. Finally she did calm down and with tears continually trickling down her face, agreed to stay and open up.

"It's what my Tommy would have wanted."

Her eyes would remain red and puffy for the rest of the day and everyone avoided contact for fear of a repeat performance. Before the week was out and while Tommy wasn't yet in his grave, Andy Marshal had laid claim to the

business. There were mutters of disapproval but no one commented until Eli at last spoke up.
"I ain't sure about that Andy, I mean who put you in fuckin' charge. Tommy didn't leave any instructions as far as we know, so personally I think we should have a vote, it's the only fair way."
About to shoot the suggestion down in flames, Andy was instantly stopped when all the men, almost in unison, began to nod their heads and mumble their agreement. It was decided that they would each put their chosen leaders name into a hat and the one with the most votes would take over, it was also agreed that once the decision had been made there would be no further discussion on the matter. Eli came out on top with five votes to one and on hearing the result, Andy Marshal told them all to get stuffed and then stormed out in a blind rage. The first thing Eli announced was the fact that the firm should have some new recruits. Fresh, energetic blood was needed and over the ensuing weeks six more bodies were, after strict scrutiny, taken on as hired help.

The funeral was a moderate affair but even though the Firm was small scale when compared to the city firms, there were still one or two main faces in attendance. As the coffin entered and the devastated family followed in behind, Suzy Day's eyes darted in all directions as she scanned the congregation trying to spot her husband's lover. Jojo had left it until the last minute and had then crept in and sat at the back but when the service was over and the family once again followed the coffin out, she was spotted. Standing on the paved walkway and as the congregation emerged, Suzy approached Jojo and hugged her.

"We both loved him sweetheart and now is not the time for grudges. He would have wanted you to be here and I want you here."

Jojo smiled but was stuck for anything to say as she hadn't been aware that Tommy's wife even knew of her existence.

The new and aptly named Carter firm rapidly grew from strength to strength, protection rackets were now a big earner and unprecedented levels of violence became the norm, with Eli often taking part himself. It was done as a reminder to them all that the boss wasn't afraid to get his hands dirty but also that it might make them think twice before crossing him. Andy Marshal never returned, whispers spread that he had moved to Manchester in the hope of joining a new firm and Eli silently wished him luck with that, the North/ South

divide was strong and he wouldn't find it easy.
As the cash rolled in and with the onset of
loansharking, things began to quickly change.
Eli was no longer one of the boys and now ruled
with an iron fist. The men still respected him
but at times wondered if Andy might just have
been a better choice, especially when Eli was
balling them out or had taken his fists to one of
the men when they'd made a mistake. Shortly
after Tommy's death, Micky Handley had
attempted another take over but when his wife
was threatened in the High street and then his
five year old daughter went missing for a day,
he backed off forever. The little girl didn't come
to any harm, that was never the intention and
she had been returned home by nightfall on the
same day. What Eli wanted to instil, was the fact
that Micky and his family could be got to at any
time. It worked and from then on there was
peace in Essex or at least it would remain that
way for a very long time.

Two years after he'd taken over, the firm moved
premises. A small unit was leased at the end of
Church Road on the Bates Industrial Estate.
Now referred to as the office, it was perfectly
positioned and being at the end of the road,
metal gates were erected which were always
kept locked. There was no through access so no

one had any reason to approach the building. If they did then it was only for business or the threat of aggravation. It didn't happen often but after close circuit monitors were erected, the men always knew well in advance if anyone was sniffing about. A tea and coffee importers sign was erected above the threshold so as to make the firm appear legit but the only deliveries ever made were under the cover of darkness and consisted of either stolen goods, dope and cocaine, the latter was something Eli had only recently decided to start dealing in as it went against the grain and it would always remain just a small part of his empire. Angela wasn't privy to what her husband actually did but she knew it definitely wasn't legal and by the end of 1984 and now six months pregnant, she had more than enough on her plate and knew that giving Eli an heir was the most important thing to her husband.

# CHAPTER THREE
## 1985

It had taken the couple five long years of trying before Morris Freedom Manfri Duke Carter finally made an entrance and no baby could ever have been loved or wanted more. Eli was now the boss of the formerly named Day firm and had taken the business far beyond what Tommy Day could ever have dreamed of. Money was plentiful and the small house on Crew Lane shone like a new pin. Angela loved her little family more than anything and never asked Eli for any of the trappings that they could now easily afford. The one constant thorn in her side was Bonnie Carter. Even on her annual visit Bonnie had tried hard to find something wrong with the home, tried to find dirt where there was none or continually insinuate that Angela wasn't a good mother. It was impossible but that didn't stop her trying. She picked holes in the food that was offered, food that her daughter-in-law had spent hours preparing and even stated that the baby didn't look Romany and hoped that Angela hadn't been playing away. Angie was bitterly hurt but knowing how much Eli loved his mother she didn't protest and would only smile sweetly in the woman's direction but the remark regarding Morris's parentage was the final straw and even though Angela hadn't shown any sign regarding how upset she was, Eli was on his feet in seconds.

"How dare you! I love you Mammie but sometimes that tongue of yours is nothing but pure fuckin' evil. I want you to leave now and don't come back. Ever!"

Bonnie couldn't believe what she was hearing. Her son, her baby boy was choosing a gorger over his own flesh and blood. The tears began to fall but Eli wasn't having any of it, he'd seen it all before too many times and reiterated his statement that he wanted her to leave, banishing his mother forever. To continually put his wife down was one thing and something they could both tolerate if only for one day per year but to insult their child's parentage was another matter altogether. Bonnie continued to plead with her son but her words fell on deaf ears as he showed her to the door. It would be ten long years before he had any contact with his family again and it had happened by chance at a traveller wedding. Just a year after, Bonnie had passed away and even though he was glad that they had reconciled, the feelings just weren't there anymore, too much water had passed under the bridge but Eli swore to still keep in contact with his community and that's exactly what he did.

By the time Morris Carter celebrated his fifth birthday the family had moved into a much larger and grander house and there was also a new addition to the family. Marcus was a beautiful child, loved by everyone except his brother who after having all of the attention for so long was as jealous as hell. Morris would take any opportunity to make his brother's life miserable both mentally and physically. He would tell lies and blame Marcus for things he hadn't done, trip him up as he walked by and even gave him body punches that wouldn't show for days but not once did his brother run to their parents. He took the punishment in the hope that one day his older brother would love him or at the very least like him. Angela was aware of the hatred her older son felt and continually tried to change his mind about little Marcus, Eli on the other hand, could never see any wrong in his first born and at times it caused arguments with the couple but things would take a dramatic turn when the boys were in their mid and late teens.

The family had left the security of their lavish home to take a week's holiday. Eli wanted his children to know their roots and get to know other travellers and the history of the family. A camp had set up on wasteland in Cornwall, just a stone's throw from the sea. It was the annual holiday for many of the Romany families and vans had travelled from all corners of the United Kingdom, knowing that by the time the courts had produced an eviction order, the holiday would have come to an end and they would all be on their way back home.  By the second day there were over thirty vans, all parked in a large protective circle with a huge fire pit in the centre. Days were spent on the beach, barbeques were held in the evenings with singing and dancing and with everyone in high spirits.  Morris was only just of legal drinking age, though it wouldn't have mattered if he wasn't as a traveller boy is seen as a man by the age of around sixteen.  Angela didn't like it, if the truth be told she hated attending these events but knowing how much it meant to Eli, she did her best to mix in with the other women which was difficult at times as she had absolutely nothing in common with them.

On the third evening Morris had sneaked a bottle of scotch into the trailer.  His parents were outside socialising with family and old friends and as Marcus shook his head with every swig his brother took, Morris became more and more agitated.

"What you fuckin' looking at you pussy?!!!!"
"Don't start Morris for fucks sake!"
"You're just a snivellin' little cunt with no balls."

"No I'm not!"

"Alright then, let's see? The tides up and I'm going for a night swim, you comin' or not?"

"No, it's too dangerous and you shouldn't go either."

"See! Just like I said, a pussy."

With that Morris staggered to his feet and after almost falling out of the van, made his way along the grass track to the water's edge. Marcus felt duty bound to follow to make sure his brother was safe and just as he'd thought, within a couple of minutes Morris was in trouble. It might have been the height of summer but the water was still incredibly cold.

"Come on you pussy! Come on in and show me you're a fuckin' man!"

Running into the darkness until his feet couldn't touch the bottom his body instantly went into shock and Morris began to flail his arms around. He managed to call out 'Help!' before he blacked out. Kicking off his shoes and with the help of the moonlight, Marcus was beside his brother in seconds and struggled, due to the difference in their sizes, to pull a now unconscious Morris out and onto the sand. Somehow he managed and wrapping his discarded coat over his brother's body, he laid on top of Morris to give warmth and at the same time began to slap his brother's cheeks.

"Morris, Morris!!! Wake you, oh God please wake up."

Slowly Morris's eye began to flicker and a few minutes later he was breathing well and was completely conscious. After a while the brothers somehow managed to stagger back to the camp with Morris leaning heavily onto Marcus for support. Able to slip back into the van without anyone seeing them, Morris swore his brother to secrecy. From that night on an instant bond between the two was established and it didn't go unnoticed by their parents. No questions were ever asked about what had happened, it wasn't the Romany way, what happened between two men was their business and no one else's but both Eli and Angela were over the moon that their boys were no longer continually trying to beat the shit out of each other.

Situated just over six miles from Romford, the house on Hall Lane in Upminster was huge and set in ten acres of land. Eli Carter had made the purchase a couple of years after his first son was born and the property had been his and his wife Angie's pride and joy. The boys had spent an idyllic childhood running around the wooded grounds and both had started their education at St Ursula's Catholic Primary School in Romford. By the time they had moved to All Saints

Catholic senior school in Dagenham their behaviour was so bad that many times they were threatened with expulsion and if it hadn't have been for Eli's generous donations, they definitely would have been. Still, the boy's futures looked bright and had already been mapped out by their parents, well at least it had been up until Morris became a teenager. Overnight they both seemed to have grown into uncontrollable monsters with Marcus being led by his older brother. Their actions became more violent, with bullying and extortion far beyond a school boy level. Their conduct was called into question over and over again but as usual Eli paid for things to be swept under the carpet. This continued even after finishing their education and they were soon totally out of hand and would listen to no one and that included their father. Morris joined the family firm on his sixteenth birthday and Marcus would do the same five years later. His nature was much kinder than that of his brother and school wise, he seemed to settle down without Morris's bad influence, well at least during school hours.

Reclassified and ceasing to actually be a part of Essex since 1965, Morris and Marcus still saw themselves as Essex boys and desperately wanted to be included in the growing notoriety that came with the location. By 2007 both boys were firmly established in the firm but it wasn't smooth sailing. The old man was stuck in the past and things had to change if you wanted to be a leader in the underworld. It was hard going as neither would toe the line and the favouritism shown in front of the other men didn't make for a good atmosphere. It was all about to change and on Morris's twenty third birthday, when his mother had spent all day preparing a celebratory meal, things finally escalated. Just as Angela was about to serve up dinner, she was informed by her eldest son that he was going out so not to bother doing him a plate. Eli had seen the trouble his wife had gone to and a row instantly broke out between Morris and his father. When Eli had taken a swing at his son Marcus had felt duty bound to intervene. It was something you never did especially in the traveller community but as Marcus didn't see himself as a gypsy, he went in all guns blazing. It turned into a free-for-all and both men, young men who could easily handle themselves, ended up taking a severe beating from their father. Angela was screaming at her husband to stop but Eli knew he needed to be hard to bring them both back into line and strangely it had worked. Neither realised just how vicious their father could actually be until now and from that day forward they toed the line and did as they were told. It still didn't stop them from dreaming big and making plans for when the day finally arrived, the day they could at last take charge of the Carter firm and as far as the boys were concerned, it couldn't come soon enough, even if that meant the cost would be their father's life.

Shortly after the showdown, Angela became ill. She had been complaining for weeks that she was short of breath and after continually being chastised by Eli, she finally made an appointment to see a doctor. Without hesitation she was referred to the local hospital and from there the situation progressed rapidly. In little under a month she had been diagnosed with inoperable lung cancer. Breaking the news was heart breaking and Eli just wouldn't accept it. He looked into treatments from abroad, homeopathic remedies, anything that would stop the love of his life leaving this world. Angela allowed him to do whatever he thought necessary just to appease him but her years of heavy smoking had finally taken its toll and she knew it. Six months later, surrounded by her husband and sons, Angela Carter took her last breath. The boys were distraught but it was nothing compared to Eli's grief. After the

funeral, a funeral attended by the gypsy community at her request even though it wasn't her heritage, he locked himself away in their bedroom for days on end. The only time he made it outside was to visit his wife's grave, as not being able to bring himself to burn her body in a wagon as was tradition, Eli had Angela interred at the local cemetery. Morris, never the one to miss a trick, saw it as an opportunity and after a heart to heart with Marcus, the boys agreed that it was probably now their time to shine. They both excitedly made plans regarding moving their business into the city, Morris wanted to be a real player and that was never going to be possible if they remained in Romford. Their dreaming didn't last long as Eli soon got word of what was happening in the firm. Dave Kinnock, known to all as Tall Dave, had taken it upon himself to visit the house while the boys were away from home. Milly Garrod the housekeeper, had opened the door to him and after explaining that Mr Carter wasn't receiving visitors, she had finally allowed the man inside when he began to plead with her. Wearily Milly made her way upstairs and hesitantly knocked on the bedroom door.
"Mr Carter, there's a man here to see you and he won't take no for an answer."
A few seconds later Eli opened the door and it

was obvious to Milly that he'd been crying.
"Did he give you his name?"
"Yes he did and it's very strange Mr Carter, he calls himself Tall Dave?"
Eli couldn't be off smiling when he saw the quizzical expression on her face.
"Tell him I'll be down in a minute."
Fifteen minutes later and after Tall Dave had explained all that the boys had been up to, Eli Carter was on his way to the office. Needless to say, the big plans that Morris and Marcus had been making, were once again put on hold.

# CHAPTER FOUR
## 2018

Built in 1961 and consisting of five magistrates and one Crown Court room, it had been many months if not years since Chelmsford Court had seen such a high number of public spectators as it had today.

"Stand up straight and take your hands out of your pockets when in my court young man!" Morris smirked at being called a young man, he was thirty three but compared to the old trout sitting in judgement he guessed he was young. The public gallery was full to bursting with what the local newspaper would later report as 'Congregated under one roof, the most notorious of the Essex criminal world'. Several derogatory shouts then went out in the direction of recorder Judge Camilla Baron-Spires. Now only working part time, Camilla hated these kinds of cases and the Crown v Carter had been a particularly nasty affair. Not one to scare easily, Camilla glared at the gallery, her expression was cold and stern even if today that wasn't what she actually felt inside but no one would ever have been able to tell. Banging her gavel down hard onto the surface of her bench, her voice was loud as she bellowed.

"If I do not have order in this court immediately, then I will have no other option than to clear the room!"

Instantly there was silence but Morris Carter only smirked again and for his smug attitude, though unbeknown to him, six extra months was promptly added to his three year sentence.

"Mr Carter, you have been brought before this court for the brutal, unprovoked and racially motivated attack on Philip Myers. There was no rhyme or reason to the assault and in police interview you simply stated that 'you didn't like blacks'. Mr Myers was unable to carry out his work for over three months, his mental health has suffered because of your assault and he is permanently disfigured. This kind of behaviour will not be tolerated by this court and indeed by the general public as a whole. You were cowardly in your actions and you have been cowardly here today by not admitting your guilt in connection with that act. You have wasted the courts time not to mention many thousands of pounds, which will not reflect well on your sentencing. The good men and women of this jury have found you guilty as charged and if it wasn't for the fact that this is your first appearance before me, though I very much doubt it will be your last, I would have been far more severe in my sentencing. As I have stated, it is your first offence and as such I hereby sentence you to three years and six months imprisonment. A word of warning Mr Carter, if you are ever brought before me again, I will not be so lenient regarding the punishment imposed. Take him down officers."

The gallery went into uproar and the noise of feet kicking on the wooden panelling and shouts from the general public, mostly by friends and supporters of Morris, were deafening. Recorder Judge Baron-Spires was advised by her usher, for her own safety, to make a hasty retreat to chambers and for once she listened.

Outside, Marcus Carter made his way around to the rear of the building where the prison escort van was waiting to transport his brother. Slipping the guard a ton as he'd done on numerous occasions before when seeing one of the firm's employees, he was then let on board to have a few minutes with Morris before he left to begin his sentence. The aisle walkway was narrow and lining both sides of the van were white metal cages. The door to Morris's confined space was open and Marcus could see his brother was sitting down, eyes closed and with his head resting on the adjoin mesh wall. Hearing someone enter Morris smiled broadly when he saw who it was.

"Hi there little bro!"

"Why the fuck didn't you toe the line Morris? I'm convinced the old cow added several more months because of your attitude? Your brief is in agreement but you never fuckin' listen, do you?"

"Fuck the silly bitch. I'll only do three of 'em in any case, maybe even less."

"That's if you fuckin' behave yourself!"

"Moi? I'm a good boy I am."

Marcus could only raise his eyebrows and slowly shake his head. Being the youngest, most of the time he looked up to his elder brother but sometimes Morris was impulsive and that impulsiveness often brought trouble down on the two of them.

"Well it's your life but try and stay out of bother Morris, you know the old man ain't too clever at the minute so everythin's goin' to fall on my fuckin' shoulders till you get out."

"You'll be fine so stop worryin' Mar! Now give us a hug before the bastards cart me off to the depths of hell."

Doing as he was asked Marcus hugged his brother to him, he loved Morris with all of his heart but most of the time his sibling was a hot head and acted before he'd thought things through, something Marcus never did.

"I aint goin' to come visit, those places give me the creeps so I'll see you when you get out. Any idea where you're going?"

"The Scrubs for now but those cunts will probably ghost me someplace at the arse end of nowhere so I don't get any visits."

"Well look after yourself, any message for the old man?"

"Tell the old cunt to hurry up and die!"

Morris began to laugh and his brother joined in but then suddenly Morris became serious.

"I mean it Marcus, we need to start dealing big time, it's where the real money is but while that old cunt is still alive it ain't goin' to happen!"

Marcus nodded his head, turned and descended the steps, grateful to be back in the fresh air. He knew he would struggle if he was ever made to do any real time and hoped that it would never happen. As for his brother, Morris would be like a pig in shit because of all the men and again Marcus Carter started to laugh. Back in his range rover he took a few moments to think about things. This whole sorry mess had begun on a simple Friday night out in Brentwood. The Sugar Hut was a favourite of Morris though Marcus found it too showy and full of the types seen on TOWIE. He liked women, had tested out more than a few in his time but Marcus was picky and the fake blonde tango examples at the Hut, were definitely not his type. Morris on the other hand loved to spend time in the company of women but they were not his sexual preference in the least. Knowing that he could only admire the toned, well-dressed young men from afar frustrated him at times and though he was aware that his brother knew of his bedroom escapades, there was no way he would act on an invite whilst in Marcus's company. The brother's notoriety preceded them and the entrance fee was waivered as they were led straight inside, much to the grumbles of the large queue that stretched along the High Street. One glare from Bobby Fortnum the head doorman and the complaining instantly stopped. Inside the men were shown to a VIP table in the relaxation area and instantly a chilled bottle of Moet Chandon and two long stemmed glasses were brought over.

"This is the life Mar, treated like fuckin' royalty we are!"

Mick Sizewell, manager at the Hut for the last five years walked over and shook hands with both men in turn.

"Nice to see you again boys. If you want anythin' and I mean anythin'! Just give Kirsty over there the nod."

"Will do and thanks Mick. See Mar, told you, fuckin' royalty."

Marcus could only roll his eyes. He had to admit, his brother was a bit of a legend in Essex

but it never bode too well to get big headed about these things. There was always some little tosser on the way up who wanted to make a name for himself and topping one of the Carters would do just that. The Ibiza tunes pumped out through the ceiling speakers and after necking half of the bottle, Morris was ready to cut some moves on the dance floor.
"You comin'?"
"Nah, I'll sit here and watch."
"Please yourself you miserable sod."
By one am Marcus was flagging but not through drink, it had been a long week and all he wanted was his bed. Morris on the other hand was more than a little oiled and his brother had to almost drag him from the dancefloor.
"Come on Morris, time to go!"
"Oh fuck off Mar, I'm only now getting' in me fuckin' stride! Come on! Let your hair down and get in the groove for once."
Now Marcus was annoyed, he'd come here tonight under duress but now it was time to go and he wasn't going to allow his brother to pressurise him into staying. Morris had done several lines of Charlie throughout the evening and the powdery white residue was still evident around his nostrils. Leaning forward, he gently wiped under his brothers nose with the tip of his fingers.

"It's up to you but I'm outta here and as I'm the driver, it will be a long fuckin' walk home. Choice is yours?"

Reluctantly Morris followed his brother and the pair were almost at the exit when a man of around twenty five stepped into Morris's path.

"You're that fuckin' faggot hard man ain't you?"

The comment was said to evoke anger and by God it didn't disappoint. Phil Myers, a wannabe gangster had come prepared and within seconds was brandishing a three inch paring knife. Not long enough to cause death, well hopefully at least but long enough to do some serious damage and make Philip a name for himself. There was just one problem, he had no prior knowledge of what Morris was capable of.

"You black Cunt!!!"

Seconds later and Philip Myers was on his back with all of Morris's sixteen stone weight straddling him. Grabbing the knife Morris sliced the man from his right eye down to the corner of his mouth. Moving his face in close he then bit down and spat out a mouthful of his assailants left cheek. Philip screamed out in agony as Morris got to his feet, totally unfazed by the man's pain. Marcus tried to pull his brother away but Morris used all of his weight to then stamp down on his attackers ankle. The sound of bone snapping was audible to all in the foyer

and Marcus knew there would be a shit load of trouble now heading their way.  They made it to the Range rover and the drive out of Brentwood was taken in silence.  By the time they crossed over the M25 Marcus couldn't hold his tongue any longer.
"What the fuck was all that about?"
"You heard the cunt, he called me a faggot!"
"And?"
"Look, you know what I like but that ain't common knowledge to the whole fuckin' world.  That cunt was tryin' to shame me, well he'll think fuckin' twice in the future."
"Look Morris, you ain't gettin' away with this one.  There were too many witnesses and plenty of cameras in and out of the place.  Why don't we go and pay the Old Bill a visit and get this over with?"
"No fuckin' way!  Take me home."
Doing as he was told Marcus drove the remaining four miles but as they entered through the tall ornate gates, the police were already waiting outside the house with blue lights flashing.  Eli Carter stood on the front steps in his dressing gown and his expression spoke volumes.  As they got out of the car and Morris was immediately placed in handcuffs and read his rights, Eli stared coldly at his youngest son before turning and going back

inside.

"Give my brief a ring bro!"

Marcus stood on the steps and watched the flashing lights dim as the cars disappeared. He wasn't looking forward to the third degree that he knew was coming once the front door was closed.

"Now what's he done and why the hell didn't you stop him?"

In their fathers eyes Morris was the golden child, the apple of his eye, the one to take over the empire some day and he expected his youngest son to look out for his brother at all times.

"I ain't his fuckin' keeper Pop's. You know what he's like when he's on the Charlie and tonight he did it big style. Nearly ripped the face of some poor cunt and he ain't goin' to get away with it, not this time. I'm goin' to bed!"

That had all happened three months ago and now punishment had been handed down and in Marcus's opinion it had been more than fair. Not feeling like going home and being the bearer of bad news just yet, Marcus headed for the Drill on Brentford Road. He knew a couple of the firm would be in there and only now beginning to actually feel the loss of his brother, he just wanted to see a few friendly faces. The pub was one of the few remaining old school establishments, it sold good food and still had a pool table which is where he spotted Denny Shannon and Smiter who were both arguing fiercely over which pocket would be the best bet for the black.

"No not that one you twat! Middle pocket I said."

"Oh fuck off Smiter you don't know what you're fuckin' talkin' about."

"Leave it out you pair of muppets!"

Both men instantly stopped arguing and turned to see who had made the comment.

"Marcus me old son, how'd it go?"

"Three and a half and the old man ain't goin' to be too pleased when I break the news to him Denny."

"Maybe not but with all due respect, you ain't your brothers fuckin' keeper Mar."

"You try tellin' Pop's that! In his eyes Morris can do no wrong and he won't hear anything' said against him. Sometimes I think he could commit murder in front of the old man and Pop's would say they deserved it and that they must have wound Morris up."

Denny Shannon nodded his head in agreement, he'd worked for the firm for a little over five years and while he liked and respected Marcus, he loathed the man's older brother.

The Carter firm may have run out of Romford

but the boys had high hopes of moving right into the city once the old man had finally popped his clogs. Morris might well have been five years older but the boys were as close as twins and were the diamond's in their father's life, Morris a tad more than Marcus. Even though Eli Carter had started the firm and still ran it successfully without too much interference from the Old Bill, the boys had plans far and beyond anything their father could have dreamed of. There was just one problem, they would have to wait until he died as any talk of expansion or suggestions regarding branching out had, in the past, fallen on deaf ears. That hadn't stopped Morris setting up a little side-line unbeknown to his father, or so he thought. Part of Eli's business dealings included prostitution but it had only ever been on a small scale. The three street Toms Morris secretly ran out of Kings Cross, brought him in a healthy income and allowed him the finer things in life without having to keep asking his old man. When the time was right, when he was at last finally in charge, he had plans to expand on this. Morris wanted high class call girls who visited the top hotels and brought in big bucks and not the skanky street whores who probably carried more diseases than the average sewer rat but for now he couldn't afford to be choosy.
"What you drinkin' Mar?"

"Thanks Smiter I'll have a Guinness but make sure it's cold, nothin' worse than a warm Guinness in my book."

The three men took seats at one of the tables and spoke of Morris and his past escapades.

Suddenly it felt like a wake and Marcus didn't like it.

"I'd better be off now boys."

Standing up he swiftly said his farewells, reminded the men to be at the office early the next day and then made his way back to the family home where both brothers had, up until today, still resided. He wasn't looking forward to it and was well aware that his father would hit the roof but he couldn't put off the inevitable any longer.

# CHAPTER FIVE

The large detached house known as 'Timbers', was situated at the end of Streamside Close in Edmonton and it oozed class and sophistication. The wooden mock Tudor façade had been tastefully done and from the road the house looked much older than it actually was. The furnishings were expensive and of the best quality and the house was Jeans pride and joy. When the family were in residence it was a golden rule that work was never mentioned. Jean had been married to her childhood sweetheart Derek, known to all as Del, for almost thirty two years but knew very little of what he did for a living. However, she was aware that it was illegal and in all honesty it wasn't what she wanted. If the truth was told she actually hated it but it provided all the luxuries of life so she wasn't about to complain so long as she didn't know any of the finer details. Unbeknown to the couple, Jean was already pregnant on their wedding day and a little under eight months later the first of their three children was born. Allison was as headstrong as her father, it hadn't been an easy birth and she was a difficult child to raise, so when her sister Dawn came along four years later it was a blessing. Dawn was quiet and compliant and those two facts endeared her mother to her after the nightmare of her older sister. Del was desperate for a son but after ten years and two miscarriages, the couple had almost given up hope. When Kenan finally arrived in the winter of 1996 Del was elated, his family was at last complete.

Allison Foster slammed the front door and marched into the kitchen. It was the weekly get together and none of them ever dared to cancel. Allison was manageress at the local travel agents and had her own flat situated above the shop. She had been desperate to leave home and none of the other family members had put up a fight, in fact since she'd left almost two years earlier there had been peace at Timbers for the first time in as long as anyone could remember.
"That fucking moron!"
Jean Foster still maintained the petite figure she'd had on her wedding day. Immaculately dressed with a short blonds bob, her husband was so proud that he'd managed to capture such a beauty. Rolling her eyes upwards when she heard her daughter's voice, Jean didn't turn around and just continued stirring the saucepan of gravy that she'd spent most of the afternoon preparing.

"Now who's rattled your cage?"
"Kenan! That little sod always parks his car so that I struggle to get close to the house. It's raining and my hairs wet now thanks to golden balls."
"I doubt he did it on purpose, you know young boys Allison, their brains are firmly in their trousers at his age and they think of no one but themselves."
Rubbing her hair with a towel that she'd grabbed from the downstairs loo as she'd walked through the hall, Allison sighed heavily, would either of her parents ever see any faults in her brother? Kenan could do no wrong in their eyes and at times it frustrated her beyond belief.
"Dawn here yet?"
"No, she rang a while ago to say she was running late, problems at the Bank I think."
Dawn Foster worked as a cashier for Barclays over on South Mall but she had always declined any promotions offered. Earning a living was important but that was as far as it went and Dawn had no aspirations to climb the career ladder. She was a real home bird, had no interest in boys or getting her own place, for Dawn all that mattered was her family and spending time with them.
"I'm just going to pop up to her room and see if she's got a top I can borrow because if I have to

sit through dinner in damp clothes, that little arsehole will get the sharp end of my tongue. Dad here?"

"No, but he did ring to say that he wouldn't be late."

Allison made her way up the stairs and walking the length of the galleried landing she had to pass her brothers bedroom. Kenan was lying on his bed engrossed in some stupid computer game and knowing that she wouldn't get any sense out of him, she decided not to vent her anger on him just yet. Entering Dawns room she felt just a pang of jealousy. All of their rooms, her old one included, had been decorated in sumptuous furnishing and fabrics. Her own flat was nice but couldn't compare to Timbers and since she had left, her room had been redone for guest use and it wasn't to her taste. Rifling through her sisters wardrobe she grimaced at some of her siblings fashion choices, tops and dresses she wouldn't be seen dead in. It was just as well as they wouldn't have fitted her, Allison was a tad on the large side after inheriting her build from Del's late mother and it had always been a thorn in Ally's side that her sister was pencil thin. Finally she grabbed a plain beige cashmere sweater, it was a snug fit but it would just have to do.

The front door again slammed and this time Jean

let out a loud sigh of irritation at the tirade she knew was about to start any second.

"Fuckin' traffic! Do you know I left over an hour ago? It should have taken under thirty minutes but oh no! Some twat down the council decided that Friday would be a good day to have the road up and make the A406 stretch between South Woodford and Pymmes Park, single fuckin' file! Can you believe it?!!"

Jean had stopped listening as soon as she'd heard the words 'fucking traffic', it was the same every Friday and she was bored with his constant complaining. She loved her husband with all of her heart but he could try the patience of a saint at times and she imagined he must be murder to work for. Del Foster's mood instantly softened as he leaned over the stove and took in the aromas before kissing his wife on the cheek.

"Smells great babe and I'm Hank Marvin, what time we eatin'?"

Jean tenderly touched the large scar that ran down her husband's right cheek, it was something she did whenever he was close to her, something she'd done for many years and it was a constant reminder to her of how he had put his life on the line to save her.

"As soon as Dawn gets in but she's running a little late."

With that the front door opened for the final

time but unlike her sister and father, it closed quietly. Dawn walked straight into the kitchen and kissed her mother tenderly on the shoulder.
"Good day mum?"
She was the only one who had bothered to see what kind of day she'd had and Jean smiled warmly in her daughter's direction.
"Just fine beautiful and you?"
"Oh you know, okay, nothing to get worked up about. We managed to find the shortfall so everyone's gone off for the weekend with a spring in their step. Have I got time to get changed mum?"
Jean nodded her head and then began to lay the table and then dish up the vegetables. Five minutes later and the whole family were seated in the dining room and tucking into one of Jeans famous roasts. There was a lot of light hearted banter around the table and it wasn't until desert had been finished that Del turned towards his son.
"I need a chat with you later Kenan, come to the study while the girls are clearing away."
He winked in his son's direction and it didn't go unnoticed by Allison. Sighing heavily she threw her spoon down onto the table, once again her brother was being treated differently to his sisters. No one took any notice which angered Allison even more but she wasn't about to kick

off any further, it never got her anywhere and would only cause even more bad feeling not to mention it would upset her mum.

Del's study resembled a gentlemen's club with its dark heavy wallpaper and oxblood leather chesterfield chairs. He hardly did any work at home but still liked to use the room if he wanted a private word with one of his kids or just to have a few moments alone if he was getting it in the neck from his wife. Glancing at his fortnightly subscription to Private Eye, he was stopped when Kenan tapped on the door and then walked in.

"What's up Dad?"

Kenan Foster had opted out of college and university and after finishing sixth form had dossed around for a year getting under his mother's feet. Finally he was given an ultimatum, get a job or go back into education. Opting for the latter he had completed a two year course in maths and English literature before announcing he was taking a year off to go travelling. It hadn't gone down well with his mother as Jean always worried when she couldn't see her children at least twice a week and even then that was pushing it. If she'd had her way they would all still be living at home with her fussing and taking care of them, just as she'd always done.  Doing the traditional gap year thing, even though he had no plans to attend university, Kenan had travelled to India, New Zealand and then on to Australia.  It had been a wild time and he'd enjoyed it but suddenly getting homesick he had returned to England eight months into his travels.

"Take a seat son.  Now we need to discuss your future, we've, me and your mum that is, we've gone along with all that you've wanted but now it's time to knuckle down and start workin'.  You're twenty two and now I want you to follow in my footsteps and come and join the firm."

"Sorry Dad but I don't want to."

Del slammed his fist down onto the desk and the pure rage he was feeling was evident on his face.  He rarely showed aggression to or in front of his family but on the odd occasion when it did happen, they all knew to take a step back.

"You will do as I fuckin' say, do you hear me?  No son of mine is going to be known as a sponger and that's exactly what you've become, well it stops now!!!"

The look of horror on Kenan's face was evident be he knew better than to complain further.  His father loved him, that went without saying but Del had one hell of a temper if you wound him up.  Kenan didn't want a life of crime and mixing with muscle bound halfwits but it seemed he had no say in the matter so after a few seconds more of thinking about the job, a job he had Hobson's choice in taking, he reasoned that it might not be that bad, he was the boss's son after all.

"Okay, if that's what you want."

Del smiled broadly and the tense atmosphere immediately disappeared. Opening up the highly polished humidor on his desk he removed a large King Edward cigar. Proceeding to light it and puff out clouds of billowing smoke disgusted and annoyed Kenan and he waved his hand in front of his face. The rest of the family couldn't stand the smell any more than Kenan and this was the only room in the house where it was allowed and only then after Del had promised Jean that he would always have the window open. On this occasion it had strangely and conveniently slipped his mind.

"Right, I expect you up bright and early in the mornin'. You can travel to work with me for a couple of days until you get a feel for the place."

It appeared strange that none of his children had ever visited his place of work but it had been written in stone from the day Allison had been born and something, even as the years passed, that Jean wouldn't relent on.

"Does mum know?"

The question instantly wound Del up again just

as Kenan knew it would.

"Don't try and pull that one and you leave your mother to me. Well, that's all so off you trot sunshine and remember, up bright and early!"

Going up to his room for a while, he resisted the chance to stir the shit by letting the cat out of the bag to the others. It would kick off on its own later when his mother found out, of that he was sure.

The rest of the evening passed without event and Dawn was the first to turn in for the night, swiftly followed by her brother. When Jean yawned loudly it was a signal for Allison to either stay over or get off home.

"Alright mum, no need to be so bloody blatant. I'm surprised you ain't handed me my coat!"

"Don't be so dramatic love, you always have to turn everything into an argument. I'm tired that's all, me and your father aren't as young as we used to be."

"You speak for yourself Jeanie!"

Her husband had just woken up from napping on the sofa and his eyes resembled piss holes in the snow. Shaking her head and thinking of the words she'd just uttered, she began to laugh at him and mockingly added.

"Of course not love, I bet you could still boogie away until the early hours couldn't you?"

"Too right I could and don't you forget it lady!"
Allison shook her head, stood up and after kissing her parents goodnight, reluctantly left the place she still called home.

When Del and Jean were finally tucked up in bed and had begun one of their late night chats, something they had always done from day one, Del turned to face his wife wearing a serious expression.

"What?"

"I've got something to tell you and you ain't goin' to like it!"

"What, what is it?"

"Kenan's joinin' the firm."

Out of bed in a second she began to pace the floor and her voice was raised. In the adjoining room Kenan had his ear to the wall and grinned as he waited for world war three to start. There was no way she would allow him to join the firm, he was banking on it.

"Over my dead body he is!"

Del hauled himself up the bed and rested his back on the designer headboard.

"I'm sorry darlin' but that's exactly what's happenin'. We've pandered to him long enough, he's twenty two for Christ's sake and has never done a day's work in his life. Both of our girls support themselves and its time he did the same!"

"What turn into a criminal like you and that good for nothing brother of yours?"
"Don't fuckin' bring Jimmy into all of this. You can be a right bitch at times Jean but this is one battle you will not fuckin' win."
Jimmy Foster, Del's younger brother, was currently serving an eighteen stretch for armed robbery and even the mention of his name was a sore point for Del as he'd always blamed himself for Jimmy getting banged up.
"You just watch me Mr bloody big shot!"
"Look! I very rarely put my foot down but I am this time, so like it or lump it he's comin' to work for me!"
In the room next door, Kenan removed the glass from his ear and sighed heavily. That really hadn't gone as he'd expected and his life was about to drastically change and not for the better he feared. He would just have to try something different, maybe if he was a disappointment in the firm his dad would relent and leave him to his own devises.

The following morning Del entered the kitchen to find his wife cooking breakfast.
"Where is he?"
Jean was still upset and angry from the previous night and without turning around she just shrugged her shoulders, that was until she heard

her husband storm up the stairs. If he laid a hand on her son there would be murders. Slamming the door to Kenan's room wide open, Del marched over to the bed and grabbing the duvet with both hands, proceeded to throw it to the floor. Kenan slept naked and instantly he covered his manhood with his hands.
"What the fuck?!!!!"
"I want you out of that pit, washed, dressed and ready to go in ten minutes and God help you if you're not!"
Del stomped back down stairs and when he saw his wife he held up his open palm.
"Don't alright, just don't!"
Jean placed the plate of eggs and bacon down onto the table and didn't utter a word, she knew her man better than anyone and today he really wasn't in a good mood. Jean prayed that Kenan would do as he'd been told and show a good front this morning or she just didn't want to contemplate the consequences. There was no need as a few minutes later her boy appeared bright eyed and bushy tailed.
"You ready then or what?"
Before he turned and made his way into the hall Kenan winked at his mother and she gave a wry smile, her boy was fine and as far as she was concerned, all was right with the world. Del could only shake his head, this wasn't how he

liked to start the day and he would now be in a mood for the remainder.

"Sometimes I think we were handed the wrong fuckin' kid down the hospital Jean, really I do." Kissing her tenderly Del left to join his son and walking over to the radio, Jean switched it on to 5 live. Finally she could have some peace, even if that peace would only last for nine or ten hours.

# CHAPTER SIX

The Foster Firm ran out of a small terraced house at the end of Roach Road in Bow. The road was a dead end but had a footbridge to the east which crossed Hertford Union Canal and another to the north crossing Hackney Cut. Should the need ever arise, it was perfectly situated for a quick getaway and Del kept two small inflatables, complete with outboards, in ramshackle sheds that were open ended onto the banks of the canal and cut. Everyone in the vicinity knew who they belonged to, they also knew that if they wished to keep their legs, not to go near them. The boats were for emergencies only but luckily as yet that hadn't happened. As soon as they'd been put into place the locals were warned off of trying to steal them and Del's name was feared enough in the area that not once did anyone even try. If there was ever a swoop by the Old Bill, a chase could only be carried out on foot and with 25hp outboards on the boats, it would be almost impossible to apprehend the men once they were actually on the water. Dealing in large quantities of Heroin, cocaine and more recently spice, the returns were fantastic but the firm were also all aware that if caught, the punishment would be long sentences at her majesty's pleasure. Del's dealings were mostly direct with the importers and then selling on to other firms on a large scale. His men on the other hand were a different matter; they purchased wholesale from Del and had their own small crews who sold them on from street corners. Personally Del viewed what he did as having a low chance of being caught so he was happy for others to take all of the risks while he just coined in the money.

Back in his early twenties Del Foster had been an active member of The National Front. While he no longer participated in rallies or marches, his loathing of minority groups and not just colour or creed but queers and lesbians still remained. His workforce consisted of eight men who in turn all ran small crews consisting of three or four dealers each. They were all, with the exception of one, white Caucasian. Mad Tony, Stevie Hunt, Steve Lennon, Carl Ransom, Sammy Bird, Freddy Wentworth and Gordon Mayes, hailed from all over London. The exception to Del's rule was Levi Puck, a six foot West Indian who knew how to take care of himself. Levi was able to provide an open door for the rest of the firm to deal with the black crews who were scattered throughout London. Unable to see himself as a hypocrite, to Del it was business pure and simple but over the years he had become fond of the man. It was a joke amongst his men, though no one dared to speak openly, that Del had long since modelled himself on Ronnie Kray. He would watch and read anything he could that would give him further insight into the man. He dressed in sharp suits, and though not gay or a paranoid schizophrenic like his idol, there was definitely something amiss. His younger brother Jimmy, until he'd been banged up, had worked alongside Del but at times he had been more of a hindrance than a help but just like Ronnie Kray, Del knew the importance of family. If things continued as they had been and now with Kenan standing beside him, Del knew it wouldn't be too long before his notoriety far exceeded that of the Krays or at least that was what he was hoping for.

By now Kenan Foster had been in his father's employ for a little over two weeks but only a week after joining the firm Kenan had started to drive himself to the office. It was less time that he had to spend with his father and alone in the car, he was able to listen to his music and get his mind ready for the day ahead. The guys he worked alongside were friendly but he was well aware that he wasn't included in many of the hushed conversation they had. Kenan didn't blame them, after all they probably thought he would go running back to the old man but nothing could have been further from the truth. Hating what he had been forced into, Kenan was starting to dislike his father. He hated being a criminal, though he was yet to be asked to actually carry out anything illegal but he knew that in the not too distant future it would definitely be on the cards. His parents were now constantly fighting which had previously been unheard of but Jean could see how unhappy her only son had become. Every night she would plead with Del but he wouldn't even discuss the subject let alone change his mind on it. After one particularly nasty row, when Jean had actually threatened to leave, something she had never done in all their years of marriage, Kenan was summoned to his father's study.

"What's up?"

"Take a seat Son. I want all this fightin' between me and your mum to stop but that won't happen while you have a face like a smacked baby's arse. For fuck's sake pull yourself together and just fuckin' get on with it. Tomorrow I want you to take a step up in the firm. There's a shipment to be paid for and I think you should be the one to do it, looks good as far as the men are concerned. I never want to ask them to do

anythin' that I or my boy isn't prepared to do."
That was a joke and Kenan knew it, his father took minimal risks but expected maximum gain. Nodding his head, he also knew that there was absolutely no point in arguing the fact.
"I'll give you the details tomorrow, for now just go and give your mum a hug and for fuck's sake put a smile on your boat, no wonder she's depressed the poor cow."

The following day after he'd been told to pull his socks up, Kenan entered the house on Roach Road and he could feel all eyes were upon him. Carl, Steve, Stevie, Levi, Sammy, Freddy, Gordon and Mad Tony were all in situ which was strange as they usually appeared at different times or at least staggered in within a span of half an hour. Today it seemed as though they were all in early on purpose, almost like an initiation and Kenan felt uncomfortable. Levi was the only one to smile but he was so huge that even after knowing him for years, his smile was still enough to intimidate Kenan.
"Boss wants to see you."
Kenan nodded in Levi's direction but didn't say anything and instead made his way towards Del's office. Sighing heavily, he really wasn't looking forward to this but after taking a few seconds to compose himself he, like everyone

else he knocked and waited to be invited inside.
"Come! Argh there you are son. Take a seat and listen to what I have to say. The people you will be payin' a visit to tonight are right nasty cunts so you need to be on your guard. They know you are my boy so there shouldn't be any aggro but you never know. You want to go tooled up?"

Kenan just stared at his dad not really knowing what he was talking about and Del just shook his head in frustration.

"Tooled up? A gun or a knife?"

"No I don't and if you're fuckin' sendin' me into a situation where I might need weapons then you can think again!"

Kenan was handsome but slight in build and he definitely wasn't a fighter, in fact unlike his father he hated violence of any kind. Del stood up and walked from behind his desk, stopping when he was standing directly in front of his son.

"Do you really think I would knowingly put you in any kind of fuckin' danger? For a start your mother would skin me alive. All I meant, look, some blokes find it a comfort to know they have backup at hand. Now these blokes know the score, know that if they harmed a single hair on your head it would mean a full scale fuckin' war!"

Kenan was bricking it but would never admit that to his father as it would show weakness, something Del would hate and make his son pay dearly for.

"Have it your own way then but personally I have always felt that it makes you feel more at ease. Now the meet is at nine so come home have your dinner as usual and then make your excuses. Your mum will be none the wiser and you should be home again by midnight. You need to go over to Berwick Street Market in Soho to an Indie shop that's situated on the corner. Go round to the back and knock on the door. They will be waitin' for you. Don't get into any conversations, just hand over the cash and get out of there. Oh and Kenan, don't try and drive, more chance of being seen and the parkin's a bitch at the best of times let alone at night when the place is heavin' with fuckin' queers and Toms."

With that Del walked back over to his desk, a silent signal that he had done talking. As Kenan joined the rest of the men, Levi was the only one to speak. Guiding him away from the others by the shoulder he leaned in close so that he wasn't overheard. Kenan stood at five feet nine but Levi still seemed to tower above him. The whites of his eyes were amazingly bright and when he smiled, he showed the most spectacular set of teeth Kenan had ever seen.

"You okay kid? I know the first time out is a little dauntin' but you'll get used to it."

"What if I don't want to?"

"Don't want to what?"

"Be here, do this? I ain't no gangster Levi but the old man won't fuckin' have it. I'm being forced into this and I hate it, I fuckin' hate it!"

Levi Puck inhaled deeply. This wasn't good, wasn't good for Kenan, the firm in general nor any of the blokes that worked here. They played a dangerous game, your mind had to be focused and your heart had to be in the job, if it wasn't you were libel to make slip ups.

"I get you man but you need to get your head in gear, get caught and you bring trouble down on all of us."

Levi's eyes were now wide open and he studied the young man as he waited for an answer. Kenan closed his eyes and at the same time slowly nodded his head.

"Good lad."

That evening was the weekly family get together and though he was quiet, Kenan still tried to engage over the dinner table but he wasn't that convincing and Jean was watching her son like a hawk. As per normal Allison was kicking off about something and nothing but he didn't have

the energy to get into a debate with his sister. Her mood was dark and she was spoiling for a fight so Kenan just stayed tight lipped. It didn't stop Del interjecting and within seconds they were going at it like hammer and tongs.
"Ally! Why do you always have to fuckin' start?! For once can't we just have a nice family dinner?"
"Oh that's right, it's always my bleedin' fault……………"
Sitting next to Dawn, Kenan suddenly felt her hand on his under the table. The others were too busy arguing to notice when she whispered.
"You okay hun?"
Her kind words made him feel like crying and not wanting to appear a sissy and risk his father's wrath, he smiled and then excused himself from the table. Jean had been watching and now also getting up from the table she followed her son up to his room.
"Are you alright darlin'? Only you ain't yourself."
"Yeah mum I'm fine thanks."
"You're not, a mother can tell but I won't pry. Just remember Son, don't do anythin' in life that you don't want to do no matter whose puttin' pressure on you and that includes your dad. Whatever happens I'm here for you, please don't ever forget that."

Jean placed a kiss upon her baby boys head before leaving him alone, it did no good to keep harping on. Her children's happiness was paramount to her and none more so than her boy. When and if he wanted to talk then he would go to her, until then, she would just have to wait.

At precisely eight that night Kenan went into his father's study and collected the small backpack that had been left out for him. Taking a sneaky peek inside his eyes were out on stalks when he saw the bundles of fifty pound notes and for a fleeting second he considered doing a runner and never coming back. Quickly realising that it wasn't an option he zipped up the bag and headed out of the door.

Catching the tube from Edmonton Green to Oxford circus, the journey took roughly twenty minutes and would give him enough time to locate the premises and have a nose about before the meet. Exiting the station Kenan walked along Regent Street and then turned left onto Marlborough. It was a bit of a hike but finally he came to a junction where Berwick Street crossed his path horizontally. He'd been to this area before but it had always been in the daylight and suddenly it seemed like Soho had come alive

with hordes of people moving in all directions. Reaching the end of the road he saw 'Indie Creations' situated on the corner just as his dad had told him. The window was full of what Kenan could only describe as hippy gear and he wondered if anyone actually ever bought the stuff or if it was just a total front for illegal activities, activities he had been forced to be a part of. A narrow alleyway ran between 'Indie Creations' and the shop next door and cautiously Kenan made his way down to the rear of the shops. It was a dead end and his destination seemed to be the only premises with a back yard. Pushing the latch down on the gate he stepped onto a concrete pad of no more than twelve feet square. Tapping on the back door he waited for it to be opened and looking down at his hands could see them visibly shaking. Kenan had had enough and decided there and then that after this his old man could go and fuck himself. Hearing a bolt slide he put his thoughts to the back of his mind knowing he was about to come face to face with whoever he was supposed to be meeting.
"Yeah?"
"I've been sent to make a payment."
The man standing in the doorway was almost touching the header and if Kenan had thought that Levi was big, he was nothing compared to

this bloke. The man didn't offer his name and only gave a nod of his head for the visitor to come inside. There was little light as Kenan stepped over the threshold but having difficulty seeing would turn out to be the least of his troubles. Before the door had been closed all hell broke loose. Armed police burst inside and bundled the two men down the hall and into the front of the shop which was totally void of stock, Kenan's initial assumption had been correct. A single trolley suitcase sat in the centre of the room and it wasn't rocket science to work out what it contained. Del had told him it was just a visit to make a payment but Kenan now realised he was also there to collect as well.

Now surrounded by officers, Detective Inspector Ian Dudley began to speak to the man and then Kenan.

"I am arresting you on the charge of supplying class A drugs. You do not have to say anything but, it may harm your defence if you do not mention when questioned something which you later rely on in court. Anything you do say may be given in evidence. Graham, take them away and make sure they don't fuckin' talk to each other!"

D.I Dudley had been waiting months for this opportunity and tonight he had hopefully hit the jackpot. After much debate and a long wait to get a warrant, listening devices had been installed just a week earlier and it had paid off. Opening up the case he was somewhat disappointed with the haul, oh there were drugs inside but nowhere near the quantity Ian had been hoping for. Grabbing the rucksack that had been wrenched from Kenan's back Ian unzipped the top and was pleasantly surprised to see bundles of notes. At least he would have two collars tonight but he had to admit that not only did the kid seem very young, he in no way looked like a typical dealer. He was smartly dressed, was amenable and had been polite when asked his name and address. With a good brief he could possibly get away with a three stretch but Ian supposed it was better than nothing. Peter Hanson, the guy who had opened up, wouldn't be so lucky and when Ian did a mental calculation and came up with at least a stretch of fifteen years, he smiled. All in all it had been a good day's work but he still wished he could have collared whoever was in charge because it certainly wasn't the kid who'd been arrested.

Over in Edmonton Del was like a cat walking on hot coals. He continually snapped at Jean which really wasn't like him. By two am he was pacing up and down with worry but there was no one he could call, well at least not until the morning so he had no choice but to wait it out. Sergeant Tom Jones was, he'd heard all the jokes a million times before, on Del's monthly payroll. It wasn't much and he was the only bent copper Del knew but the man was able to put feelers out at any station to find out what was going on. Luckily he actually worked out of Charring Cross nick which was where Kenan and his accomplice had been taken.

As soon as Jean woke she went straight into her sons' room and instantly knew something was wrong. Kenan's bed hadn't been slept in and he never stayed out all night without letting her know. Entering the kitchen she saw her husband sitting at the breakfast bar. Del had dark circles under his eyes through lack of sleep and his hair was standing on end from continually running his fingers through it in frustration.
"What's going on Del?!"
"The boys been arrested."
"Kenan? Oh my God why?!"
"I'm not exactly sure as they haven't officially charged him yet but it doesn't look good so prepare yourself for the worst."
"What on earth are you talking about? Del? Del!!!!"

There was no reply as Del Foster was already half way out of the front door.

# CHAPTER SEVEN

Morris Carter had now been incarcerated in prison for just over six months. Initially he had been sent to Wormwood Scrubs and had struggled with the regime and constant noise. Complaining daily did no good whatsoever and only resulted with him being ghosted over to Wandsworth within a fortnight of his arrival. It hadn't bothered him and strangely, though the surroundings weren't that different to the Scrubs, he'd settled in well, at least he had after paying out for protection. It was something that had really gone against the grain but at least he was relatively safe from assault. Finding out who ran the wing had been easy and after asking for a visit, a meet was granted two days later. Jono Parker, a high profile drugs importer, ran the wing and even though he was aware of exactly who Morris was, he wasn't about to make an exception for anyone. Jono was serving twenty to life so knowing he wasn't going to get out any time soon or ever come to that, he didn't take any notice of a person's reputation on the outside. Morris swaggered straight into Jono Parkers cell without knocking and was as usual full of self-confidence and bravado.
"Hi Jono, I'm Morris Carter."

"I know who you are and it's Mr fuckin' Parker to you! So what do you want?"

"I've been told that you're the guvnor and I would like to ask for a bit of protection while I'm in here please."

Jono eyed the stranger suspiciously, it was obviously his first stretch as he didn't know how the system worked. Was he being setup? For several seconds Jono didn't speak as he mulled the situation over in his mind. Confident that there was nothing to worry about he continued.

"It can be arranged for a price but if you ever deviate from our fuckin' arrangement then it stops instantly and you will be left to your own devices. I might also add that anyone who tries to cross me is not looked upon very fuckin' kindly by the others, namely the blokes on my payroll."

"Understood Mr Parker and I'm a man of my word."

"Oh and Carter? Never come into my pad again without waiting to be invited!"

Morris' face reddened with embarrassment and after apologising profusely, he shuffled out of the cell with his head down and made his way back to his own abode.

Marcus made sure that every week two hundred was paid into an anonymous bank account just to keep his brother safe and it appeared to be working. Morris was hot headed at the best of times and Marcus was of the opinion that he had probably already kicked off several times by now. It was something you just didn't do, not if you valued your health, so when he'd been contacted by one of Jono Parker's men on the outside, he agreed without hesitation. Two hundred quid wasn't much by the Carter's standards but it soon mounted up over the months but still Marcus never missed a payment. He didn't discuss the arrangement will Eli as he knew his father could go either way on the matter. It was likely that he would tell his son to make sure that it continued but there was also a slim chance he would say no and that Morris was a Romany and Romany's weren't bullied by anyone. To say nothing was easier than to have confrontation and just like his dear late mum, confrontation was one thing Marcus hated. It was the one thing that actually set him apart from the rest of his family.

With prison food such as it was, Morris had gained an enormous amount of weight. To begin with, well at least for a couple of days, he had refused the stodge that was dished up but hunger got the better of him and now spam, potatoes and all things fattening were the order of the day. Arriving at Wandsworth it had been a bit like Christmas for Morris when he saw all of the men, many who were exactly his type but it turned out to be a lot harder than he thought to get off with someone.  You had to be very careful not to approach anyone that wasn't queer or gay for the stay or you were liable, with or without protection, to get a severe beating.  Instead his days were spent reading and writing letters to his father.  It wasn't something he'd had much experience of in the past but for now it at least killed some time.  The days could really drag if you didn't occupy yourself and as he'd never been one for pumping iron, there weren't many alternatives.  Sharing a cell with Timothy Gilmore, a seventy something former safe cracker, really cramped Morris's style and he longed for a younger, sexy pad mate.  Initially the old boy had been interesting with his tales from the past but after you'd heard a story for the fifth, sometimes sixth time, it became not only boring but annoying.   As he was paying for protection, Morris wasn't asked to do anything for Jono in return and initially he had refused to carry out any kind of work for the Prison service, sighting a bad back or a sprained wrist, anything rather than get his hands dirty.  After his initial six month revue he was deemed as lazy and told that if he didn't comply, then all canteen entitlements would be stopped.  Morris couldn't imagine living without his deodorant and soap, let alone not having access to his favourite barley sugars. With a great deal of animosity he reluctantly agreed and was put to work in the Prison laundry. For the first couple of days he hated it but by the end of the first week, when he knew the ropes, it actually became enjoyable. Hot and steamy, the work actually helped him to lose the weight he had gained and within a month he was eight pounds lighter.

Robbie King strutted onto the wing a few weeks after Morris had begun his laundry duty. Standing six feet in his stocking feet he was built like the proverbial brick shit house. Looks wise he wasn't much to write home about but his physic was exactly Morris's type. Their eyes locked in the canteen over the evening meal and Morris couldn't stop staring. Unaware that Robbie was gay, he could only admire the man from a distance until a chance encounter in the showers would change their lives. After a particularly busy day, Morris was relaxing, just standing and letting the hot water run down his body but when he momentarily opened his eyes for a second he saw Robbie washing himself further along in the stalls. As he rubbed soap over his biceps and licked his lips suggestively,

Morris was no longer in any doubt. Without a care of being seen, the pair were at each other in seconds and Morris received and gave the rutting of his life. This led to as many encounters in the showers as they could get away with but still it wasn't enough. For someone so strongly built, Robbie King was extremely effeminate, he wanted to take care of his new partner and they both wanted to be together all of the time. Morris knew he had to go cap in hand and ask for a favour, a favour that would no doubt be very expensive. Walking along the landing he stopped outside Jono's cell, tapped on the door and waited, compulsory for anyone who wanted to speak to the wing King, to be invited inside.
"Enter."
"Hi Jono, I wonder if I could have a moment?"
Jono Parker motioned with his hand for Morris to take a seat and at the same time a flick of his head told the other two inmates, who had just been in to settle a canteen payment in lieu of past credits, to make themselves scarce.
"How can I be of assistance Morris?"
"It's me and Robbie. We've kind of, well we've kind of gotten into a relationship. You probably don't like queers and …."
"My dear Morris, I have no opinions on who you should or should not be sticking your cock into.

Now what do you want from me?"

"I would like old twat Gilmore moved on so that me and Robbie can share a pad."

Jono sucked in air between his teeth and at the same time as the annoying sound could be heard he slowly shook his head.

"That's a big ask, I mean it ain't going to be easy or cheap come to that. A lot of palms will need greasing and I reckon it will set you back about five grand give or take."

"I don't care Jono, I'll pay whatever it takes. Get your man to contact my brother and he'll sort it for me."

Jono did just that though Marcus wasn't very happy with the price tag. If it wasn't for the fact that he had to keep his father happy he would have refused but Eli had taken the sentence badly, his health was declining and Marcus didn't want it on his conscience should anything bad happen while Morris was locked up.

Six days after the request saw poor old Timothy Gilmore physically manhandled from the cell. His personal items were thrown out onto the landing and as the old man began to gather up his books and clothes Morris just watched and gave a wry smile.

"I thought we was rubbing along nicely Morris so why have you done this?"

"Oh fuck off you old cunt and get your stuff out of my way. You bore me fuckin' senseless with you incessant stories and it weren't as if I was ever gonna fuck you now was it?"

Timothy just stared open mouthed, it never ceased to amaze him how people could be nice to your face one minutes and treating you like shit the next. He'd thought he had a good friend in his cell mate but now he was being discarded like a piece of rubbish and it hurt the old man. With his problem now firmly out of the way Morris welcomed his lover with open arms. Sourcing fury throws and soft furnishing at an exorbitant price via Jono, the two lovebirds soon had the place looking more homely, Robbie seemed to have a natural flair with design and Morris liked being taken care of. The sex was off the scale and if it hadn't have been for his lost liberty Morris wouldn't have minded staying here forever. Everything was fine for a few weeks until the couple had their first argument. It had started out as a moan by Robbie about how untidy his boyfriend was but within a few minutes the row had escalated to a full blown fight. Screaming and punches being thrown could be heard throughout the landing and many of the inmates stepped out of their own cells to listen and get a better view. Morris was a hard man but Robbie was no push over and had a good height advantage. They were both spoilt queens and neither was about to give in, the result, Robbie ended up with a black eye and Morris had scratch marks down his cheek. The brawl was halted when two of Jono's men intervened, much to the disappointment of the onlookers who were cheering and baying for the two men to go in harder. There was nothing like a good scrap on the inside to get the men excited and now their enjoyment had been stopped but one look from Sid McNamara, Jono's second in command, saw them all retreat to their cells without further complaint. If screws had been in the area or at least any that were not receiving back handers from Jono, then Morris and Robbie would have been separated and no longer allowed to share a cell which would have devastated them both. While Morris just wanted a relationship that only revolved around sex and of course being waited on hand and foot, Robbie had become infatuated with his lover and jealousy was now the order of the day. If Morris so much as looked at another man let alone speak to him, there would be murders when the two were alone in their cell, so much so that Morris was called into Jono's pad when there had been complaints from a couple of the screws. Being summoned wasn't a good thing and even Morris was nervous as he tapped on the steel door.

"Come!"

"You wanted to see me Mr Parker?"

"Take a seat Morris."

A chair had been strategically placed in the centre of the room and doing as he was told, Morris was on edge as he sat down.

"Now it has been brought to my attention that you and your boyfriend are having far too many domestics and it stops now!"

"But I ......"

"I said, it stops now!!!"

In a fleeting second Jono was out of his seat and was now standing directly behind his visitor. Moving swiftly, he had the man in a headlock and jerking his forearm under his victims chin he roughly forced Morris's head upwards.

"Do you know how easy it would be to snap your fuckin' neck right here and now?"

Swallowing hard Morris managed to slightly nod his head.

"You might be a someone on the outside sunshine but in here you are nothin'! If I say jump, you say how fuckin' high Mr Parker? Do I make myself understood!?"

Again Morris managed to nod and then as quickly as the assault had taken place it was over.

"Now get out and if I have to fuckin' call you

back in here a second time, the outcome will be far different."
"Yes Mr parker understood and I'm sorry to have caused you any trouble."
Walking back to his cell Morris was seething. On the outside that cunt Jono would have been toast for what he'd just done and having to suck up to the bloke really went against the grain. Still, Morris realised he was lucky, he had sex on tap and was, for a price, able to get his hands on almost anything he desired. He knew his old man would do anything to keep him happy while he was inside and Morris had taken advantage of that ever since his cell door had slammed shut. From now on he would be nice to Robbie but he was damn sure he would make him suffer when he shagged him. Anal sex could be tender and loving between two men but also rough and very painful and tonight Robbie King was going to find out just how painful it could be.

# CHAPTER EIGHT

Just a few weeks after Morris Carter had begun his lustful affair, Kenan Foster was to have his day in court. Del had paid for the best criminal lawyer in London and Felix Montgomery, because it was the first time Kenan had ever been in trouble, had fought hard to secure bail, albeit on a tag. For Kenan, the past few weeks had been a nightmare, with constant questioning by his father and constant crying by his mother, at times he felt like screaming. Finally when Del was sure that he had his story straight and wouldn't crumble under cross examination, he moved onto his boy's fitness. The barrister had forewarned them that a custodial sentence was most definitely on the cards and Del wanted Kenan prepared. Three times a week father and son, along with Mad Tony and Levi Puck, would stay late at the office. A physical programme was worked out and weights were installed. Up until that point Kenan had always been on the slight side, tall but thin in stature. Now he had bulked up nicely and after Del had insisted on a course of steroids, of course unbeknown to Jean, a good shape and muscles had formed. Initially Kenan had outright refused to take the drug but if he was totally honest, he was now really

pleased with the results.
The night before his trial he had his last meeting at the office.  Mad Tony and Levi Puck had been asked by Del to have a talk to his son.  Being the only two men in the firm who had actually done any real time, they were in a perfect position to put Kenan in the picture of what would happen and any pitfalls he was likely to experience.
Entering the office Kenan was surprised at the welcoming committee but there were no smiling faces, whatever was about to happen was deadly serious and Kenan could feel the knots begin to form in the pit of his stomach.
"Take a seat Son, the lads want a word with you."
Suddenly Kenan was scared, he didn't know if he'd done something wrong but he'd had enough of people giving him shit and any second now he was about to bolt and make a run for it.
"Don't look so worried Son.  I asked the fellas to have a chat with you, get you ready for life on the inside and forewarned is forearmed or so they say.  Levi?  Do you want to start?"
Kenan instantly calmed down and took a seat at the table.  He was keen to hear anything that could help him as he was now just hours away from being locked up and he didn't mind admitting that he was scared shitless.  Levi's

voice was deep but his tone was unusually soft, he could see how scared the kid was and he didn't want to make matters worse but he had to be honest if his advice was to be of any use.
"I ain't gonna sugar coat things Kenan, what you're about to go through will be rough. You need to keep your head down, don't tell anyone your business or about the firm or it could be used against you. Someone will challenge you, they always do and you have to stick up for yourself 'cause the fuckin' screws sure won't. You might come off worse but once the bullies know you ain't an easy target they will leave you alone. The second bit of advice I have is stay clear of the fags, you're a good lookin' boy and they will be on you like flies round fuckin' shit. You have to let them know you ain't anyone's bitch!"
Kenan could be seen to visibly swallow hard, he hadn't given that side of his sentence a second thought and now, well now he felt sick to the stomach.
"Don't sign up for the induction course."
"What's that?"
"It allows a prisoner to find out what will happen inside on a day to day basis."
"Ain't that a good thing Levi?"
"For fucks sake! No it ain't."
"Why?"

"It straight away tells the blokes on the wing that you're a newbie and you'll also be seen as a fuckin' sissy. Try and pal up with someone, never go to the showers alone or allow yourself to be in a situation where they can get to you alone. It ain't easy but you must try. You'll get those that are just gay for the stay and they will probably leave you alone but the real queens on the wing will all want you for their own and they are the ones you have to watch. They go about in fuckin' packs, just like hyena's the dirty cunts!"

"Okay Levi, I think you've made your point." Del was worried and if he had to be honest even he hadn't thought too deeply about the sex side of prison.

"Tone, what you got to add?"

"Well, I've done a few stretches in my time, I wasn't much older than you on the first one and I always found it easier if you seek out the wing guvnor."

"I thought you said the screws won't help you?"

"Not the fuckin' governor you soppy little twat! I mean the guvnor, the top bloke who rules the wing. You didn't think the guards control anythin' did ya? Fuck me Del! Your boy ain't half lived a sheltered life. As soon as you're settled you have to seek him out, it shouldn't be hard. You then have to ask for protection."

Mad Tony then looked in Del's direction.
"It ain't goin' to be cheap by the way but if you don't want a hair on his pretty little head touched, then that's the only way forward."
"I don't give a shit what it costs, who do I need to contact?"
Tony started to laugh and Levi Puck soon joined in. It was obvious to both that Del had never done a stint at her Majesty's either.
"You don't, they will get in contact with you. That's about all we can offer you advice wise kid. Keep your head down, do as we've told you and you'll be out in no time."
Mad Tony didn't believe his own words for a second but there was absolutely no point in putting any more pressure on the kid than was necessary.

The family showed a united front and were all at the Court by nine the following day. Jean was in floods of tears even before sentencing and Allison was her usual stroppy self.
"How much longer do we have to wait, I've got a job to go to you know!"
Not one to normally say boo to a goose, Dawn turned on her sister with venom.
"For God's sake Ally, think of someone other than yourself for once. Our baby brother is about to lose his liberty, the least you can do is

support him!"

"I am supportin' him it's just………"

No one was listening and motioning with her eyes in the direction of their mother Dawn then turned and walked towards the court bailiff. Del was pacing up and down with no real purpose he couldn't think straight and selfishly just wanted this all to be over with. Dawn was the only one who was really trying to find out what was happening and when she returned her face was sombre. Kenan had been taken down to the holding cells as soon as they'd arrived and there was little information available other than that her brother was already in a meeting with his barrister.

At ten on the dot they were all called into the court room and told to stand until the Judge, Redvers Cottington, had taken his seat.

Expecting a two day trial the family were shocked when Kenan's plea of guilty was read out. Instantly Del was on his feet and shouting in the direction of his son.

"Kenan, what the fuck have you done!?"

"Order! Order in this court or you will be held in contempt."

Jean grabbed the sleeve of her husband's jacket and yanked him down into his seat.

"Would the defendant stand. Kenan Miles Foster, you have admitted to your crime and for that you are commended. You have saved the government purse and I will therefore take that into account in my sentencing. As there was no evidence put forth by the prosecution other than you being in the vicinity where drugs were held, I will sentence you only in respect of the enormous amount of cash you had upon your person. I am in no doubt that this money was to be used for the purchase of drugs and as you are unable or unwilling to tell the court where this money originated, I have no other option than to sentence you to custodial incarceration for a length of two and a half years. Bailiff, take him down."

Jean began to scream uncontrollably, her boy, her baby was going to be locked away with murderers and villains. Del tried to take her in his arms but Jean pushed him away roughly and at the same time glared at him in such a way that it sent a shiver down Del's spine. He decided to see if they could at least see Kenan before he was taken away but was informed that a short visit would be allowed but Kenan had asked solely to see his sister Dawn. As Dawn was led into the bowels of Wandsworth Crown Court she felt the total degradation of the place. Oh it wasn't dirty or anything but it felt almost as if the shame, rage and futility of life seemed to emit from the very walls that now held her brother. Guided into a small holding cell that consisted of a bench, table and two chairs, she was asked to take a seat. A few minutes later Kenan was led in wearing handcuffs, a sight that made her heart break.

"Hello my little darlin', how you holdin' up?"

"I'm okay Dawnie, its mum I'm worried about."

"She will be fine, she has us lot but you, why Kenan, why did you plead guilty?"

Kenan lowered his head but he hadn't been quick enough to hide the pools of tears that now filled his eyes.

"My brief told me that if I got found guilty and that was a forgone conclusion, I would be looking at a five maybe six stretch. How could I fight it Dawn, they had me fuckin' bang to rights girl. It's okay for the old man to blow a gasket but he ain't the one doing the time. I made up my mind about this a few days ago but decided to keep it to myself. Judging by the old man's reaction in there I think I made the right call don't you?"

Inappropriately and out of nowhere they both burst out laughing, you had to know their father well enough to see the funny side and the light relief definitely brought a moment of respite from what was about to happen. They both stopped when the door was unlocked and two uniformed officers entered the room.

"Time to go Sonny."
Dawn stood up and hugged her brother.
"Stay safe and stay strong Kenan. No matter what's thrown at you remember, its thirty months that's all. It sound much less like that and I for one will be counting off the days."
"Maybe I'll get lucky Sis and be banged up with Uncle Jimmy."
With that he was gone and she slowly made her way upstairs to face the barrage of questions that she knew was imminent.

Built in 1851 and previously known as Surrey House of Correction, HMP Wandsworth is famous for being the prison that Ronnie Biggs escaped from in 1965. Even though the last execution was carried out at the prison in 1961, the gallows still remained until 1994. The building itself is stark, built of grey stone and brick there is absolutely nothing inviting about the place but that was probably the intention when it was constructed. Twin towers flank the arched and gated entrance but luckily this is not the first view of the prison that new inmates get to see.

As the van pulled through the gates, Kenan was oblivious to his new surroundings until he stepped out into the cool midday air. Glancing all around he saw the harsh brick buildings that were austere and cold. Inmates could be heard calling from the barred windows but these were not greetings of welcome. There were three other new arrivals in the van that day but none of them looked at each other, preferring to keep their eyes on the ground so that they couldn't be challenged by anyone. Led single file through an unassuming metal door, they were taken one at a time into a side room and told to strip. A body search was then carried out and when it was over Kenan felt violated. He was then photographed, had his fingerprints taken and was offered a shower which he declined. A sweat top and pants were thrust at him. He was then given a prison number and his personal property was recorded and boxed ready for his release date.

"You want to sign up for the induction programme?"

The guard was eyeing Kenan suspiciously looking for any sign that he could tell the wing boss that there was fresh meat on the block.

"Look pal, all convicted prisoners are given the opportunity to participate in the induction programme. It allows you to see what will happen within the prison. Well, on a day to day basis at least. There are programmes and activities available and you'll be told about visiting entitlements and the roles of certain staff

within the prison. So?"
"No thanks."
"Please yourself. Follow me."
Taken to the 'first night block' a dedicated bank of cells for all new prisoners, Kenan was told to step inside. He was roughly handed sheets, a pillow and blanket and the door was then slammed shut. Throughout the night the hatch was lowered hourly in case he was suicidal and that and the constant sound of muffled voices and even screams, stopped any chance of real sleep.

The following morning at six on the dot the cell door was opened and after being shown where to go for breakfast, Kenan was led into the main prison area. Wandsworth contains eight wings on two units. The smaller of the two contained the three wings that were originally designed to house women. Unluckily for Kenan he was allocated to the larger, C wing to be exact. If he had thought that the first night cell area was noisy he was now in for a rude awakening. The cell door on the upper landing was unlocked and he came face to face with an area smaller than his en-suite had been at home. Handed his bedding and a fresh set of clothes, he was told in an abrupt tone to get inside. Two bunks were situated on the right hand wall with a table and

two chairs on the opposite. A man of around forty lay on the bottom bunk so Kenan supposed he was on top. About to introduce himself, he momentarily stopped when the cell door slammed shut making him jump slightly.
"Hi, I'm Kenan, Kenan Foster."
The man, who Kenan would later learn was called Terry Oaks, ignored his new pad mate and turned over to face the wall. It was only just after nine and Kenan knew he was in for a long day so when his door was again opened around four that afternoon he was grateful to see another face. It was another prisoner pushing a trolley who handed Kenan two breakfast packs for the following morning. Handing one to his cell mate he then climbed up to his bunk to inspect the food. The bag contained breakfast cereal, milk, tea bags, coffee whitener, sugar, brown and white bread, jam and margarine or some type of butter spread. Nothing he picked up looked remotely appetising and what there was, wasn't much and while it was certainly enough to sustain a man, it wasn't anything compared to his mother's food. Placing the bag at the side of his pillow Kenan laid back and closed his eyes, desperately trying to imagine a place, any place other than where he was. Hopefully he would be allowed out of the cell tomorrow as he was desperate to find out who

ran the wing and ask for the man's help.

# CHAPTER NINE

Since Morris had been locked up business on the outside was failing dismally. Eli had decided to take a back seat and had put Marcus in charge. He wasn't a born leader and without his brother he was struggling. He had tried his best but finally when the monthly accounts were well and truly below par, he knew he had no option but to inform his father, before they had no business left. Entering the grand dining room for breakfast his face spoke volumes as he took a seat opposite Eli. Milly Garrod, a local woman who came in daily to clean and cook meals had just placed a plate of eggs and bacon in front of her employer. Turning to Marcus she asked what he would like to eat.
"I'm okay thanks Milly, I'll just have a piece of that fine looking toast."
Milly smiled warmly, Marcus was such a sweet man unlike his bully of a brother but she could tell that something was wrong and not wanting to be in the vicinity if the old man hit the roof, which he did almost daily, she made a hasty retreat back to the safety of the kitchen.
"Morning Son, how are things going?"
Marcus swallowed hard, he knew how this was going to pan out but there was no other option.

"Dad I'm strugglin', really strugglin' and I just can't seem to get to grips with things."

Eli slammed his aging hand down onto the table top.

"I fuckin' knew it! You ain't a patch on your brother. So now I have to come out of fuckin' retirement to sort out your mess?! Get the car."

"I didn't mean straight away Dad, I just need a bit of advice that's all."

"Fuckin' advice?! You couldn't run a fuckin' piss up in a brewery. This needs sortin' and sortin' today. You know its Appleby next week and I ain't about to miss it. I have attended that fair for as long as I can remember, can you imagine the shame I would feel tellin' the family that I won't be there because my twat of a son can't manage without his big brother. Phone round, I want everyone present and if they argue, tell them no fuckin' exceptions if they want to hold onto their jobs! Oh, and tell them I want the meet at the Bull not the office."

Marcus didn't argue further, he knew better and for him and the blokes it was now going to be uncomfortable. His father had run the firm with military precision, it was probably the reason that the Carter Empire had been so successful but the men wouldn't like it. Morris was a good boss, firm but wouldn't let anyone pull the wool over his eyes, plus he was more relaxed than their father and since Eli had chosen to go into semi-retirement, the atmosphere had vastly improved. Getting up from the table Marcus made his way into the hall and then began to make the calls.

Thirty minutes later and Eli and Marcus pulled up outside the pub. Business was still carried out at the office but Eli had purchased the Bull when it had come up for sale a few years earlier. It reminded him of the past, the good old days spent in the back room when he had first started out. It was where Tommy Day had introduced him to the underworld, it was special and Eli saw no reason not to use the premises. The unit was good for business but the pub, to him at least, still felt more comfortable. Jojo Murrow had long since left as barmaid, in all honesty she'd never been the same since Tommy died but in an age old tradition, her daughter young Jo and then her granddaughter Sally, had taken her place. This time there had been no shenanigans, Eli was a one woman man and that's the way it would stay for the rest of his life. Pushing open the front door, Marcus had walked in but the usual cheers and boisterous comments immediately stopped when Eli Carter followed his son. Gus Walker, who'd been in the firm longer than anyone and that included Morris and Marcus, realised that the proverbial shit was about to hit the fan. The old man no longer ventured here or the office so there must be something seriously wrong! They were then all invited to take a seat at the large table situated in the centre of the room.

"Right, because my inadequate son can't run this business without his brother, I will be back in the saddle for the foreseeable future. Since the two clowns I fathered have taken over things have begun to slide and I ain't havin' it, I ain't fuckin' havin' it, do you hear!!!!!?"

Gus was about to interrupt but thought better of it. He had only challenged his old boss once but after the beating he'd received, he knew he didn't want to risk history repeating itself. Eli might be getting on in years and according to the boys his health wasn't the best but he was still a mountain of a man and even after all these years, Gus really didn't fancy his chances if it came down to a confrontation.

"You will all pull your fuckin' socks up or suffer the consequences. Gus, you're in charge of the girls, pull them in and order them to work their skinny arses harder, if it takes a few slaps to make your point then so be it. Smiter, you can up the pressure on the loan sharking. I've had a butchers at the books and several of the fuckin' muppets are late with their payments, take Jack with you."

Eli reached into his Crombie coat pocket and pulled out several folded pieces of paper.
"Chester, have a butchers at these and let me know what you think. It was somethin' Morris had been working on. Its regardin' a plan he had for a security firm over Dagenham way but keep it low key, if it's a goer I don't want the Handley firm getting wind."
"Ain't that gonna be steppin' on a few toes guv?"
"Possibly Chester but work is work and if we get any fuckin' beef we'll deal with it or have you lot gone fuckin' soft?"
Everyone at the table, including Marcus, lowered their heads.
"Good. Now I'm away for a few days at Appleby, when I get back I want to see a vast fuckin' improvement or heads will roll. Marcus, take me home."
When the door closed behind them, the men were grinning from ear to ear. The adrenalin was pumping, this was what they had signed up for in the first place and of late things had become boring and mundane. Maybe it was a good thing that Morris was banged up after all.

Appleby horse fair, Appleby in-Westmoreland Cumbria, is held on the first week in June. It runs from Thursday through to Wednesday and is an annual coming together lasting for a day short of a week, with the main events happening on Friday, Saturday and Sunday. First started in the late 1600's, it is a chance for many travellers of the Romany community to come together. Horses are taken down to the sands, an area near to Appleby town centre where deals are struck and friendships are made. Ridden into the water to be cleaned and to show off their prowess, the horses are washed before being tied up outside the Grapes public house. There have, in the past, been many accusations of animal cruelty but the very great majority of horses at the fair are well looked after, well treated, and in good condition. Closed to vehicle traffic for the main days of the fair, the event is relished by the Romany community. Stalls line the road and contain fortune tellers, palm readers, buskers, music stalls as well as a vast array of clothing stalls for the youngsters. Tools, hardware, china, horse-related merchandise including harness and carriages are all on offer and many will fill their vans with items to sell on in the ensuing months.

After a little shy of a four and a half hour drive, Eli finally pulled up in the Castle car park at just past midday. He had long since given up taking a trailer himself, well ever since Angie had passed away. Now on visits Elli slept in a small annex van that belonged to his elder brother Duke and his daughter Kezia. Never having married, Kezia's sole purpose in life was to care for her father and it was job she took very seriously, fussing over the man to the extent that at times he felt as though he couldn't breathe. The Carter's still travelled on the road in a troupe of six vans, relatively small compared to some groups but it was also well known and accepted that Duke was Shera Rom, head gypsy of the extended Carter family and spokesman for the whole Romany community in the united kingdom. He had never been challenged for that title even with his aging years it just wasn't the done thing with travellers. They respected each other, their traditions and loyalties. Again, as was tradition, Eli knocked and waited for the van door to open, you never stepped foot into a travellers home without first being invited. As soon as she saw him, Kezia wrapped her arms around her uncle in a loving embrace. It was something, the warmth and show of love, that Eli still missed but only since the death of his beloved wife had he ever considered selling up and re-joining his community. Now every year it was becoming more and more difficult to leave his family when the fair came to an end.

"It's good to see ya again Uncle Eli, come on in

and I'll make you some tea."
Stepping into the trailer was like going back in time. Whereas the youngsters now all wanted the most up-to-date vans with all mod cons, Duke's was just the opposite. Traditional in every way, the small area shone like a new pin. High gloss floor to ceiling units filled one side and housed a vast selection of Royal Crown Derby china that Dukes wife had collected for many years until her death a decade earlier. White leather sofas covered in heavy clear plastic to stop any dirt, were positioned along the other side and at one end was a dining table and four chairs, once again upholstered in white leather with the plastic still intact while at the other end was a double bed, covered in the most elaborate white lace bedspread. Duke looked up from what he was doing, re-stitching a small bridle that one of the children would be using the following day when she took her pony down to the river. Smiling from ear to ear Duke stood up and embraced his brother.

"Good to see you Eli and I'm glad you made it."
"I wouldn't miss Appleby for anythin' brother."
"Me neither but we ain't gettin' any younger and none of us know what tomorrow will bring. How are the boys?"
"Don't get me started on those two muppets. Morris is banged up doing a three and a half

stretch and Marcus is about as much use as a chocolate fuckin' tea pot. He's got a good nature I can't deny that but when it comes down to business he's fuckin' useless. My Morris though, well he's a right hard bastard but he's got a short fuse, never a good combination. I tell you Duke, I'm ashamed of the pair of them!"

"That's harsh brother."

"Is it? You tell me when a Carter has ever gone to prison?"

"Well we've had a few near feckin' misses."

Eli laughed at his brothers words. Duke was right it was probably more down to luck than judgement but still, he wished it hadn't been one of his sons to be the first in the family.

"Anyway, enough about me, how are you doin'?"

"Not a lot changes in this community brother. We still travel the roads and get looked on like a piece of shite by most gorger's but that's never goin' to change. The youngsters seem agitated most of the time but I ain't got a feckin' clue what it is they want. They don't really want to travel, don't want a permanent home or to pay taxes but cry like babies when they are looked down on. I tell you Eli, I don't half hanker for times gone by, you know when Daddy and Mammie were still here, you know what I mean?"

Eli touched his brother's shoulder tenderly.
"I do Duke, I do indeed. So what's the plan for this weekend?"
"The usual, horses down to the sands tomorrow, always an enjoyable sight. A few beers and a bit of a barbeque are planned for Sunday to celebrate the end of another, hopefully peaceful Appleby and then that's it for another year. You stayin' till Sunday?"
"Do you really need to ask, Appleby is in my blood. Where's Kezia sleepin' tonight?"
"She'll take the couch as usual."
"It makes me feel uncomfortable Duke. Why don't I take the couch and let her have the annex van?"
"Not a chance! She wouldn't hear of it and you know it ain't our way. You are a guest and as such you will be treated royally."
Eli knew that the conversation was over, he admired his brother's love of tradition and for a second he wondered just what it would have been like if Angela had been prepared to join his family and become a traveller. The boys would have turned out so differently and for a second but only that, he resented their life together.
The next two days were spent enjoying the entertainment and reconnecting with old friends and family members, even if that family was

very distant. In the Romany community you never forgot your roots or the people you were connected to and as usual it had warmed Eli's heart when he was introduced to the younger generation and they were welcoming and respectful. Gorger's, especially the younger generation could learn a lot from these if only they would stop looking down on Gypsies and tarring them all with the same brush. As the fair came to a close Eli was feeling exhausted. The few days he had spent at Appleby had been full on and he didn't know how many more years he would be able to attend but seeing his brother and niece made all the fatigue worthwhile.

# CHAPTER TEN

Kenan was beginning to feel stir crazy and it was only his second day. Nights were the worst, men screaming and calling out for their mothers, hard men who were probably experiencing nightmares of guilt. Kenan had tried to cover his ears with his pillow but nothing was able to blot out the horrendous noise. Terry Oaks still hadn't opened his mouth which was unnerving. It would take until later that day for Kenan to find out that the man was in for sexual crimes against a minor but had refused to go onto rule 43 as a vulnerable prisoner. He'd received beating after beating, one of them almost fatal but still he continued to profess his innocence. It wasn't only Kenan he was ignoring but the whole population, loose lips and all that, if he kept his head down and didn't mix with the others maybe they would finally leave him alone.

When the cell door was at last opened, Kenan was told where the showers were but he politely declined and instead washed his face, hands and under his arms at the small sink situated in the corner of the room. The door remained locked until 12.30 when he was finally let out and told to make his way to the canteen for lunch. Terry Oaks lunch was delivered to the cell and Kenan would learn that the man never left the tiny room except to shower when everyone else had been locked up for the night. It wasn't special treatment, only a wish by the governor to avoid another death on his watch. As Kenan pushed on the double swing doors of the canteen he felt as though all eyes were on him, fresh meat and pretty meat at that. Thankful that he had decided against a shower, he picked up a tray and then slowly moved along the serving area. The choice was Potatoes, Chicken breast or fish, veg, soup and unlimited bread but none of it looked appetising, still, he had to stay strong so filling his tray he looked around for a seat. Morris Carter hadn't been able to stop staring at the young Adonis and it hadn't gone unnoticed by Robbie King who slammed down his cup, glared at his lover and then marched out of the canteen in a strop. Morris beckoned for Kenan to join him and just happy to be acknowledged, Kenan walked over as fast as his legs would carry him.

"Hi, Morris Carter, pleased to meet you?"

"Kenan, Kenan Foster."

"What a pretty name."

Suddenly Kenan realised what was happening and although the older man didn't come across as camp or effeminate, there was no doubting that he was gay. The two ate in silence and when the food was gone Kenan asked the question.

"I need to find out the wing Kings name, can you help? Maybe get me an introduction?"

This was music to Morris's ears, if he did the lad a favour then Kenan would owe him and oh how much fun they were going to have.

"It's Jono Parker but I will need to go and see him first. What cell you in?"

"First floor landing in the corner, I'm sharing with Terry Oaks."

"Oh dear that's not good. I assume you know what he did?"

Kenan shook his head so Morris went on to explain about a five year old girl who would, thanks to Oaks, never become a mother. The revelation made Kenan sick to his stomach and he knew the first request he was going to make was to be moved.

At 4.30 Kenan again took a seat beside his new found friend and stared down at his tray in disgust. The offering was exactly the same as lunch only this time Kenan had opted for fish instead of chicken. He was unsure of exactly what fish it was but it definitely wasn't cod or haddock and the taste was strong, almost as if it was starting to go off.

"Disgusting isn't it? You'll get used to it kid, either that or you'll fuckin' starve. Now about that meet you asked me to arrange, Jono will see you first thing in the mornin' so make sure you opt for a shower."

Kenan's face broke into a smile, it was such a small thing but just maybe this Jono bloke would be able to help him out.

"Thank you Morris, thank you so much!"

Entering his cell for what he hoped would be for the last night, Kenan looked at Terry with utter contempt and Terry realised that the new bloke must have been informed of his so called crime.

"I didn't do it, didn't do what they're saying I did."

At the same time as climbing up to his bunk Kenan almost spat out his reply.

"Well you would fuckin' say that wouldn't you. You're a real piece of shit you cunt!"

Within seconds Terry was out of his bed and now standing, he was chest high to Kenan's mattress.

"Listen here you little wanker. You know nothing about me, about why I'm in here. Do you really think if I was fuckin' guilty I would put up with all the crap that these twats dish out at my expense? I could have gone on the 43's and been protected but why the fuck should I

when I didn't do anythin' to that little girl."
Terry stopped talking then and just stared daggers at Kenan who suddenly felt guilty. Maybe the bloke was speaking the truth, he wasn't sure what to believe but the one thing he did know was the fact that it wasn't any if his business and he had to stop following others like a fucking sheep.

"Look, I'm sorry okay? I'm new and this is all like a fuckin' mind field for me. If you don't want to accept my apology that's up to you but it was sincere."

Terry didn't reply and just ducked down onto his own bunk.

The next morning when the cell door was unlocked and left open, Kenan stepped onto the landing and came face to face with Morris.

"Ready for your meet?"

"I ain't showered yet."

"I know, I was waitin' for you in there. Never mind that now, it doesn't bode well to keep the bastard waitin' so move that pretty little arse along!"

That last remark sickened Kenan and he swallowed hard. He was as nervous as hell and was desperately trying to remember all that Mad Tony had told him. He couldn't recall a thing and when they reached Jono's cell, he could feel

his whole body begin to shake. Morris knocked
and waited for the word 'enter!' to be heard.
"Mr Parker, this is the young lad who would like
a word with you."
"Thank you Morris, you can go now."
Morris was more than a little put out, he wanted
to hear what was being said and hoped with all
his being that Jono would move the kid into his
cell. He hadn't given a second thought to Robbie
King and his lover was still sulking over the
interest that Morris had shown over Kenan. He
may have been built like the proverbial brick shit
house but Robbie was a queen and his over the
top campness was blatant. He had definitely
been the woman in the relationship and as such
he had a vicious tongue but bitching and
moaning to his lover had never got him
anywhere so this time he was trying the silent
treatment but that wasn't having much affect
either.
"Take a seat Kenan, now how can I help you?"
"Thank you Mr Parker. I was wondering if it
would be possible to get a cell move? I'm happy
to pay but I need to be away from Terry Oaks,
not that I'm sayin' he's guilty or anythin', what
he did or didn't do is none of my business but I
would feel a lot happier if I was away from him
and a single cell would be even better."
Jono Parker laughed out loud as he mocked the

innocence of the young man.

"I bet it fuckin' would but singles are scares and at a premium. If I can swing it you're looking at the best part of five grand, think you can cover that?"

Kenan vigorously nodded his head. He hadn't bothered to ask for the protection that Tony had advised him about, thinking if he got a single cell he wouldn't need it, now he just had to convince his father to part with the cash when he came to visit in a fortnight's time. It all turned out to be irrelevant as the one and only conversation Kenan had with Terry Oaks turned out to be the last. A prisoner lying on his bunk was at his most vulnerable and two days later Terry was found in bed, his face battered to the point that it was unrecognisable. The only piece of evidence found was a blood soaked sock containing a PP9 battery. The entire wing was put on lockdown while an investigation took place. Police were brought in from outside but as usual nobody saw anything so it would go unsolved. While the act of murder wasn't common place, it did happen on occasion but the men on this unit didn't let it bother them too much. Kenan on the other hand was traumatised by the event and he was glad that he wouldn't have to share a cell with anyone for the foreseeable future. He also didn't think to tell Jono that he no longer needed a single so the wheels were now in motion and he would soon realise, that he was still expected to stump up the cash or pay the consequences.

Del pulled into the carpark at ten on the dot. The visit with his son was scheduled for eleven and he wasn't relishing having to wait for an hour with all the low life's that filled the small canteen on visiting day. Jean had handed him a list of questions she wanted Kenan to answer, such as was he eating properly, were they treating him well? Now as Del sat in the waiting area he scanned the piece of paper, sighed heavily and then screwed it up and hurled it into a small metal waste bin in the corner of the room.
"Visitor for prisoner 28563 Carter?"
Immediately Del got to his feet and made his way through to security. He hated being frisked and having to stash his personal belongings, all but a few quid, into an allocated locker. The whole thing took just under twenty minutes but finally he was sitting at the table waiting to see his son for the first time in two weeks. As Kenan walked towards him Del could see the boy had lost weight and had dark circles surrounded his eyes, circles that had never been there before. Deciding to keep up a cheerful front and not

mention it, Del stood up with a wide grin on his face.

"Hello there kid, how you holdin' up?"

"I'm okay Dad thanks, it ain't no holiday camp but it's not as bad as I thought it would be."

"Cuppa and some chocolate?"

Kenan nodded his head and then watched his old man head over to the small serving area that only visitors were allowed to approach. A few minutes later he returned with two steaming paper cups and enough bars of chocolate to keep a hoard of kids happy for a week.

"Dad! You do know I can't take any back in with me and there's no way I can eat that fuckin' lot."

They both started laughing and for a split second it was just as if they were back in the kitchen at home sharing some good old banter. At exactly the same time they both stopped laughing and looked at each other with serious expressions.

"It won't be for long kid, you'll soon be home tuckin' into one of your mums roasts."

Kenan's eyes filled with water and conscious that others could see him, he wiped his eye with the cuff of his sweatshirt.

"I need some cash Dad, well not me but to be paid to Jono. He runs the wing."

Del frowned, this was just what he was afraid of.

"This Jono geeza giving you grief, 'cause if he is I'll…."

"No, no it ain't anythin' like that. They stuck me in with a kiddie fiddler or so the rumour goes. Anyway, Jono can get me moved but at a cost."

"Let me have the details and I'll get it sorted."

The relief on Del's face was evident and Kenan could visibly see his father's shoulders relax. Del wasn't the only one to relax and even though he knew his father would never say no, all the same it was good to hear that it would be dealt with.

"It don't work like that Dad, they will contact you."

The rest of the time passed quickly with talk of his mother, sisters and what had been happening. Even tales of Allison kicking off didn't bother him and when the bell rang to signal the end of the visit Kenan wanted to wrap his arms around his dad and never let go.

Within two days of seeing his father, Kenan Foster was on the move. It was only three cells further along the landing but it was still a move and to top it off the cell was a single meaning there was no chance he would have to share with anyone in the future. His new found friendship with Morris Carter was flourishing even if at times Kenan didn't like how touchy feely the man could be. Making sure to never encouraged Morris, he was at least grateful to have someone looking out for him. Things sadly changed a week later when the two men were in the shower at the same time. Kenan noticed Morris give the only other person in the room the nod and seconds later he and Morris were alone. This time there was no innuendos or touching that could be misconstrued as a mistake. Morris walked straight over to Kenan, roughly pushed him up against the tiled wall and as he tried to kiss him and force his tongue into Kenan's mouth he grabbed hold of the youngster's penis and began to masturbate him but Kenan fought hard and managed to push Morris away.

"What the fuck are you doin'?!!!"

"Come on pretty boy, you know the fuckin' score! I've helped you out now it's time for you to return the fuckin' favour."

"Over my dead body you fuckin' poof!"

"If that's what it takes but I had rather hoped for a bit of a relationship."

Kenan snatched up his towel and shampoo and ran from the shower room. Still half naked he quickly made his way to his cell and pushed the door closed. His heart was rapidly beating as he paced up and down not knowing what to do next. The following day it was the exact same scenario only this time Morris held on for dear life and managed to painfully insert a finger into Kenan's rectum before he escaped his assailants clutches. Back in his cell he yet again wracked his brains trying to think of what to do but in reality he knew there was only one thing for it, he would have to approach Jono and yet again ask for the man's help. Not waiting for an invitation, Kenan quickly dressed, made his way to the upper landing and rapping hard on the steel door, waited to be invited inside.

"Hello young man, didn't expect to see you again so soon. What can I do for you?"

"Please Mr Parker you gotta help me."

Jono began to laugh, if he had a quid for every time he'd heard those words from a newbie.

"I ain't got to fuckin' do anythin' sunshine. I ain't a fuckin charity and whatever you want will have to be paid for and that's only if it's achievable. Now what's the problem?"

"Morris Carter is trying to fuck me and I ain't interested. That ain't my bag Mr Parker, not even for the stay but he won't take no for an answer."

Jono walked over and placed his hand on Kenan's shoulder.

"I'm sorry kid but that's one avenue I never go down. Sex is a very strong desire and somethin' I don't get involved in. True, this prison, well this wing at least, does belong to me but even I

draw the line when it comes to relationships. I'm strictly a money man and there's little cash in tellin' someone who they can or cannot give a portion of the old pork sausage to. We don't tolerate a nonce in here but anythin' else is just categorized as being queer and in here that's just what Morris is, another queer no more no less. Now he's from the Carter firm and on the outside that means somethin', carry's clout if you know what I mean. It's down to you to protect yourself and the best advice I can give you is to never be alone with the cunt!"
Jono felt sorry for the kid but the blokes in here wouldn't appreciate being dictated to regarding their sex lives. They toed the line when it came to obeying orders but who they were or were not shafting was their own concern. Kenan returned to his cell a nervous wreck. He was determined to fight off Morris at any given opportunity but he realised it was only a matter of time. There was no point in asking the screws for help as he would be seen as a grass and on the outside there was jack shit his old man could do to help him. Of all the things that could happen when you're banged up, this had to be the worst.

# CHAPTER ELEVEN

For three long weeks Kenan fought off Morris's advances as hard as he could but when he was at last assigned work duties in the laundry he knew he wouldn't be able to survive much longer. A day's work in the laundry started at 8am with a lunch break at noon and by the end of the first day he was worn out. On the second day at five on the dot the inmates were slowly led two by two back to their cells and when only Kenan and Morris were left, Kenan knew he had been set up. The guard seemed to be taking an age to come back to the laundry and for Kenan Foster his time dodging Morris's advances was finally up. His heart was racing and he was scared beyond belief but he wasn't going down without a fight. It was pointless, he was no match for Morris Carter who was twice his weight, not to mention the fact that the man also towered head and shoulders above him. Morris sauntered over to where Kenan was standing in front of the laundry table.
"Time to pay your dues pretty boy!"
"Fuck off you queer cunt!"
Kenan ran around to the other side of the ten foot stainless table and a game of cat and mouse ensued but it didn't last for long. Unaware that

the guard on duty, Steve Mason, was as bent and corrupt as any guard could be and the fact that he often did favours for Morris in return for a blowjob, Kenan prayed that the screw would soon come to his rescue. Morris lunged forward and at the same time Kenan reached for one of the long wooden poles that were used to lift the boiling sheets from the drum of the washers. He would rather die than let the pig in front of him have his way but it was futile and as he tried to raise the pole upwards to get a good swing, Morris grabbed it from his hand, spun him around and roughly pushed him down over the linen folding table. Everything seemed to be happening in slow motion but within seconds Kenan's jogging bottoms and pants had been ripped down exposing his young naked buttocks. Sweat poured from his brow as he fought with every bit of strength he could muster. Reaching out he managed to grab a metal measuring scoop and bending his arm backwards he rammed it as hard as he could into Morris's side. Momentarily it halted the assault as Morris cried out in pain but then filled with rage, he grabbed Kenan's wrist and slammed it down onto the metal with such force that the bone snapped in two. Screaming in agony Kenan could now do little but accept his fate. With one hand holding down his victim, Morris

released his rock hard penis with the other and forcibly raped his victim. As the skin of his anus ripped and tore Kenan screamed out in agonising pain but was silenced when Morris slapped his open palm over the young man's mouth. With every thrust the agony was excruciating and silently he thanked God when it was over pretty quickly. As Morris withdrew, Kenan thought his ordeal had finally come to an end but Morris wasn't done yet. Having had his enjoyment he was now nursing a painful injury to his side and he rained down blow after blow to the back of Kenan's head. With ease and still filled with rage, Morris proceeded to flip Kenan over and began to pummel the youngsters face.
"You scrawny little cunt! You've been leading me on for weeks and now you go cold on me and have the fuckin' cheek to assault me?!"
Blood poured from Kenan's nose and mouth, not to mention a large wound on the side of his head. He could feel the room begin to spin and as his eyes started to flutter, Morris allowed Kenan's body to drop onto the cold concrete floor with a thud. Kicking out at his victim, the tip of Morris's shoe made contact with Kenan's temple.
"That'll fuckin' teach you to lead me on!"
By the time the guard returned the attack was over and nodding his thanks in the Screws

direction, Morris casually stepped over the crumpled and bleeding body of Kenan Foster and strolled from the laundry back to his cell. Officer Mason gazed down at the hurt inmate and knew that Carter had gone too far this time. The kid needed to go to the hospital wing and reports would now have to be filed. It wasn't anything Steve couldn't cover up but it was unnecessary hassle and he would be having words with Morris as soon as he'd got this all sorted. Calling loudly for assistance Steve then knelt down beside Kenan and attempted to pull his trousers back up.
"Okay Son, we'll soon get you sorted."
Kenan went to mouth something but the words just wouldn't come out of his mouth. He felt the room begin to spin again and suddenly he fell into unconsciousness. Now Officer Mason began to panic, a bad beating was one thing but a death on his watch was an entirely different matter and something he wouldn't be able to cover up. Worried beyond belief, he sighed in pure relief when seconds later two additional officers joined him in the laundry room.
"Get a stretcher now!!!"
Kenan was rushed to Wandsworth healthcare wing and within minutes all hell had broken loose after the duty doctor, Sam Carmichael, examined his patient.

"What in God's name happened to him!? On second thoughts don't bother but this inmate needs to go to hospital immediately!"
The guards that had moved him had finally managed to pull up Kenan's trousers up on route but they couldn't conceal the blood than now covered the stretcher where he lay and Doctor Carmichael, along with the other injuries, was concerned about internal damage via the young man's rectum.
"I'll call an ambulance."
"There isn't any time, you will have to transport him yourselves."
This had suddenly escalated out of hand and Steve Mason began to panic again.
"We can't do that Doc, we have to follow protocol."
"Officer, for once you either ignore bloody protocol and take him to hospital now, or explain to his family how he died!"

A little over two miles away, St Georges Hospital on Blackshaw Road was the nearest to the prison and the van screeched to a halt outside the accident and emergency department in less than eight minutes. Officer Mason was ordered by the doctor to remove the handcuffs and reluctantly Steve did as he was told. Kenan was rushed for a CT head scan which revealed swelling on the brain but it was a further twenty four hours before Del and Jean were informed. Immediately Del contacted his Solicitor and he was finally allowed to see his son a few hours later. Filled with rage and with tears streaming down his face he could only stare down at Kenan's motionless body. Tubes were coming out of his nose and mouth and the dried blood of almost two days ago still remained so taking a moist tissue, Del tenderly began to dab his son's face. Furious at the situation, he wanted answers, but no one was talking so after the threat of legal action and when his solicitor intervened, an appointment was at last made for Del to see the governor the following day.

Davis Holmes had been the Governor of Wandsworth for the past ten years and in that time he had experienced many threats by inmates, gang members and also the families of those incarcerated. Nothing really bothered him, it was par for the course but the story regarding what had happened to Kenan Foster, as a first time offender, was horrendous. Del was shown into the governor's office by a prison guard and marching over to the man's desk, he promptly began a tirade of abuse directed at the lack of care and security given to young men incarcerated for the first time. Del threatened

violence, legal procedures and going to the press but it was the latter that bothered Governor Holmes more than anything.  Breathing deeply, the governors' tone was soft as he spoke.
"Have you ever been to prison Mr Foster?"
"That's got fuck all to do with it!  This is about my son and how you allowed him to be beaten by some fuckin' maniac.  You had a duty of care and you fuckin' failed dismally!"
The governor slowly nodded his head.
"I cannot agree more Mr Foster and the only reasoning I can give and it is in no way an excuse, is simply the fact that my men are over worked, under paid and the prison service, this prison in particular, is badly under staffed.  Obviously there is no way that Kenan can be released until he's served his sentence but I will personally make sure that nothing happens to him for the remainder of his stay."
Del was a little taken aback by the response, it wasn't what he'd been expecting and he now felt relief that at least he was being heard.
"While my boy is in the hospital I want visitin' access to him with no screws in the room."
"That can be arranged, though of course officers will have to be posted outside of the room.  I will make the call as soon as our meeting is over."
Still enraged, Del nodded his head and then turned to leave.  As he reached the door the

governor spoke again and his words confused Del but he was too angry to ask what the man meant.

"I really am sorry Mr Foster, no man, young or old should ever have to experience what Kenan went through, it was a debauched and sickening act!"

Completed in 1976 and with almost eight thousand employees, St George's hospital became part of the trauma network in 2010. Dealing with many horrendous traumas, there was a need for privacy and as such there were many individual private rooms that led off of the wards, one of which now housed Kenan Foster. Day after day Del sat by his son's bedside only returning home to wash, change his clothes and to eat. Jean was beside herself and pleaded with Del to let her visit with him but he refused. He was adamant that no mother should ever have to see her son in that condition and besides, he was the only one who had been given permission for visits. On day five of his admission and after Del continually willed his son to wake up, Kenan finally opened his eyes. Seeing his dad he gave Del the broadest of smiles but within a few seconds, when he remembered what had been done to him, he began to sob. It was a heart breaking sight and one Del had never witnessed before, well at least not from one of his own children.

"Come on boy, you're okay now. I've sorted it so that you finish your sentence without any more aggro."

Still the sobbing continued and Del started to worry that his son might have received brain damage.

"Please Kenan, you have to put the beating behind you. We all get a pasting in life at some time or another, especially in our game but it's over now."

"It ain't that Dad it's....."

Kenan searched his father's face, he wanted to share what he'd been through but he also knew how Del felt about queers. Would he now view Kenan as one, would he be disgusted with his boy rather than see what he had suffered at the hands of that pig?

"What is it Son, come on, you can tell your old man anythin' you know that."

"Anything, really?"

"Anythin' no matter how bad, I'm your Dad for fucks sake!"

"He raped me Dad, pinned me down and raped me and when he'd shot his fuckin' load in me he decided that I hadn't suffered enough so he tried to kill me."

For a few seconds Del couldn't speak, couldn't

really take in what he had just been told.  Of all the things he could have imagined, this most definitely wasn't one of them.  Now he understood what the governor was on about at their meeting and inside he could feel the rage begin to build up.  Moving forward he took his only son in his arms and held Kenan as tightly as he could while his son just sobbed and sobbed.  "Now don't you worry about it, it's over now and I will sort that cunt out.  You mark my words, the bastard will pay and pay dearly!" Remaining in hospital for a further three days until the doctors were happy that he wouldn't relapse, Kenan was returned to prison but not before his dad had spent that time questioning his boy.

"So that queer cunt, what's his name?"

"Morris Carter but he's protected Dad.  Jono Parker takes care of him on the inside and when Carter first came onto me I asked Jono to make it stop but he wouldn't get involved.  On the outside Morris is a known face."

"A fuckin' known face!  He won't have a bastard face left when I've done with him.  So where's he hail from?"

"Essex and by all accounts they are a right nasty crew Dad.  Can we just leave it, I'm struggling to come to terms with what happened to me let alone deal with anymore aggro."

"Sorry Son but I can't let this one go."

"Please Dad, please don't tell Tony or Levi, I'm so fuckin' ashamed."

"Okay, okay, whatever you want but you have nothin' to be ashamed of kid, you didn't ask for this to happen."

Del had no intention of keeping his word, if the men knew exactly what that cunt had done to Kenan it would fire them up even more and that's exactly what was needed if they were going to go to war with another firm. He decided to take his time and find out as much about the Carters as he could before he went into action but one thing he was certain of, they would pay and pay dearly for what had been done to his boy.

On his return, Kenan was placed in solitary confinement for his own safety. He didn't mind, the single cell and having no contact with others made him feel safe. Not having to carry out any work duties either, he knew Morris couldn't get to him. The Officers who had been on duty the night of the assault had received a severe dressing down from the governor and there was even mention of losing their jobs should it ever happen again, the threat was specifically directed to Steve Mason. Now they all treated Kenan with compassion and respect, even going above the call of duty to get him anything he asked for. By the time of release, Kenan Foster had a television, a play station and more books than he would ever be able to read.

# CHAPTER TWELVE

A week after Kenan was returned to prison Del was still having trouble coming to terms with what had been done to his son. Some animal had violated his little boy in the worst way imaginable and it felt to Del as if a piece of his heart had been ripped out. If he could have gotten to Carter himself, then Del would have had no problem exacting his revenge, of that he was sure. He hadn't yet shared the information with Jean as he couldn't judge how she would handle it. He doubted that she would, so deep down he knew he'd done the right thing so long as his son didn't breakdown in front of her. Kenan was the light of her life, she loved the girls dearly but there is no bond like that between a mother and her son. He also hadn't yet shared his troubles with his firm either as he didn't know how to go about it, would they think his son was gay? Now he was angry and had a short fuse most of the time with anyone he came into contact with and that included his own loyal men. Finally when he'd snapped at Levi for the umpteenth time over absolutely nothing, Mad Tony took him to one side. He was taking a risk but if someone didn't have the balls to speak to the guvnor, then sooner or later he was sure that blood would be shed, whether it was the boss's or another employee he didn't know but either way, this had to stop and stop now!

"I might be speaking out of turn and I don't know what the fuck is goin' on with you Boss but you have to stop this or the guys are gonna end up fuckin' walkin'."

Del just stared at the man and as he did so his eyes filled with tears, something Tony had never seen before. Normally Del Foster was as hard as they came and would die before he showed any emotion to anyone and at times that even included his own family.

"Do you need to talk Guv?"

Slowly Dell nodded his head and the two made their way into Del's office where Tony walked over to the filing cabinet, removed a bottle of scotch and poured them each a large measure. Sitting behind his desk, Del now had his head in his hands.

"So what's goin' on Del? You're angry and apart from that you've hardly been here for the last couple of weeks and when you are it seems like you don't want to be?"

Raising his head Del wiped his palm across his mouth as he sighed heavily. It felt as if he had the weight of the world on his shoulders but he knew he had to share his burden, that or he was going to totally lose the plot, not to mention his entire workforce.

"Kenan's in solitary for the remainder of his sentence."

"What the fuck did he do?!"

"Please Tone, just let me finish and don't say anythin' or I don't think I can do this mate."

Mad Tony, real name Anthony Morgan, had been a member of the firm for over fifteen years and was as loyal to his boss as any man could be. To see Del acting like this actually caused him emotional pain. Placing his palm in the air was a silent gesture telling his boss to continue.

"My boy did fuck all wrong! Some dirty cunt took it upon himself to rape Kenan and not happy with tearin' the poor little sods arsehole to shreds, he then proceeded to beat him almost to death. He's been in the hospital for the last nine days, actually in a coma for a while with fluid on the brain. I've been with him for most of that time but now he's back in Wandsworth and in protective custody for his own safety. There ain't been any charges brought nor will there be so it's down to me to get justice but the cunt has got another six months to go yet and to top it all off he's a face and part of a serious firm by all accounts."

When he was sure that Del had finished talking Tony spoke.

"It ain't just your justice Guv, it's all of ours. That kid is like a son to us and it goes without sayin', we're all in this together. I've got a pal in Wandsworth, Earl Delaney, well he ain't really a pal, more of an acquaintance actually. Anyway, Earls serving twenty to life so not much chance of getting' out, as such there ain't anythin' he won't do, for a price of course. You want me to sort it?"

Del thought the offer over for a few seconds.
"Yes but that ain't all Tone, as this animal is part of a family firm I want to hit 'em where it hurts as well."

A week later and Tony Morgan paid a visit to Wandsworth Prison. The attack on Kenan wasn't gone into in any detail, only what was required of Earl and strangely it wasn't murder. In his conflab with Tony, Del had been very specific, he wanted this Morris guy to lose his manhood. A fee of ten grand was mentioned and once payment had been made to Earl's wife, he would take action as soon as he could. It hadn't bothered Earl, he hated faggots, especially the ones that preyed on the innocent or vulnerable. Tony hadn't needed to explain what had happened, purely by what they had asked Earl to do spoke volumes.

Returning to the Roach Road headquarters, Tony

walked in to find the whole crew, including the boss, sitting around the large conference table. Del looked up, his face tortured and desperate to see an acknowledgement that at last something was about to happen.

"All sorted Guv, well ten large and it'll be sorted."

Del smiled and clapping his hands together the meeting got under way.  Explaining in exactly the same manner as he'd done with Mad Tony, Del revealed all that Kenan had been forced to endure.  When he'd finished he looked each of them in the face, trying to see if there were any expressions of disgust but all he saw was pain. Levi couldn't contain himself and was out of his seat in seconds.

"The dirty, filthy, fuckin' cunt!!!  What are we gonna do about it Boss?"

"It's okay Levi, calm down.  I've taken measures to have him sorted but I want to hit his firm as well.  All I have is a name and the fact that he runs out of Essex somewhere, so it's goin' to take a bit of plannin'.  That said, there's no rush as we have to make a fuckin' impact and I'd rather we take our time and get it right.  The cunts name is Morris Carter and I want you all to put your ears to the ground and find out anythin' you can. Our usual collections and deliveries will continue but for the foreseeable, no new

business until this is sorted. Come on then, move your fuckin' arses!"
In silence, everyone slowly left the building but their lack of conversation wasn't anything to do with fear or what they were about to undertake. Each of them was thinking about Kenan and what he'd been through. He would be out in just over four months and they all wanted to be able to welcome him home with open arms and tell him that he would be okay and that the monster that attacked him would never do it again.

It was almost a week before any news came through and for the entire time Del was on tenter hooks, not only at work but at home as well. As he hadn't confided in Jean she didn't have a clue what was going on and they'd had several arguments regarding his attitude and snappy way with the girls, especially when Ally visited but still he revealed absolutely nothing. Early one Monday morning he arrived at Roach Road to find the building unlocked. Cautiously entering he was met by the sight of Gordon Mayes who was sitting at the table waiting for him.
"Fuckin' hell you soppy twat, you almost gave me a bleedin' heart attack!"
"Sorry Boss but I wanted to speak to you before

the others got here."
"What's troubling you?"
"I've got some news and it ain't good. Seems this Carter crew are right hard bastards and…"
"You goin' soft or somethin'?"
"No Guv, please sit down and just listen."
Del raised his eyebrows but did as he was asked, he just hoped none of his other blokes were starting to get cold feet.
"Fire away, I'm all fuckin' ears!"
"As I was sayin', they ain't just an ordinary firm. There's another, young brother named Marcus and the old man is called Eli."
"Fuckin' Eli! What an earth sort of a name is that?"
"A gypsy name boss."
"Not fuckin' pikey's please!"
Del wasn't stupid, he knew dealing with travellers was a whole different ball game. They could be right slippery bastards and as cunning as the foxes they often hunted but regardless of who they were, he wasn't about to chicken out of getting vengeance for his boy, he would rather die than let this crime go unpunished.
"No boss, not exactly. The old man was born in a wagon so it goes but now they live in a mansion in Upminster. Their business is run out of an in industrial unit in Romford. Apparently, if my source is right, it's like fuckin' Fort Knox."

"And?"

"I get what you're sayin' and Kenan needs his vengeance but this ain't goin' to be easy Boss."

"Nothin' in life is fuckin' easy Gordon if it was then we'd all be fuckin' dead, at least those in our game would be. So what do they deal in?"

"Protection, loan sharkin', street Toms, robbery, about anythin' you can think of really. Not much business done in our line of work, seems the old man has an aversion to drugs for some reason."

"Probably why our paths have never crossed. Right, before that cunt gets released we hit the firm where it hurts, in the bastard pocket! Find out about any collections, dates, times etcetera. Also have a look into where his Tom's work"

Gordon stood up and began to walk towards the door when Del suddenly spoke. Expecting to be given another task, Gordon waited for instructions.

"I don't have to remind you, tight lips and all that?"

Nodding his head, he walked from the room and without another word, left the house. Del remained at the table mentally making plans, he was going to make them pay so badly that they'll wish Morris Carter had never been born.

At the end of that day when Del returned home

he was like a new man and didn't snap anyone's head off just for speaking. It was the weekly family meal and even though it wasn't the same without Kenan, it was something Jean would never allow to stop, not even temporarily. Allison had dared to raise the subject just once and had immediately been shot down in flames by her mother. Jean hardly ever raised her voice, least of all to her children but on this occasion Allison saw just how angry her mother could be when pushed to her limits.
Walking into the kitchen he spied his wife sitting at the table peeling vegetables and bending low he kissed the top of her head.
"What was that for?"
"Can't a man kiss his wife if he wants to?"
"Certainly but from the way you've been behaving lately I would have expected a punch in the back of the head more likely than a kiss."
Her words cut like a knife but he supposed he deserved them, probably deserved more in fact. His behaviour had actually been so bad, that most women would have packed a bag and left by now.
"Low blow but you have every right. I'm sorry babe but I've been under a lot of pressure of late, it's no excuse I know but I think I'm finally beginning to make some head way."
"Well I'm pleased about that thank the Lord,

now are you goin' to get washed before dinner? The girls will be here soon and you'll ruin the food if you keep us waitin' too long."
Smiling lovingly he made his way into the hallway, these weekly meals killed him emotionally. Sitting with his family at a table where a place had been set for his absent son was like a stab through the heart but he hadn't, even at his angriest, dared to mention it to his wife. Jean was coping in the best way she could and who was he to try and spoil that. If this was how she reacted just because Kenan wasn't here, he couldn't imagine what she would be like if she knew the truth. His choice to keep the gruesome facts from her had been the right decision, he was sure of that now.

# CHAPTER THIRTEEN

Since the attack on Kenan and despite Robbie trying to get back in favour with his ex-lover, Morris had kept himself to himself. He wasn't in Jono's best books and knew it, the wing had immediately gone into lockdown and business had come to a complete standstill for twenty four hours. Morris knew he had overstepped the mark and that he would be made to pay in some way or another but he had desired Kenan for so long and when he was rebuffed, he just lost the plot. In hindsight he knew he had probably gone too far but the kid hadn't died and Morris was at least grateful for that, not for Kenan's sake but purely down to the fact that he could have been on a murder charge and ended up being banged up for years. As it was, he surprisingly hadn't been charged with anything and was still on schedule to be released in just under six months' time.

Now balding, Earl Delaney stood over six feet tall and weighed in at twenty one stone. Born in Kingston Jamaica, he had come to England with his aunt some forty five years earlier at the age of six. His mother Missy, a single parent, had thought that it would be best for her only son and he would be able to make a good life for himself but nothing could have been further from the truth. Living in the East End and mixing with others of the same colour but not of the same intentions, Earl soon found himself on the wrong side of the law. His aunt Hannah, a God fearing woman of good standing in the community warned her nephew time and time again but at the age of seventeen when he had once again been brought home by the police, she had finally told him to leave her house. If he changed his ways he would be welcome to return but that was never going to happen. Hannah had duly informed her sister of what had occurred but stuck in Jamaica, there was little Missy could do about things. A heated telephone conversation had resulted in a stalemate and the end of a mother and sons relationship. Earl didn't believe in God, he also didn't believe in being good, preferring to make a living taking what he could from whomever he could. By the age of twenty he was running with the Manga Gang, a name chosen by Devon Williams the leader, after his liking for the famous Japanese comic books. For a couple of years the gang had terrorised the area and gang wars were common place, especially with the Shadwell crew who were trying to muscle in on Devon's lucrative heroin trade. One almighty set-to on a Saturday night on White Horse Lane when knives were pulled had resulted in Earl's first stretch in prison. It would turn out not to be his last and over the next twenty plus years, he spent many of them locked up courtesy of Her Majesty's Prison system. Finally two years ago things had gone too far and a double fatal stabbing had seen him receive a twenty five to life sentence. On one of his few times of freedom over the years he had met Monica Brown and after a very short courtship, Monica had fallen pregnant but Earl had once again been locked up before the birth. This scenario repeated itself three more times before he received his final sentence and he knew he would never be with his baby mama again. Somewhere deep inside there was a small piece of goodness left and he knew that he had to provide for his family, so he began to hire himself out on the inside and now he was being paid by Del Foster.

As a longstanding inhabitant of B wing, it had taken a large payoff to Malcolm Smith, a guard almost as corrupt as Steve Mason, for Earl Delaney to get himself moved to C wing and for the past few days he had monitored Morris at every given opportunity. Keeping himself to himself as most newbies on the wing tended to do, he was left alone to settle in so when he walked around as much as he could taking in the sights, no one took any notice. Earl had soon realised that the man he was to target had a very regimented routine, far more regimented than the prison usually required. He didn't know why but could only put it down to the fact that Morris Carter was scared, scared because of what he had done. The man always went for a shower at precisely six forty five, let out by Officer Mason of course and was then in the canteen ready for breakfast by seven on the dot. Due to the strict time schedules, Earl decided that the shower block was his best and probably only option, so now he just had to sort out a weapon and plan the details of his attack. If successful, he knew he would be made to pay dearly but at least his family would be secure for a while. No wanting to alert anyone by asking for a favour weapon wise, he decided to make his own shank. The complete ban on disposable razors was yet to come fully into force so Earl was able to break open his last remaining one and carefully remove the blade. Cutting the bristles from his tooth brush he used his disposable lighter to melt the plastic and insert the blade into half of its thickness. Next he began to rub the handle on the concrete floor until it resembled some sort of point. It was a crude attempt but all the same would make a double ended weapon and would definitely be effective. Deciding not to wait too long as things on the inside could change in a matter of hours, he would strike the following day and if all went to plan, then Monica would be able to hold onto the five grand she'd already been given and not give him any grief on her next visit. Sometimes Earl had thoughts running through his mind that the cash he earned on the inside was the only reason she visited but then again, if it wasn't for seeing her twice a month, then there would be no visits whatsoever. His aunt didn't bother with him and besides she would be well into her eighties by now, that's if she was even still alive. His no contact with his mother continued but that was irrelevant anyway as she still lived in Jamaica, as far as he knew.

After asking for an early shower he set his alarm clock so that he was already in the block five minutes before Morris arrived. Earl was getting nervous, not because he was scared of the outcome but simply down to the fact that he didn't want to mess things up. His family needed all the help they could get and having to hand the cash back and not receive the final payment would be heart breaking and that was only if she hadn't already spent the down payment. If Earl knew anything of Monica, it was the fact that she could spend for the entire country and not bat an eyelid. From the first day they had met, his Monica had always been a spender and she didn't care who's money it was but if this went tits up and she ended up owing Del Foster, well he didn't even want to think about that scenario. No one in prison liked to get up in the mornings and most would leave it until the very last minute which meant the shower block was empty and the only sound was that of running water. When he heard someone enter Earl was certain it was his man. Turning his back so that Morris couldn't see what he held in his hand he waited to be joined in the large stall. Eyeing the tall, thick set dark man, Morris thought all of his Christmases had come at once. Licking his lips in anticipation at what he hoped might happen he discarded his towel revealing his fully erect penis. Moving towards the man, he was momentarily taken aback when Earl turned and smiled. Morris reached out but didn't expect what would happen next. In a flash Earl produced his home made weapon and slashed out wildly. With water running down his face and into his eyes Earl's timing was off and trying to aim for Morris's groin he missed badly and instead the blade made contact with his victim's cheek. The razor was so sharp that the wound cut down to the bone and Morris screamed out in pain as blood gushed from his face. Luck was on his side that day as Officer Mason was at that second passing the shower block. Running inside he had Earl up against the wall in a matter of seconds. When he'd managed to cuff the culprit he then turned to Morris while at the same time calling out for assistance. Earl's towel was used to stem the blood flow and after getting Morris to his feet, his own towel was wrapped around his body before he was swiftly escorted to the medical wing.

The wound was stitched but not so neatly that it wouldn't leave a massive scar. Sam Carmichael was again the duty doctor and whereas he'd felt pity for Kenan, he felt only loathing for Morris Carter. Unaware that he had been the one to hurt the young inmate, Sam knew that there was usually only one reason why men would be in the shower block this early in the morning. Well he would make sure that this queer bastard wouldn't be so attractive anymore. Always a vain man, Morris was desperate to see his face and when handed a small mirror he screamed out at the image staring back at him.

"Oh my God!!! What the fuck have you done to me?!!!"

"I have done my job, no more, no less. Now get this piece of shit out of my department."

On the outside Morris knew that his father would have paid for top surgeons to make sure that the damage was at a minimum. Now he would be badly scarred for life and there was nothing he could do about it. By lunchtime his face had swollen so much that he had difficulty eating or even drinking anything and when he phoned his brother, Marcus initially didn't recognise the voice on the other end of the phone.

"Who is this?"

"It's me Marcus, I'm hurt bad and you need to come see me as soon as possible. I think I can get a special visiting order under the circumstances. As soon as it's arranged I'll call you back."

Marcus didn't like the sound of this, he also knew that for the time being, the worst thing he could do would be to tell their father. As hard as it was for Marcus to accept, Morris was the apple of Eli's eye and as such all hell would break loose if anyone dared to touch a hair on his precious son's head. Deciding to stay quiet until he'd found out the details and had at least seen his brother, Marcus tried to put the call to the back of his mind.

Earl Delaney had been told to dress and then remain in his cell until he was called by the governor for an interview. It wouldn't go well of that he was certain but in all honesty he wasn't bothered. When an extra ten months was added to his sentence he just shrugged his shoulders, what was ten more months added to the end of twenty plus years anyway. Earl was also moved from the landing and sent back to B Wing, again he wasn't bothered, and at least there he had a couple of friends. All in all it had turned out well and he knew Monica would be off of his back, at least for a while. Now he just hoped that the damage would be enough for Del Foster. He didn't expect the finally instalment and prayed that they wouldn't ask for their money back.

Just as he'd said, Morris was able to obtain a special VO and the visit was to take place in a private room. The injury was so bad that the governor didn't want the other inmates and their families upset by prisoner Carters appearance. When Marcus entered the room his brother was already seated but had his back to Marcus.
"What the fuck's happened Bro?"
Morris just shrugged his shoulders and as he turned, Marcus was speechless at what he saw. The sheepish expression on his face also told Marcus that his elder brother was holding something back.

"Don't shrug your fuckin' shoulders Mo, what the hell happened and I want the truth!"
Morris took a deep breath, this was uncomfortable and he was going to have to admit that he'd rapped a man, in the cold light of day that sounded horrendous and although he didn't care what others thought of him, his brother was a different matter.
"I got mixed up with this young bloke, things went a bit too far and this is the result. Mind you, it could have been a whole lot fuckin' worse."
Morris let out a nervous laugh and then instantly covered his check with his hand as the movement was causing him pain. Marcus could only stare in amazement as his brother just gazed at him wide eyed.
"This ain't no laughin' matter Mo. So what you sayin', you raped the poor bastard?"
Now Morris went on the defensive as his brother's words and tone insulted him and made him feel like a monster, which in his eyes at least, he definitely wasn't.
"Oh fuck off Marcus, you make it sound worse than it was."
"Worse than it was?!!! You tell me, how can raping a bloke be any worse? So this geezer paid you back then?"
"No not really. Seems his old man is a bit of a

player and he organised something from outside. I think he was planning to have me done in but luckily things didn't work out that way. I mean the kid survived, it might have been a bit touch and go but he's back inside and serving out his time in solitary so why would they want to top me?"

"Survived! What else did you do Morris, what the fuck did you do?"

"Look! I fucked him okay and then the little toe rag started insulting me and I admit that I lost it a bit, well a whole lot actually. As far as I know the kid was in a coma for a while but it's over now so can we just move on from it and whatever you do don't tell the old man."

Standing up Marcus began to pace up and down and at the same time ran his hand through his thick black hair. Once again everything was being put on his shoulders and he was sick to the back teeth of it.

"Impossible! For one, that scar runnin' down you face is a complete fuckin' giveaway. Let me do some diggin' and find out if this is really over or if we're lookin' at further repercussions. Who's the old man?"

"Del, Del Foster, runs a firm out of Bow."

"Never heard of him but that means nothin'. Leave it with me and I promise I won't tell the old man until it's really necessary."

"Thanks Mar, you never let me down."
"Don't fuckin' thank me you moron, this is more aggro and I really don't need it."
With that Marcus Carter walked out of the room with a feeling of foreboding regarding what was to come.

# CHAPTER FOURTEEN

On his drive back to Essex, Marcus couldn't get the image of his brother's disfigured face out of his mind. Morris had always fancied himself, actually thought that he was drop dead gorgeous in fact and had voiced that view on several occasions to anyone who cared to listen but that certainly couldn't be said now. Marcus also kept thinking about the poor soul that had been the object of Morris's sick desire and just what all this could turn out to mean. Wasting no time he drove straight to the office. He wasn't about to share what had happened with the blokes, at least not yet but he needed time to think before returning to Upminster and the barrage of question he knew he would be in for from his father. Waiting until just before midnight to go home, when he was sure that Eli would be tucked up in bed, Marcus spent the next couple of hours trawling his father's ledgers and making a list of underworld contacts that could possibly give him information on the Fosters.

At breakfast the next day Marcus, just as he knew would be the case, was bombarded with questions.

"Why were you so late last night? How was my boy? Why did he want to see you so urgently? Is he okay? How….."

"For fucks sake Dad! Give it a rest will you. Golden balls is fine, you know Morris and he always comes up smellin' of fuckin' roses even if he's fallen in shit! There's nothin' to tell he just wanted to see his baby brother. I have to get off now, got a couple of promising business meetings. See you tonight."

With that he grabbed a slice of toast and was out of the room before Eli could comment further.

Pinky Hamilton was coming up to his seventy fifth year but was still very active in the London underworld, if only in an informative capacity. Over his career he had worked for many of the top firms and there weren't many people he didn't know of or much he wasn't aware about, regarding what was happening crime wise. Eli Carter had known Pinky from way back when he was working for Tommy Day and while the two had never been bosom buddies, they had a long standing mutual respect for one another. Years earlier Pinky had started running a small crew out of Bethnal Green and had kept his antics to street robbery and small scale theft so as not to tread on the toes of any other firm. Eventually he had moved up to the Forman firm and even though one firm was based in Essex and the other in the East End, at times mutual business had been carried out between the Carter's and Foreman's, especially when either wanted to borrow bodies that were not well known to the Old Bill in a particular area, hence the paths of Eli Foster and Pinky Hamilton crossed on several occasions.

Marcus drove over to Bethnal Green and parking up outside the block of flats on the Cranbrook Estate he surveyed the surroundings. The area was poor and run down to say the least and spying several youths milling about, he singled out one and beckoned him over.

"You want to earn a quick score?"

The boy, dressed in jeans and a grubby T-shirt that looked like it had been worn for several days without being washed, eyed Marcus suspiciously.

"You some kind of fuckin' nonce Mister?"

"No I am not! But I'm particularly fond of my motor and as such I would like it even more if it still had four wheels when I come back."

The boy nodded knowingly but still eyed Marcus warily as he was handed a crisp twenty pound note for the car to be watched until the man returned. The boy, who obviously hadn't been taught any manners, snatched the money without a thank you and then stared long and hard in Marcus's direction.

"How long you gonna be Mister 'cause I ain't standin' here all fuckin' day?"

Marcus couldn't help but chuckle, the kid couldn't have been much more than ten but he spoke like a seasoned villain. It was sad really but in this neck of the woods they had to grow up fast or be eaten alive by their peers.

"Twenty minutes tops and there hadn't better be a fuckin' mark on my motor kid!"

With that, he made his way up to the first floor landing, stepping over laundry baskets and scattered toys on his way as he searched out his destination. The area was so rundown and as he tapped lightly on Pinky's front door Marcus couldn't work out why an earth the man still resided here. A few seconds later the door was opened just a tad, enough to see who was calling but not enough to be fully visible or vulnerable. From the two eyes that peered around the wooden door Marcus wasn't able to recognise if this was Pinky or not as it had been years since he'd been in the man's company.

"Pinky, Pinky Hamilton?"

Pinky looked the visitor up and down and didn't think the man was a copper, dressed far too expensively for that.

"Who wants to know?"

"I'm Marcus, Eli Carter's son."

Suddenly the door opened fully and Marcus immediately recognised even with the badly wrinkled face and thinning grey hair, that this was exactly the man he was looking for.

"Well bless my soul, ain't seen you since you was a nipper. Come on in son and I'll put the kettle on."

Shown into the small front room, Marcus took a seat on the dilapidated old sofa while his host made tea and he was taken aback with how barren and sparsely furnished the place was. Pinky was living like a pauper which was strange as he remembered his father telling him how much money had been made, especially in the early years. The two china cups clinked in their saucers as the old man shuffled back into the room and it was a pitiful sight.

"So Son, what can I do for you?"

"I'm tryin' to find out about a London firm. My twat of a brother who is presently doing a stint at her majesty's, has got himself in a spot of bother. The old man don't know yet, I think it's best to leave him in the dark until I know what we're getting into. You ever heard of the Foster Firm?"

"Sure have. Del Foster is a bit of a cunt, albeit a very successful one. Runs his firm out of a house on Roach Street, deals mainly in the supply of class A or that's what he was into.

Nasty fuckin' business, weren't like that in our day. Anyway, how's the old man keepin' these days?"

Marcus wasn't there to talk about old times but at the same time knew he couldn't be rude so the next ten minutes were spent reminiscing the tales of villainous acts that had happened over three decades earlier.

"So Pinky, is there anythin' else you could tell me, anythin' that might help us if we come up against any trouble?"

"I know he lives outside of the East End, over Edmonton way. Big house at the end of Streamside Close, called it Timbers though fuck knows why? He's got a wife, two daughters and a son as far as I'm aware. Ronnie Kray is his hero and the soppy twat models himself on big Ron, even down to the sharp suits and greased back barnet, though he ain't queer, well not as far as I'm aware. He's got a right nasty scar on his right cheek, some wide boy fronted him up years ago and left him marked, mind you, I think I would rather that than what happened to the other bloke but that's a long story for another time. Ain't much more I can tell you kid, he has a tight crew, keeps himself to himself and is a right nasty bastard by all accounts."

"No, that's great you've been a big help and I'll be sure to pass on my best to the old man for you."

About to walk out of the front room, Marcus stopped and hesitated for a second before he spoke.

"If you don't mind me askin', why have you never moved Pinky?"

"It's me home Son, only place I've ever lived."

"Good enough reason I suppose. Well you take care of yourself."

With that Marcus left and didn't hear the heavy sigh that came from the front room. Pinky wasn't about to admit to anyone that he had gambled away every illegal pound he had ever earnt. Now with only his state pension and living from hand to mouth each week his addiction had long since ceased as he just couldn't afford it. Making his way into the hall to be sure that the street door had been closed properly, Pinky saw a bundle of cash had been laid on the telephone table. He smiled, the bloke was kind and although not a good trait in their game, it was a lovely gesture from him so Eli must have raised him right.

The car was intact when Marcus reached ground-level though the kid from earlier was nowhere to be seen. Starting up the engine he called Eli to see if he was at home or at the office before making his way over to Bow. Parking up behind several other cars he watched the house on Roach Street. His luck was in as a short while later a Merc pulled up and as the driver got out Marcus peered through the windscreen and could clearly see the scar that Pinky had told him about. Well at least he now knew what the man looked like so deciding to return to Upminster, he sighed heavily at the thought of the raised voices and anger he knew he would have to endure from his father.

Milly Garrod was dusting the ornaments in the hall as he entered the house and she didn't look too happy.
"You okay Mill's, look like you've got the world and his wife on your shoulders?"
"Not really love, he's in a right bloody strop, near on bit my head off earlier and all I did was ask him if he wanted a cuppa."
"Don't let him get to you darlin', you should know by now what a miserable bastard he can be. Where is he by the way?"
"Sittin' in the conservatory but I'd avoid him if I was you."
"Sadly I can't Milly, wish me luck."
With that Marcus walked along the length of the thirty plus feet entrance hall and stepped into the large Victorian style conservatory. He couldn't deny that his late mother had good taste and every one of the fifteen rooms in the

house was decorated with classy and very expensive furniture and soft furnishings.
"I need a word Dad."
Eli's eyes narrowed, it was unusual to say the least when either of his sons came to him with a problem and only then when it had gotten to a point where they couldn't sort things out themselves.
"I want you to listen to all I have to say before you blow a fuckin' fuse okay?"
Eli slowly nodded his head in anticipation of what was to come.
"Morris has caused a situation and please don't interrupt. He raped and near on beat a young kid to death. Now I know you've never accepted that he bats for the other side but whether you like it or not, he does!"
Eli went to speak but was silenced when his youngest son held his hand up.
"He appears to have gotten away with it on the inside but it's not over by a long way. Seems the kid is the only son of a known face. Now I went over to Pinky Hamilton's to find out as much as I could and this geezer can be a handful, deals in class A in a big way so I think we might be in for a shit load of trouble. I mean, would you let it go if it was one of us?"
Eli didn't reply for a few seconds as he mulled over all he'd been told. It had always angered

him to think that his eldest was queer but now he had to openly admit it and it really went against the grain.

"What did your brother say?"

"It was him who told me, that's why he wanted me to pay a visit. Do we sit back and wait until this bloke takes revenge or go in all fuckin' guns blazin' but with no real reason?"

Eli rubbed his head with the palm of his hand, he felt stuck between a rock and a hard place. If he acted before anything kicked off he could be making a mistake but if he waited it could turn nasty.

"Let it ride for the moment but put a plan into action should this Foster geezer come after us. I would imaging he will wait until your brother is released so that will give us a bit of time to get ready. Explain to the men that they need to be on their fuckin' guard but don't let on about your brothers sexual habits okay?"

Marcus smiled and slowly shook his head, would his father ever see his brother in a bad light? The old man hadn't even asked about the poor kid and what damage he had received.

"They already know Dad, have known for years in fact but what Morris does or doesn't do in the bedroom is his concern. The only problem we have this time is the fact that it wasn't consensual and he raped and nearly killed someone."

The words made Eli bow his head in sickening shame but it was useless to protest and try to once again deny the truth.

"Drive over to the office and get things sorted, we need to be ready for whatever is headin' our way and Marcus?"

Marcus turned to look at his father.

"You're a good kid and I'm proud of you. You're handlin' this well and lookin' out for your brother, a lot would have turned their backs on him long before now."

Marcus walked from the room wearing a look of astonishment on his face, not once in his life had his father ever praised him. Maybe because Eli was being forced to admit the truth, he would see his youngest son in a more favourable light from now on.

Two days later and Marcus returned to the prison to let Morris know what was happening. He also informed his brother to up his protection for the remainder of his sentence and the firm would foot the bill. Morris didn't think another attempt would be made on his life but it wasn't worth taking the risk and he was sure that Jono Parker would be happy for more income. Morris needn't have worried as after the initial failed attempt, Del Foster had decided to wait until the evil bastard was released from prison before extracting his revenge.

# CHAPTER FIFTEEN
## FOUR MONTHS LATER

On the day of Kenan's release, the whole Foster family had been up with the larks. Even Allison had taken the day off from work and was at the house by seven that morning. Jean and Dawn were busy putting banners up and baking a cake and it felt as if the dark cloud that had hung over the house for so long, was finally about to be lifted. Del was due to collect his son at eight thirty, the governor had made sure that Kenan was the first to be released and there would be a gap of fifteen minutes to allow him time to leave the prison grounds without being seen or coming into contact with any other inmates that were also being released. It was common knowledge regarding what had happened, though the authorities still couldn't prove who had actually carried out the atrocious act as Kenan had remained tight lipped. Governor Holmes imagined that the young man was full of shame though he really had nothing to be ashamed of, still it was best to allow him some privacy as the governor knew from past experience that Kenan's mental health would suffer greatly in the ensuing months. It had been agreed that only Del would go to the prison, the women would wait at home as they

still had lots to get ready and besides, Del told them that after being locked up it might all be a bit too much for Kenan.  Just as he pulled into the visitor's car park at HMP Wandsworth, the small door in the vast roller shutter opened and he saw his son step over the threshold with a clear plastic sack slung over his shoulder.  Kenan stopped for a moment and glanced all around and Del thought that maybe he was taking in his first breath of fresh air in many, many months but when he didn't head towards the car his father became concerned.  Suddenly it dawned on Del, he had changed his vehicle six months earlier so Kenan wouldn't recognise it.  Gently beeping on the car horn he waved from the open window.  As his son approached Del stepped from the car and then flung his arms around his heir in a desperate attempt to feel that father son connection again.  Kenan's body suddenly went ridged and he sharply pulled himself away.  He couldn't be off noticing the look of hurt on Del's face but neither could he tolerate physical contact of any kind and the latter was far stronger than that of not wanting to hurt his father's feelings.
"You okay Son?"
Kenan didn't reply and as he stared down at the ground he just shrugged his shoulders.  Del opened the passenger side door and gently

taking his elbow, guided his son into the car. It was as if his boy was now so very fragile, something Del hadn't experienced since his children were babies. The drive home was taken in almost silence, Kenan didn't want to talk and Del didn't have a clue what to say to a young man, his son, who just a couple of years earlier had been so full of life, so ready for a bit of banter but was now a shadow of his former self and so very broken. As they pulled into the drive Del looked at Kenan and thought he could see just the smallest hint of a smile.

"Glad to be home Son?"

Kenan just stared at his father blankly and Del was starting to get worried about his boys state of mind. Maybe he just needed time to settle in and find his feet, the small family gathering didn't seem to be such a good idea now and Del decided to forewarn his boy.

"Now your mum, Ally and Dawn are waitin' inside to see you, made a cake and everythin' but…."

Kenan suddenly spoke, cutting his father off mid-sentence.

"Please Dad, I can't face any of that, I just want to go to my room and be left alone if you don't mind."

Del roughly grabbed his son's arm and the action stunned Kenan and for a second he shrunk back into his seat in fear. The look on his face hurt Del but not enough to stop him saying what needed to be said.

"I fuckin' well do mind! I know you've been through the mill but don't forget they have too. Your mum, who by the way doesn't know the full extent of what you went through, has cried herself to sleep every night since you were sentenced. Dawn has become even more introvert, if that's possible and Allison, well she's as much at war with the fuckin' world as she's always been so it's hard to tell if there's any difference there."

Del was hoping that his last few words would at least make him laugh a little but all he got back was the same blank expression of earlier.

"I'm sorry they are hurtin' but that's not my fault it's yours!"

"What the fuck are you on about?"

"If you hadn't have forced me to work for you, then none of this would have happened, would it?"

Del didn't know what to say, after all Kenan's statement was true even if his words felt like a stab to his heart. They both got out of the car in silence and Kenan grabbed his bag and followed behind his father. Opening the front Door and then stepping aside to let Kenan enter first, they were met with the usual 'Surprise!!!' and instantly Jean was in floods of tears as she moved forward to hug her son, something she'd been planning since the day he was sent away and if she had her way she was never going to let go. As Jean moved closer, Kenan took a step back. Tears now filled his eyes as he slowly indicted 'no' with his head. Looking at Dawn and then to Allison his brow furrowed and dropping his bag on the floor he ran as fast as he could up the stairs. No one said a word but Jean looked pleadingly at her husband for some answers.

"Just give him time babe, this must all be a massive head fuck for him. I think he's in shock, it was only a couple of years for us but for him it must have felt like a bleedin' lifetime."

No knowing what else to say Del disappeared into the sanctity of his study and closed the door, a silent signal for him to be left alone as well. Jean sighed deeply and then gesturing to the banners and balloons with her hand, told her girls to take them all down.

Alone in the kitchen she sat down at the table and sobbed her heart out, whatever had happened to her gorgeous boy as it now felt like a stranger had walked through her front door. She decided to leave him for a couple of hours and then alone, she would go to his room and try to get some answers.

As it was a weekday, Del made the decision to go back to work and Allison chose not to waste her day either so she went for some retail therapy. The only one who was more worried about her mother and brother than herself was Dawn. As per usual she had been left to finish the clearing up on her own and it had taken her a lot longer than anticipated as one of the glitter filled balloons had burst scattering its contents all over the expensive Persian rug. Thirty minutes later she had at last finished and after one final inspection, she quietly made her way to the kitchen. Stopping in the doorway, she studied her mother for a few seconds before she spoke. Jean had always been the backbone of the family but now she looked old, far older than her years and to Dawn, so very vulnerable.

"You want to come for a walk in the park Mum, maybe cheer you up a bit?"

Jean turned to her daughter and as she smiled at the small act of kindness, Dawn could see that the tears were still wet on her cheeks.

"Oh thanks darlin' but I'm okay, you go though, it will do you good. If I'm being honest, I could do with a little alone time to get my head straight, you don't mind do you?"

Dawn smiled, winked at her mother and then silently walked from the doorway. With them all finally out of the house it was the perfect opportunity to check on her boy and she wasn't about to waste a second.  Making a fresh pot of tea and then pouring Kenan a large cup, she checked her face and hair in the ornate hallway mirror and then climbed the stairs to her boy's room.  After tapping gently on the door but when there was no reply, Jean turned the handle and went into the room.

"Thought you might like a drink darlin', no one makes tea like your old mum hay?"

There was no reply but she could see his form under the sheets so placing the cup onto the bedside table, Jean gently pulled back the fabric which covered his face.  His cold eyes stared back at her and she felt a shudder run through her entire body.

"Leave me alone!"

He had never spoken to her like that before and the pain his words and tone caused was immense but she wouldn't give up.

"Okay babe but drink it while it's hot.  I'll check on you later. I love you Son?"

The words were not reciprocated and that above anything, broke her heart.

Over at Roach Road Del was pacing up and down in the front room which the firm used as a communal space to gather every day for a briefing.  The rest of the men were yet to show an appearance and Del didn't know if he was glad of that fact or if he wanted them here right now so that he could vent his fear and anger. Hearing the front door open he turned to see Stevie Hunt enter, followed only seconds later by Levi Puck.

"Alright Boss?"

The question had been asked by Stevie and Levi knew it was a stupid thing to say. Of course Del wasn't alright, one look at his face and any idiot could see that. Stepping past Stevie, Levi walked right up to Del and placed his hand onto his boss' shoulder.

"How's the kid? I take it he did get released today?"

Del flopped down wearily onto the brown leather sofa, somewhere he never usually sat and then placed his head in his hands.

"Yeah but he's in a right fuckin' mess."

"It'll take time Guv, just give him time."

"I ain't got any fuckin' choice now have I? To be honest I don't think it will make a shit's worth of difference anyway. I've lost him Levi, I know I have. That dirty sick bastard has emotionally killed my boy and no amount of time will ever fix that. You know he blames me for it all, said I forced him into the firm and if I hadn't then none of this would have happened and you now somethin' else? He's right!"

"Then he at least needs to know that we are going to extract some kind of fuckin' revenge. When do we start?"
"As soon as that cunt is released. I have it on good authority that he's got time off for good behaviour, what a fuckin' joke! He's out in three weeks."

Back in Edmonton, Jean had given it a couple of hours and then gone back up to Kenan's room. Once again she gently tapped on the door and once again there was no response, so she quietly opened the door and went inside but the bed was now empty. Looking in his en-suite, which was also empty, she slowly searched the rest of the house. Making her way back down to the kitchen she was becoming more and more anxious when she couldn't think of anywhere else to look for him. Momentarily glancing out of the kitchen window she suddenly noticed that the shed door was slightly ajar and running from the kitchen she made her way down the long expanse of grassed lawn but stopped just short of the wooden building. She had a bad feeling in her gut, something was telling her not to go inside. Slowly she placed her hand onto the latch and then for a second closed her eyes before attempting to push the door open. The large shed, it had been there since before the family moved in, was old and the wood had sagged and dropped in places. Jean didn't usually go down there and Del had constantly complained that it needed replacing but as usual hadn't done anything about it. Putting her shoulder to the wood she used all of her might to push as hard as she could and gradually it began to open further. She could feel the bottom scraping on the floor as it finally gave way and it sounded like nails on a blackboard which made her shudder. The first thing she noticed was the rear window, which she hadn't been able to see from the front and it was now wide open. Scanning the space with the help of the light that the open door had allowed to filter inside, she suddenly stopped dead in her tracks unable to breathe. Kenan's lifeless body hung from an old rafter that spanned the right hand corner of the room. Jean suddenly ran the twenty foot length but on reaching her son she knew he was dead. His body hung limply, his open eyes bulged and she was able to see the red, purplish tinge to his once beautiful skin. Letting out the most pitiful scream she dropped to her knees and was still there ten twenty minutes later when Dawn returned from her walk. After entering the hall and calling out for her mother and when there was no answer, Dawn walked through to the kitchen and opened the back door.

"Mum? Mum are you out here?"
Dawn quickly glanced around the garden and was about to go inside again when out of the corner of her eye she also spied the shed door was open. That was strange, her mother didn't go onto the garden that much let alone go into the shed. Walking over the manicured grass she made her way down the garden but as soon as she stepped inside and saw her mother crumpled on the ground and then saw her baby brothers lifeless body, she knew life was never going to be the same again. Pulling out her mobile as fast as her shaking hand would allow, she tapped her contacts list and then her father's number. Del was still sitting on the sofa talking to Levi when his phone rang and he smiled when he saw who the caller was.
"Hi sweetheart, how's things goin' now?"
"Dad you need to come home."
"Why darlin', what's happened Dawnie?"
"You just need to get back here as fast as you can!"
With that the line went dead and Del could only stare at Levi with panic filled eyes.

# CHAPTER SIXTEEN

As Del's car, driven at speed by Levi, screeched to a halt in the driveway, the two men could only sit in silence for a second when they saw the two police cars and an ambulance parked outside the house.  Suddenly the front door opened wide and two paramedics emerged pushing a stretcher which plainly had a covered body on top.  Del could feel his stomach instantly knot up and he felt physically sick.  Opening the car door he leant out and threw up onto the drive as he cried out.
"No, no, fuck me no!!!!"
Levi reached over and touched Del's arm in an attempt to calm his boss.
"Don't jump to conclusions Boss, we don't know what's happened yet or who they have just brought out.  Come on, get yourself together and we'll go and find out."
When Del stepped from the car his feet felt like lead weights, he was desperate for information but at the same time he was dreading what he was about to be told.  Each step took a mammoth amount of effort and when they finally reached the front door they were met by a uniformed officer who attempted to bar their entry.

"I'm sorry Sir but you cannot come in here."
Del inhaled deeply and it took all of his resolve not to punch the copper in the face.

"Can't fuckin' come in! It's my bastard house you twat!"

The officer stood his ground and about to argue further, Del stopped when the door again opened and Dawn emerged. Spying her father she almost fell into his arms as she began to sob.

"Oh Dad, I'm so sorry."

Gently pushing Dawn away from him Del grabbed her by the elbows and stared deeply into her eyes.

"Now listen to me Dawnie, I want you to tell me what's gone on. What's happened? Is it your mother?"

Dawn, who had momentarily stopped her tears, began to cry again and as he pulled her to him in an attempt to comfort her, Dawns next words were like a stab in the heart.

"It's, it's Kenan Dad and he's dead! Mum found him hanging in the shed."

Del took a step backwards, his mouth dropping open in utter dismay. His face was set in a frown of disbelief as he slowly shook his head. Speechless and in shock, he couldn't seem to form any words, or at least none that his mouth would allow him to say as tears instantly began to drop down onto his cheeks.

"Dad? Dad, say something please."
Just then Jean emerged being supported at the elbow by Allison who for once was lost for words as she just stared in her father's direction. Jean seemed spaced out almost as if she'd been sedated which she hadn't, that would come later in the day when she had a complete meltdown in front of her family. As she spied her boy's body in the back of the ambulance she broke free from Allison's grasp and ran over to the vehicle. Like a woman possessed which of course she was, possessed by sheer and utter grief, she attempted to climb inside. One of the police officers barred her way but he didn't get a chance to physically stop her as Del was by her side in seconds.
"It's okay, it's okay officer, I can handle this."
Suddenly she let out the most horrendous scream, it was almost an inhuman sound and Del felt as if his heart was being ripped out of his body.
"Come on darlin' let the men do their jobs."
"My boy! My baby boy!!!!"
"Mine as well Jeanie but there's nothing' we can do for him now sweetheart."
Jean fell into her husband's arms and sobbed uncontrollably, her whole body shaking with each racking eruption of howling. When her outburst began to subside just a little he led her

back into the house followed by Allison and Dawn. Levi stood outside, he knew it was best to let the family grieve in private and to be truthful he wouldn't have had a clue what to say to any of them, the boss included. A few seconds later and they all heard the rear doors of the ambulance slam shut and the vehicles drive away. Seated on one of the sumptuous sofas, Jean Foster seemed to have shrunk before his very eyes and Del could only stare at his wife in disbelief. Turning to his daughters he asked what had happened but Allison just shrugged her shoulders. Looking to Dawn even she wasn't able to add much more than he already knew.

"I went for a walk Dad. As far as I knew Kenan was still in his room. I asked mum if she wanted to come along but she said no, that she wanted some time alone. I got back after about a half hour to find her down the shed, she was just kneeling on the floor and I, I......."

Del held up his hand, he could see that talking about it was difficult and that she was about to breakdown.

"He wasn't in his room."

They all turned to look at Jean who was staring into space but had suddenly now begun to speak.

"I searched everywhere, his bed was empty so I

looked all around the house but it was like he'd disappeared. Then from the kitchen window I saw that the shed door was open. That fuckin' shed! Why didn't you get rid of it when you said you would?!!!!"

Her eyes narrowed and were now totally focused on her husband and she was looking at him with such hatred as her words came out like venom.

"Darlin' it ain't my fault, he could have done it anywhere. He obviously chose the shed as he wouldn't be easily found."

"Excuses Derek, always fuckin' excuses. You killed my boy, it was your fault!"

"Mum!!"

Dawn couldn't believe what she was hearing but just as she was about to scold her mother, Jean ran from the front room. Making her way up to Kenan's bedroom she threw herself down onto the bed and sobbed into his pillow. She could smell him on the fabric and could clearly see his handsome face as she imagined running her hands through his curly brown hair. Her hand unknowingly slipped under the pillow and instantly she could feel something rough as it crumpled beneath her touch. Sitting bolt upright she opened up the folder sheet of paper and slowly began to read.

'I'm so sorry Mum but I just couldn't stay any

longer. When that animal raped and beat me he tore my soul out. The shame I feel is beyond words and I know I will never get over it. Don't be sad, I'm in a better place now. Love you to the moon and back.
Your boy Kenan xx'
By the time she reached the end Jean had stopped crying and was now angry, angrier than she had ever been. Snatching up the note she stomped down the stairs and throwing open the door to the front room, she marched inside. Del could instantly see that she was filled with utter rage but he didn't ask what had caused this outburst and instead waited for her to start on him, which he strangely knew was a certainty.
"And just when were you goin' to tell me, you bastard?"
"Tell you what babe?"
Jean thrust the paper towards his chest and didn't stop until her fist made violent contact with his shirt.
"This!!!!"
Del slowly read the note but stopped at the word rape. Now he knew what she was so irate about and in all honesty he couldn't blame her.
"I was tryin' to protect you sweetheart. Tell me, what good would it have done you knowing, knowing what had happened to him and knowing that he still had time to serve? Well?"

Jean could only stare at her husband blankly, she felt as if she didn't know him, after thirty plus years she didn't know Del Foster at all. Walking from the room she quietly closed the door, there was no more slamming or shouting, there was nothing left to say. The girls stared at their father waiting for an explanation but none was forthcoming.

"Keep an eye on her and if you think it's necessary, phone the doctor."

Dawn nodded, she knew what he meant and before the day was over Jean Carter would be heavily sedated. Del made his way into the hall and then out of the front door. Walking straight past Levi he got into the car and waited for his man to join him.

"Take me to the office I have calls to make," Although it was less than a thirteen mile trip, the journey, via the north circular, still took a good thirty minutes. It was carried out in silence and from the look on his boss' face, Levi knew there was big trouble brewing. While he'd waited patiently outside the house Levi had phoned in and told Mad Tony what had occurred, well as much as he knew. He also told Tony to let all of the others know so that there wouldn't be a lot of questions when Del next went to the office. Still in shock himself, Levi hadn't expected that they would be going back so soon.

"Phone ahead, I want everyone at the office when we get there and no fuckin' exceptions!" Levi did as he was asked and everyone was present and correct when Del and Levi walked in. None of them could look their boss in the eye and as instructed, no one said a word of condolence or even mentioned Kenan. It was easier like that and Del didn't think he would be able to cope if anyone said his boys name out loud. Taking a seat at the table Del began to speak and not one of his men interrupted, as they were usually prone to do.
"I obviously don't need to go into detail about what's occurred. When the funeral is over and my boy has been laid to rest, we go to war with the Carters. Gordon, I know that cunt gets out in two or three weeks but I want to know the exact date and time. Sammy, I want a list of all the Toms working for them, names, addresses, anythin' you can find out and you'd better take Carl with you in case anyone gets a bit fuckin' stroppy. Stevie, find out all you can about the brother, the old man and anyone who is associated with those cunts! I want to know their phone numbers, routines, likes and dislikes, I want to know what time they take a fuckin' shit in the mornin'! Tony, Levi and Freddy, you're with me, we will plan this fucker with military precision and on the day we strike,

the bastards won't know what's hit them. Anyone who has a problem with this speak now, it's my fight and I accept it if you don't want to participate 'cause it's goin' to get fuckin' nasty." Del looked at each of his men in turn and with each and every glance the men all nodded their approval.

Two weeks later and the funeral was held. The first vicar Del had approached ended up with a black eye after he stated that conducting the funeral wouldn't sit well with him as suicide was a sin against God. Luckily the second one he contacted was more sympathetic to the family's grief. On the day, All Saints church was full to capacity. A vast number of mourners were in attendance, kids who had gone to school with Kenan, teachers who had taught him and surprisingly there were even a couple of prison guards, though Del imagined that they had been told to attend by the governor. Among the congregation, along with his own men, were several known faces from the criminal fraternity. It was always the same when a Boss lost a close member of his family, the top guns would come out as a show of respect and that strangely gave Del some comfort. Jean had been distraught throughout the ceremony and when the coffin was carried out to the haunting sound of

Chicago's rendition of 'If you leave me now', she almost collapsed. Del had wanted a cremation but his wife wouldn't even consider that option, as far as she was concerned she had been robbed of her sons life and she wasn't about to let them have his body as well. The committal took place at Edmonton cemetery on Church Street and Del had purchased not only Kenan's plot but also the one at the head and foot and on either side. It wasn't anything to do with planning a family plot for the future, he just didn't want anyone else near his boy. Most of the mourners from the church had returned to the house, burial was a very personal thing and now apart from Del's men who were there because they had all come to love Kenan, it was just Del, Jean and the girls. When the coffin was slowly lowered into the grave Jean could be heard sobbing and Del immediately reached out to the only woman he had loved totally and utterly for the last thirty years but she just glared at him coldly and shrugged his arm away. Things had been this way since her outburst on the day Kenan had died and he could only hope that in time the situation would improve but something in her eyes, almost as if he was dead to her when she looked at him, told him differently. When the vicar began to say 'ashes to ashes' they each threw a single red rose onto the polished would surface of the coffin. Del held his wife's elbow trying to guide her away but again she pushed him away, the only one who eventually made her move was Dawn and as she did so she could see the depth of pain etched on her father's face. With the service at last over, everyone had been invited back to the house where caterers had laid out a magnificent spread. The table groaned with rare roast beef, lobsters, prawns, in fact there was very little in the way of expensive shellfish that wasn't on the table. Fine china and linen napkins were stacked at one end and in true Londoner style, everyone dug in and filled their plates as they commented on how marvellous the food was. The weather was warm and with the sun shining, many of the guests had spilled out onto the lawn but Jean didn't step foot outside, she hadn't since that fateful day as one look down the garden to where the shed had stood brought on a new onslaught of pain. After Kenan's death, Del had, within a day, smashed it to pieces but the memory was sill so raw that Jean didn't think she could cope with much more.

The wake came to a close at just after six and by the time the house was cleared up and the caterers had left, they all felt physically and emotionally drained. The girls sat silently at the kitchen table, Del was alone in his study just staring blankly into space and Jean was upstairs lying on Kenan's bed. The family was incomplete and life was never going to be the same again. Each of them felt utterly lost and confused about how they were going to pick up the pieces and carry on with life when one of them had now gone forever.

# CHAPTER SEVENTEEN

The cell door opened at six am and Morris, aware that today was the day he would regain his freedom, still went for his morning shower and then on to breakfast. He didn't want to exit the prison unless he was clean and well presented, though what on earth Marcus had brought in for him to wear God only knew. The weight he'd gained on the inside meant that the clothes he'd worn when he'd arrived, most definitely wouldn't fit anymore. As it turned out, he was pleasantly surprised with the outfit his brother had chosen. Escorted to the reception area Morris was handed a bag containing a new blue shirt, Navy cardigan and a pair of cream chino trousers. Luckily his feet hadn't grown so his brown handmade brogues slipped on like a pair of slippers. The previous evening he had traded a packet of smokes for a haircut and now, as he waited for the door within the main roller shutter to be opened, he felt almost human again. He hadn't bothered to say any farewells, not even to Jono Parker, as far as Morris was concerned they were all a load of wankers and he had used them when he needed to but now if he saw them on the street any time in the future, he most definitely wouldn't bother to pass the time of day.

On strict instructions from Eli, Marcus had been forced to leave the house far earlier than was necessary just in case the traffic was bad. As he'd expected, it wasn't, so he ended up sitting outside Wandsworth nick for well over an hour. When he finally saw his brother emerge he sighed heavily and mouthed the words 'thank fuck for that'. Morris glanced in all directions and for a moment thought that no one had bothered to collect him but when he spied his brother's Audi he smiled from ear to ear. Sauntering over with that big headed cocky swagger that Marcus hated but at the same time adored, his brother was at last free and they could all get back to some kind of normality, whatever that would mean. Opening the door and leaning his head inside, Morris smiled.

"Oi, oi saveloy, how's it goin' my old Son?"

Marcus rolled his eyes in annoyance, at the same time he couldn't help but laugh.

"Get in you muppet!"

As the Audi pulled out of the carpark Morris leaned forward and switched on the radio.

"That's more like it, you wouldn't believe the shit my ears have been forced to listen to. Those cunts have absolutely no fuckin' taste in music. So, where we goin' first?"

"Home."

For a few seconds Morris stared at his brother in utter disbelief.
"I've been locked up for what felt like life and you expect me to just go home? I want a few bevvies and a laugh, not to mention a bit of relief if you know what I mean."
He began to laugh but was instantly stopped by his brother's next sentence.
"No, we go home and that's the old man's orders. This sentence has taken its toll on us all and none more so than him. He came out of retirement to take up the reigns but in all honesty bro he's worn out."
"Well if you'd done what you should have then he wouldn't have needed to would he?"
Completely out of character Marcus slammed on the brakes but luckily there were no cars behind them.
"Don't you fuckin' dare Morris! If you hadn't got yourself locked up then we wouldn't be in this situation. Your little act of depravity has done nothin' to lessen the load, so for once in your pathetic fuckin' life, man up and take some fuckin' responsibility!"
"Okay, okay Bro! Don't get your fuckin' knickers in a twist. Home it is then."
Pulling onto the main road Marcus was focused with the on-coming traffic when he suddenly noticed a Mercedes carrying two people turn

into the road they were trying to get out of. It was only fleeting but he was sure the passenger was Del Foster, if it wasn't then there were two men with identical scars running down their right cheeks.

As Morris had exited the prison he hadn't noticed the old transit van which had been parked several meters away but still within viewing distance. Levi had been in the driving seat and Stevie Hunt was beside him in the passenger seat holding a long lens camera. He wouldn't normally have been used for this type of work but this was personal and Del needed all hands to the pump. He wanted to make sure that every stage of the ensuing events were carried out precisely and that meant having all of his men working on the same job. With the shutter set on automatic Stevie reeled off picture after picture of Morris and then the car with Marcus sitting inside. Del's Merc circled the carpark and Levi gave him the thumbs up that everything was going to plan. Pulling away shortly after the Audi, Levi tailed the car for a good four miles before being taken over by Mad Tony and Carl Ransom in a grey Vauxhall van which had been sign written with the words 'F Drake & Son Painter and Decorators'. Del had planned every little detail and this ruse was done to stop the tail being spotted. When the two vehicles were a couple of miles from Upminster, Del, in his black Mercedes and with Sammy at the wheel, had at breakneck speed overtook Marcus and the other cars. As the Audi came to a halt while the electric gates opened, the Mercedes was forced to drive on but not before Del had himself taken a few snaps of the imposing house.

"Nice set up Guv."

Del glared in Sammy Bird's direction and the man knew he had spoken out of turn.

"Take me back to base so I can get these processed and see what that sick cunt looks like."

Marcus hadn't mentioned who he thought he had seen when they had come from the prison and the rest of the twenty five mile journey had been taken in almost silence but as soon as they pulled up outside the house Morris got out and slammed the door hard. His brother had changed while he was away, he seemed to have grown a pair of balls for once and that could mean only one thing, more trouble for Morris in the future. About to place his hand on the door knob he was stopped when the door was flung open wide and his father stepped outside and instantly embraced him.

"Welcome home Son, you've been missed and no mistake."

"Dad, good to see you."
Eli glanced over his eldest sons shoulder in the direction of Marcus.
"Go to the office and sort the men out but be back here for twelve as I need you to do somethin' for me. Well go on then, don't just stand there with your fuckin' mouth open like a retard."
Morris turned slightly and winked in his brother's direction, golden boy was home and ready to take his place as number one.
In the dining room Milly had laid on a breakfast spread and without having to be told Morris dived in with little manners. Since being locked up, his appetite had, along with his waistline, expanded vastly. Eli smiled as he watched his first born tuck into bacon, eggs and what seemed like gallons of coffee.
"Now that you're back in the fold I want to bring you up to speed. Now I don't want to know the ins and outs of what happened in Wandsworth but I have a gut feeling there will be repercussions and I want you to be ready for that. You will have one of the lads with you at all times and…."
"Leave it out Dad, I ain't a fuckin' kid!"
Eli slammed his fist down onto the table. It was a sign both boys had often been witness too in their lives and Morris knew not to argue the

point any further.

"You will do as you're fuckin' told! This wasn't just some ordinary Joe you, well for want of a better phrase, interfered with. He was the son of a face and you know as well as I do that they ain't goin' to let that go. When you've settled in and when dozy bollocks gets back, the three of us are going to sit down and cover every scenario. Do I make myself understood?!"

Still continuing to shovel food into his mouth, Morris only nodded his head. He would go along with things for the moment, it didn't bode well to upset the proverbial apple cart so early on.

At the unit Marcus carried out his orders telling each of the men what to do for the day and he was just about to head back home when he was approached by Gus (Gary) Walker.

"Can I have a quick word Marcus, only I heard somethin' today and it might not be important but…"

"For fucks sake Gus, just spit it out will you."

"The kid that Morris, well you know, anyway, he's only gone and topped himself."

Marcus showed no reaction but internally he had gone into panic mode.

"Like you say, it's probably nothin' but thanks for keepin' me in the loop."

Just as he'd been commanded, Marcus pulled into the drive at noon and sighed heavily. He loved his brother, there was no doubt about that but after just a few short hours it seemed as though things had reverted back to how they used to be and he guiltily wondered if maybe it would have been best if Morris had stayed inside. Milly was as usual dusting away as he walked in and she smiled warmly.
"Hello love, had a busy morning?"
As Marcus passed her he touched her tenderly on the shoulder.
"No too bad thanks Mills, where's the old man?"
Milly rolled her eyes upwards as she slowly tilted her head to one side in the direction of the inner hall and Marcus knew exactly where she meant.
"He's in the study with that brother of yours."
Nodding his head he was momentarily stopped when she grabbed his arm as he walked by.
"Be careful Son, I've got a bad feeling in me water and I'm rarely wrong."
Smiling, he again nodded before knocking on the highly polished wooden door but not waiting to be invited inside. Marcus took a seat on the leather chesterfield and for a second watched his father and brother, who were both seated at the desk and were yet to even acknowledge his presence. Finally Eli looked

up.

"Right, now you're back we can get started. Morris, what did you learn from that kid about his old man?"

"Not a lot really, we were otherwise engaged." As Morris let out a giggle Marcus could only cringe. Now was not the time for sick jokes and especially in front of the old man. Noticing his brother's reaction, Morris instantly stopped laughing.

"He said they dealt in drugs but on a larger scale than just street dealing, apart from that, not much else. Oh yeah, he did say there were eight or nine bodies employed in the firm. So what have you got in mind Dad?"

Eli Carter looked at both of his sons in turn and wondered what he'd done to deserve such a couple of wankers. Marcus was the smartest but he didn't have the balls for violence, a must in their game. Morris could stand his own but he was hot headed and would go up like a bottle of pop at the slightest little thing. Pity he couldn't take the best out of each of them and have a son to be proud of.

"I'm reluctant to make a move just on the off chance that they do decide to let things lie. I can't see it myself but as yet they haven't made a move. If and when they do then it's you they will be after Morris."

"Fuck 'em, I can handle myself well enough if…."

He was silenced when he saw his father clench his fists, never a good sign.

"Maybe on a one to one, two on one at best but if they come after you it will be mob handed so don't be such a fuckin' prick and listen to what I'm tellin' you. Either Gus or Smiter will be with you at all times. I will organise a rota for them and you do not leave this fuckin' house without me or one of them by your side. Do I make myself clear?"

"Yes Dad."

"Good. Now Marcus, as you well know and it's come around all too quickly again but it's the start of Appleby the day after tomorrow. I want you to attend in my place."

"Really Dad? I hate it and besides…."

Eli stood up from his chair and at six feet tall and with them both still seated, it felt as if he towered above them.

"I have not missed a fair in my entire life and because of fuckin' soppy bollocks here, this year will be the first. Give my apologies to your uncle Duke and explain what's happened and that we might need to call on a few bodies in the not too distant future."

Marcus got to his feet and was about to leave when he suddenly turned to face his father.

It was done for effect and that fact didn't pass Eli by.
"There's also been a bit of an update, seems that Kenan kid topped himself a few weeks back."
Morris only sneered at the news.
"The fuckin' gutless cunt!"
Eli, rarely ever shocked, could only stare at his eldest. A man, a face come to that, had lost his son and far from feeling any remorse or guilt, Morris could only belittle the young man further."
"Shut your fuckin' trap you queer cunt! This alters everythin' because believe you me, in the next couple of weeks we will be at war."
Marcus had never heard his father speak to Morris that way yet alone openly admit that his eldest was a queer. Suddenly things were about to change and not for the better.
"Does that mean I don't have to go to Appleby after all Dad?"
"No it does not, as far as the world is concerned its business as usual but tell Duke we might need more than a few bodies."

Two days later saw Marcus reluctantly pack a bag and head off to Cumbria. As he hadn't been to the fair since his early teens, Eli had given him instructions of exactly where to go and as he pulled up outside the semi-circle of vans all eyes

were on the stranger. He stepped from the Audi and was immediately surrounded by four burly men and they didn't look remotely friendly. Marcus, with his sharp haircut and clothes, looked like a typical city gorger and the men were about to tell him in a non-too polite term, that he wasn't welcome. Suddenly the van door flew open and Kezia Carter stepped out into the bright sunlight. In the summer breeze, her long mane of black curly hair blew in all directions.
"What the feck are ya all doin'?"
"He's a feckin' Gorger Kezia, we're gonna see him off though so don't you be worryin' girl."
"I ain't worryin' and you will do no such thing, that's Marcus, me cousin and Dukes nephew. You bunch of thick heads should ask a few feckin' questions before ya wade in with yer fists."
With that the men nodded their heads in Marcus' direction and then quickly dispersed.
"Well ain't you a sight for sore eyes Cuz! Come on inside and I'll make us a brew, Dada ain't here but he won't be long."
Just as Marcus was about to take his first step up to the van he spied a woman walking across the site and she was the most stunning creature he had ever seen. Tall and slender with flowing golden hair that reached down to her waste, she had him momentarily mesmerized.

"Who's that Kezi?"
Kezia poked her head outside for a second.
"That's Rena Gallagher and she keeps herself to herself and she's definitely off limits. Why?"
"Because cousin, I'm goin' to marry her!"
Kezia started to laugh as she popped her head back inside the van and her chuckles were so loud that everyone outside could hear her. Even Rena Gallagher stopped for a second and as her eyes locked with those of Marcus, she coyly smiled. The tender moment came to an abrupt halt when Kezia once again came to the door.
"Get in here you soppy twat! Wait until the barbeque later and I'll introduce you but she ain't goin' to be easy Cuz. Her old man is as protective as you can get and Rena steers clear of travellers, especially the men who attend Appleby. A lot of people think she's stuck up but she ain't, she's just quiet and knows what she wants out of life."
"And what might that be?"
"You'll have to wait until tonight and then you can ask her yourself."
Suddenly Appleby horse fair didn't seem like such a bad place to be and Marcus couldn't wait for darkness to fall and the introduction that he knew was going to change his life forever.

# CHAPTER EIGHTEEN

While Marcus was enjoying his first night at Appleby, something he really hadn't anticipated, Del Foster was about to begin his reign of vengeance.

Linda Bullman had worked the streets of Southend-on-Sea for the last five years and the only person she answered to was Eli Carter or at the very least, one of his sons. Five years in the sex industry was a long time but Linda was wearing remarkably well. She also held the badge of top girl and as such gave out orders to the others. Chinese Mary, a small oriental woman who was so childlike in her appearance that no one actually knew her age, Stuttering Stacey, not that her stutter ever bothered the punters as it was a known fact that she couldn't stutter with her mouth full, a particular speciality of Stacey'. There was also Dee Dee Mason, though her surname was dubious to say the least as most of the other girls who worked the seafront knew her by a different name. Southend was a lucrative area especially in the summer months when the holiday makers were in town. By day the adoring husband and fathers did their family duty playing on the beach with their children but by night many would take an evening stroll alone and then indulge in vile acts of degrading sex, never knowing or caring what disease they could be taking back to the little woman lovingly waiting back at the hotel or caravan. Many divorces had occurred over the years after an unexplainable case of syphilis or genital warts had been caught and then passed on but it wasn't any of the Toms concern and there had only ever been a few incidents when an aggrieved punter had come looking for the dirty whore who had infected him.

Mabel Hicks ran an old fashioned Bed and Breakfast on Wilson Road just off of Clifftown Parade and for the last couple of years business had been poor to say the least. Oh there were plenty of day trippers but that didn't pay Mabel's bills so she had begun to rent out her rooms on an hourly basis. The working girls soon got to hear and now their business was keeping her afloat. Mabel didn't judge and had actually bonded with a couple of the girls, in particular Linda who always had her in fits of laughter when she occasionally popped in for a cuppa.
At just before midnight, punters with little more left than the shirts on their backs began to filter

out from the Grosvenor Casino. Eli's Toms were always ready and waiting in the hope that the men still had enough left to pay for a girl, and the Toms, especially if it had been a quiet night, really needed to make up their quota. He had taught them well and if a punter didn't have the cash, then rings and watches were acceptable and could be traded back the next night for the balance, after that they would be handed over to the boss who would either sell them on or have the gold melted down to add to his own private and ever growing stash of bullion. Dee Dee and Chinese Mary were the first to be picked up but strangely it was not from walk-by's but by two men in two separate vans. Never known to turn down a trick, they both climbed in and the vans drove off at speed in different directions. Stacey was next but unlike the other two, she was picked up on the street. Suggesting Mabel's place, which took several seconds to actually escape from her mouth, she was surprised when her punter refused and instead led her to the Clarence Road Carpark.
"You got cacacaca cash?"
Mad Tony nodded as he continued to almost frogmarch her over to the ticket machine that had been positioned on a three feet high brick pillar, behind it they would be out of sight from anyone collecting their cars although to be

honest it was so late that Tony could only see three vehicles.

"Bbbbb bit keen ain't ya sunshine? Old lady nnnnn not givin' you any honey at hhhhh home?"

Stacey began to cackle thinking what she'd just said was funny but it only fuelled Tony on, the love of his life and wife of twenty years had died suddenly eighteen months earlier so this whores comment only enraged him. Reaching into his trouser pocket he pulled out a wad of cash and Stacey's eyes were out on stalks. Seconds later she was pushed up against the wall and as she smiled she revealed rotten teeth which made Tony want to vomit up the burger he'd consumed an hour earlier.

"Ssss so what's it to be lover? I bbbb blow well, my pussy's still nice and tight and either will ccccc cost you a score. On the other hand I'm also up for a bit of aaaa anal but that's an extra ttt tenner. So what's it to be only I ain't got all nnnn night you know?"

Tony swiftly pulled a flick knife from his inside pocket and before Stacey knew what was happening he had sliced off more than the tip of her nose and run the blade down her cheek from her eye to her chin. As screams ran out he quickly disappeared into the shadows, he had to keep a low profile as unlike the others, his work

wasn't yet over. His victim staggered towards the seafront and she passed several people but not one of them offered to help her. Stacey was sobbing but her flowing tears were not only out of pain but because she knew he had disfigured her and life as she knew it was over. For most, the tasks set by the boss would have been difficult but Mad Tony Morgan thrived on violence and he had no qualms that it was a woman, after all she was only a dirty whore and to him that made her fair game. Chinese Mary didn't fare as well as Stacey, if that could be said? Picked up by Stevie Hunt, she was driven to Southchurch Park and after both of them had climbed into the rear of the van, Mary was about to set her terms when she spotted the knife glittering in the moonlight that shone through the windows of the rear doors. About to scream, Mary only managed a gurgling sound as Stevie instantly thrust a knife straight into her throat. Climbing out of the van, he rolled her body onto the shingle carpark and then drove off. There was more blood in the back of the van than he'd anticipated so he was desperate to get back to the East End and swill away the evidence.
Dee Dee had been driving around with Freddy Wentworth for what seemed like an age. She was starting to get anxious as he had a mean look in his eyes and wouldn't converse when she

tied to start a conversation. She was also losing money, a trick was usually over in a matter of minutes but they had already been in the van for thirty and the deed wasn't yet done.

"I ain't bein' funny pal but I don't charge by the hour you know so can we get down to business or you can let me out right here."

Freddy turned and stared at her and something in his eyes suddenly made Dee Dee scared. She began to open the window so that she would at least be able to scream for help but the lock was on so nothing happened as she frantically hit the button several times.

"I don't know what your fuckin' game is Mister but you can stop this van right now! You ain't got a fuckin' clue who my boss is and he ain't gonna be happy I can tell you!"

"I know exactly who the cunt is and if you don't shut your fuckin' trap you whore I'll finish you on the spot!"

Dee Dee knew she was in deep trouble but she had no means of escape so would have to wait and see what happened. If this guy knew Eli then it was probably a turf war or something so maybe he would let her go eventually, how wrong she was! Turning left after the Marine Estate onto the A13, he was able to put his foot down and gain considerable speed. Suddenly he released the door lock and leaning over, pushed the door open and shoved Dee Dee out. Her body hit the tarmac with a sickening thud and within seconds her life had been snuffed out. A short while later Freddy pulled into Hadley Park where he swapped registration plates and removed the white magnetic strips that had been concealing the logo of a kitchen supply company. Taking a few moments to have a cigarette and gather his thoughts, he then headed back to London, confident that if his attack had been captured on CCTV they would be looking for a completely different vehicle.

Having just finished servicing one of her regulars, Linda Bullman decided to check up on the girls. It was an unwritten rule that they congregated at the end of the night where they had begun, 'Bobs Café' situated on Clifftown Parade and open twenty four seven. Pushing on the door she took a seat at their usual table and without placing an order Bob's son Harvey brought over a steaming mug of coffee and two rounds of toast.
"Any of the girls been in yet"
"No sorry, it's been really quiet tonight Linda and they definitely haven't been in."
Linda furrowed her brow, for one of them to be late was not out of the ordinary but all three? She gave it until she'd finished her drink and

then laying a couple of pounds on the table she decided to go and have a look about, someone must have seen them? After twenty minutes of scouring the street and beachfront, Chinese Mary was fond of taking a punter down onto the sand, Linda turned into Wilson Road and decided to knock on Mabel's door to see if they were there. Only a hundred feet from her destination Linda felt the hairs on the back of her neck stand on end, she was being followed. Spinning around on her heels she came face to face with Tony Morgan and as he brought the knife down she quickly stepped sideways. The blade still sliced through her wrist and as blood spurted out he was about to strike again when he was interrupted by David Fayer who was on his way home from a late shift at Raymond House care home.

"Oi! What the fucks going on?!!!"

Tony turned and ran, disappearing down Alexander Road. David gave chase but there were so many alleyways between the properties that the assailant seemed to vanish into thin air. Returning to Wilson Road the woman was nowhere to be seen, David thought about calling the police but there was little point without a victim so shrugging his shoulders he made his way home knowing full well that sleep would be impossible.

While David Fayer had been giving chase, Linda had rapidly knocked on Mabel's front door and now in the warmth of the landlady's kitchen and with a towel wrapped tightly around her wrist to stem the flow of blood, she started to cry as the reality of just how lucky she'd been began to hit home. Over the years Linda Bullman had been attacked several times by punters either wanting a freebie or who had turned nasty when she wouldn't carry out some sick fantasy they had requested but this was different, that man had tried to kill her in cold blood! Pulling out her mobile phone she dialled Eli's number, he wouldn't be best pleased to be woken but something told Linda this was going to get far worse before it got better. Eli was deep in sleep and it took a couple of seconds before the phone ringing actually woke him. Picking up his mobile he pressed connect without looking who the caller was.
"Whoever you are you'd better have a fuckin' good reason to be callin' me this late at night!"
"Sorry Mr Carter but its Linda, Linda Bullman and I think something awful has occurred."
Linda relayed what had happened to her less than half an hour earlier and then the fact that she couldn't contact any of the other girls and no one had seen them. Eli was out of bed and dressed in seconds and after banging loudly on

Morris's bedroom door, told him to meet him in the dining room.

At the same time as the men had been sorting things in Southend, Levi Puck, Sammy Bird and Gordon Mayes arrived in Kings Cross. The three girls that Morris ran worked this area, especially around the front of the station in the hope of hooking up with commuters working late or stag parties arriving for a night of sin, at least they had done up until tonight but that was about to dramatically change. Black Grace, a tall thickset woman with the slightest hint of a Jamaican accent, Ginger Rachel, a rather studious looking girl who had started to turn tricks to pay her way through college but realising she looked different to the others and could make far more money, had soon given up her studies to go professional, then there was Svetlana Makarov, a Russian girl in her late teens who had fled to England illegally some three years earlier to escape her father's relentless sexual abuse. At only seventeen, though she looked much younger, she knew all there was to know about sex so her transition into the industry had been smooth and being so young, she earnt Morris the most out of all three girls. Levi was the first to approach the trio and opted to speak to black Grace on the assumption that as they were

ethnically connected, he would have more luck in getting her to go with him. Having already checked out the area and knowing exactly where he would carry out his assault, he put on his most dazzling smile. Grace would sleep with anyone for payment and some of the men were sickening not only in the acts they requested but also to look at so when she saw this six foot Adonis approach she was over the moon.
"You want to do a bit a business Sugar?"
"Sure do, what's it goin' to cost me pretty lady?"
"Forty for full but no anal and twenty five for a blow."
"Seems a fair price. I have a hotel room around the corner, nothin' fancy but it's clean. Care to join me?"
Grace was moving forwards in seconds, a bed to ply her trade in was a rare thing and compared to the usual of being fucked up against a cold wall or over the bonnet of some motor, it was music to her ears. Levi took her arm and together they walked along Euston Road before turning into Marchmont Street. Always on her guard, Grace wasn't overly concerned but she scanned everywhere looking for somewhere to escape should it be necessary.
"So where's this hotel then?"
"Just round here. The Judd, you know it?"
Grace relaxed a little, she'd turned several tricks

in the small hotel over the years. It was tired and rundown but just as he'd said, she knew it to be clean. Passing Cartwright Gardens, Levi suddenly grabbed a handful of her hair and forced her arm up behind her back until she yelled out in pain. He then frog marched her into the green common space that had ornate railing surrounding it with a small gated entrance. Filled with shrubs and bushes, at grass level it was easy to conceal what was happening on the ground. Roughly pushing her down so that they couldn't be seen from the road he slapped his hand over Grace' mouth as he leaned in close.

"I ain't goin' to kill you but I am goin' to hurt you, how much depends on the noise and struggle you make. I want you to take a message back to your boss."

Grace began to shake her head like she didn't have a clue who or what he was talking about.

"See, there you go and strike one! Morris fuckin' Carter you whore!

Graces eyes were wide open, she hated Morris but always toed the line as he could be a real nasty bastard if you upset him. This bloke was brazen to take on a Carter, so if he had the balls then he must be even worse than Morris. Removing his flick knife Levi gave her a smile she would never be proud of and as the blood began to flow Grace could only scream out in pain but the sound was muffled. By the time her attacker removed his hand and ran off, she was finally able to let out a long piercing scream but he was now nowhere to be seen. The fate of both Svetlana and ginger Rachel was pretty similar, the men's instructions had been to make the women ugly so that they would be of no use to their boss and they had all carried out their orders to the letter except for Freddy and Stevie Hunt, who had, without Del's approval, taken their attacks to the next level.

A few seconds after Eli had banged on Morris's bedroom door, Morris' mobile burst into life but the number was withheld. With the phone to his ear he struggled to pull on his dressing gown, all the time aware that he was keeping his father waiting, something you never did if you knew what was good for you.
"Yeah?!"
"Is that Morris Carter?"
"Who wants to know?"
"I'm Kenan's dad and I just wanted to tell you, you sick cunt! That you're next and it's goin' to be far worse than those dirty whores received!" With that the line went dead and Morris could only stare at the blank screen.

# CHAPTER NINETEEN

It was past three am by the time Del's men had all returned to Roach Road. Not actually carrying out any of the assaults himself, Del was waiting inside with a large bottle of scotch. They had all kept him up to date by phone as the attacks took place and when he'd received the last call, he sat back in his leather swivel chair with a wide grin on his face. Levi, Sammy and Gordon were the first to walk through the door and by the time the others had driven back from Southend, half the bottle, much to their annoyance, had already been consumed. With all glasses refilled, Del banged on the table for order.

"You all did well tonight and there will be a healthy bonus for each of you at the end of the week. This wasn't business and it wasn't your fight but you've stood up to the plate and for that you have my eternal gratitude. That said we now have to be on our guard as those cunts will be out for blood. None of us are safe so from now on and it's only in the short term, I want you all stayin' here. I've had mattresses put in the spare rooms upstairs but space is still at a premium so bunking up in two's is the only option."

"What the fuck! I ain't sleepin' with him."
Levi pointed his finger in the direction of Sammy Bird who was about to protest himself when Del again spoke.
"This ain't a suggestion Levi, it's a fuckin' order! Until this is over we need to keep our families safe and the only way we can do that is to stay away from them. I want you all to contact your wives and tell them no goin' out unless it's absolutely necessary and not to open the door to anyone. With any luck phase two can be carried out in the next couple of days and then hopefully we can all get back to normal."
"You mean you're kippin' here as well Guv?"
"Like I said Carl, none of us are safe until this fuckin' lot is over."
Stevie Hunt raised his hand asking for permission to speak.
"What?"
"I might have gone a bit over the top Boss."
"Me too."
Del looked at Freddy, who had suddenly decided to add to the conversation and then back to Stevie again.
"What the fuck have you two done!"
Freddy, having more balls than Stevie was the one to continue, though he was dreading the fallout.
"Seems like we might have killed our two

brasses Guv."
"What the fuck! Might have?"
"Well alright then, we did."
Del rubbed his brow with the palm of his hand and at the same time slowly shook his head.

In Upminster Eli was already seated at the table by the time Morris entered.
"Nice of you to fuckin' join me!"
"Sorry Dad I had to take a call, so what's goin' on?"
Eli relayed all that was said in Linda's short and hysterical phone call.
"I've sent Chester over to Southend to find out what's gone down and Gus over to Kings Cross."
"Kings Cross!?"
"Don't treat me like a fuckin' mug Morris, you think I didn't know about your little side line set up? I've known since day one but after tonight it's probably well and truly dead in the water. Now get comfortable boy 'cause neither of us will be movin' until we hear what's happened."
"Dad, I think I've got somethin' to add to all this. I was late comin' down because I got a phone call seconds after you knocked on my door. It was that Kenan kids' old man."
"The cheeky cunt! What did he say?"
"Well he didn't go into any detail regardin' what

had happened tonight but I think he's responsible and he also said that I was next!" Eli could feel his blood begin to boil, who the fuck did that cunt think he was! Rapping his fingers on the table he envisaged extracting his revenge and it wasn't pretty. The bloke had a beef with Morris and to be honest, rightly so but to hurt the Toms and then to make further threats was bang out of order. Just over an hour later his phone rang and he snatched it up, eager to hear any news. Eli's expression didn't alter as he said yes several times. Finally he asked what the level of damage was and his face grimaced when he listened to the answer.

"Get everyone over to the Bull now and no exceptions!"

"The Bull?!"

"It's safer for the time being."

Hanging up he turned to face his son who was also eager for news.

"Seems like the cunt has damaged every single Tom on our books!"

"What, like beat them up or somethin'?"

"No you moron, we ain't dealin' with a fuckin' amateur here, the bastard has carved them up. He also had Dee Dee and Chinese Mary killed and the others he's cut up so bad, that none of them will ever work the streets again, that's for sure. Get some clothes on, we have work to do."

Doing as he was told, Morris headed up to his bedroom to get dressed while Eli phoned his youngest son and explained what had happened.
"I can be back in three or four hour's Dad."
"No! I want you stay there and come back as we planned. Explain it all to Duke, he will know what to do."
With that the line went dead leaving Marcus well and truly pissed off. The old man seemed to once again be treating them both as if they were to blame when he knew fine well that this was all Morris' doing, yet again golden balls could do no wrong.

At the Bull the men had congregated as they'd been told but a few of them were grumbling that they didn't appreciate having to leave their beds at an ungodly hour but the room instantly became silent as soon as Eli and Morris walked in. Tall and thin and dressed in a classic navy Savile Row suit and camel cashmere coat, Eli Carter still looked like the hardened villain that he was. The old saying 'you couldn't make a silk purse out of a sows ear' would always ring true but there was something about the way a villain carried himself, they didn't strut or swagger but you knew not to mess with them all the same. Unbeknown to his sons, Eli's health was failing badly and the constant shortness of breath had recently been diagnosed as Chronic Obstructive Pulmonary Disease. Knowing his time was running out, he had decided to keep the COPD to himself. If anyone got wind then there was liable to be an attempted takeover by another firm, even his oldest son if he got the opportunity and Eli wasn't about to throw in the towel just yet and especially with all the shit that was now going down. In the main bar it was a full house in attendance and consisted of Gus (Gary Walker), Smiter (Peter Smith), Jolly Jack (Alan Suiter), Chester (Sam Williams), Hal (Harold Williams, Micky (Michael Gathercole), Denny (Denis Shannon) and Gal (Gary Matthews). Along with Morris and when Marcus got back, they army would total ten. It was agreed that Eli was too old but to him they'd used the term 'too valuable to take part', even though he was still capable of having a row when necessary he didn't argue the point. Explaining what had happened, Eli then gave precise instructions to each of them.

"Smiter, Jack and Denny, I want you out on the streets as soon as it's light. Find out exactly who this Foster firm has on the payroll, addresses etc. Chester, put your ear to the ground, find out about the property on Roach Road and if, how many shooters they keep on the premises? Hal,

you stay here in case anyone gets aggro and needs some help and do a bit of phonin' around and find out where the kids ashes or body is buried.  Micky, go to Kings Cross and see the girls, bung them each some cash and tell them to keep their traps shut.  Gus, go back to Southend and do the same.  I plan to strike in a weeks' time, I want to let the dust settle and see what occurs.  Marcus is attending Appleby for three or four days on my behalf and will make sure we have backup available if we need it.  Morris will stay with me, considering he's the main target it stands to reason that they will be gunnin' for him first.  Any question?"
Strangely the men all seemed to purse their lips and shake their heads in unison.
"Then let's get on it and we'll meet up again in two days' time."

At Appleby, Marcus was doing his best to put the troubles at home to one side.  He had spent his first night, all night in fact, with Rena but they hadn't done anything other than talk and as dawn broke and she bade him goodbye, he realised that he'd never met anyone quite like her before.  She was stunningly beautiful with a thick mane of blonde curly hair and a figure most girls would kill for but it was far more than that, she shared her hopes and dreams, the fact that she hated being part of the bevy of tin huts, always out on the road and open to continual harassment from anyone who thought they had a right to do so. Rena wanted her own van and to go off alone and the more she talked about what life could be like, the more Marcus was warming to the idea. At twenty five, she was old by traveller standards and her refusal to marry any of her father's suggestions was a bone of contention in the family. To spend all night with a man was a complete taboo in the community and Manfri Gallagher was an old school Irish traveller and would normally have chased Marcus from the site with a stick but he needed to get Rena married off and besides, he knew well enough that she would never bring shame to her family so just this once he had turned a blind eye. His youngest daughter had been born on English soil and as such had attended school, albeit sporadically. Rena had loved mixing with the gorger girls and was desperate to live a normal life, unlike her three sisters who had all been married off before their eighteenth birthdays and now had a hoard of kids following behind them. Sometimes Manfri and his wife Shelta despaired at their daughter and her strange ideas of what life should be like. At other times they saw just how beautiful and kind she was but that didn't bring money in and

Shelta wanted to see her daughter settled as soon as possible. When they had found out exactly who Marcus was, it was decided to give the young couple a free reign in the hope of a possible match.

The following morning and straight after Kezia had cooked a hearty breakfast for her father and cousin, Marcus was out again searching for the woman of his dreams, the woman he had spent a night with and not even a kiss had passed between them. He found her down at the Sands, in the middle of the water astride a magnificent grey colt, her blonde curly hair billowed in the breeze and he knew he had never seen such a beautiful sight in his entire life. When Rena spotted him she smiled and winked and Marcus, like a soppy love struck teenager, felt his heart beat just a little quicker as a knot formed in his stomach. Directing the colt to the water's edge, Rena bent down and said as quietly as she could so that the others didn't mock him.
"Do ya ride sweetheart?"
Marcus shook his head in embarrassment, his father had always tried to get him on a horse, after all it was part of their culture but unlike his brother, Marcus point blankly refused.
"Well we need to change that and quickly. Make yer way over there to the Hare and

Hounds. Go round the back and wait for me." He didn't question her and did exactly as she asked, all the while feeling like a silly school boy but he just couldn't help himself. Whatever she asked of him he knew he would never be able to refuse her. Expecting a riding lesson, Marcus was a little surprised when Rena dismounted, walked over to where he was standing and kissed him warmly on the lips. As she looked at him deeply with the biggest blue eyes he had ever seen, he knew all was lost. He instantly fell in love with a woman he hardly knew but who he was convinced would be his soul mate for the rest of his life.

Eli didn't have to wait too long before Del struck again. Having just had a wet shave at Mario's, his favourite barbers on Romford High Street and while Morris was standing outside having a cigarette, Eli noticed a stranger approaching from across the road. Grabbing Mario's cut throat razor Eli ran outside and as Freddy Wentworth went to pull something from his pocket, Eli lashed out. The blade cut through the man's leather jacket like butter and realising that there could be some serious damage, Freddy scarpered as fast as he could. Eli, due to meet his men in less than an hour was fuming, well the cunt had made his next move so the game was on!

At the Bull everyone was seated and waiting for the boss to arrive and as soon as Eli and Morris walked in it was straight down to business.

"Right! That cheeky cunt has just attempted to hurt Morris so you'd better have something' for me!"

Gus was the first to speak, telling his boss that he had the names and addresses of all but one of Del's men, he further added that he'd been able to find out that none of the men had been at home for the last couple of days."

"Clever, very clever, he has them holed up somewhere, damage limitation. Chester, you got anythin' yet?"

"I couldn't find out anythin' regardin' shooters but takin' into account what they deal in, there's a good chance they have a whole arsenal stashed inside. There has been a lot of comin' and goin' so I think that as you said, that's where they are holed up."

"Good work. Hal?"

"Well, it was a burial and the plot is in Edmonton cemetery. The mother visits the grave religiously every day but she's never alone though."

"Unlike that cunt, I ain't interested in hurtin' women. Morris, this is a job for you, Gus go with him and take Chester as a look out.

Tonight I want you to dig that little fucker up and leave him somewhere out in the open. This firm are like rats hidin' in a fuckin' sewer, well we'll see about that! If anythin', this will flush that bastard and his men out of their hidin' place!"

"Really Dad!? What prop a fuckin' coffin up, I don't think so!"

In a nano second Eli turned on his son with such vengeance that the whole room was on tenter hooks, it finally looked like his twat of a son had at last pushed the guvnor too far. As Eli spoke, his voice was so loud and booming that it sounded like he was shouting and you could visibly see a few of the men grimace and shrink down into their chairs.

"You will do as you're fuckin' told!!! This is only happenin' because of your sick fuckin' twisted actions. These men are stickin' their fuckin' necks out for you, though God above only knows why! Gus, you okay with this?"

"I've done worse boss."

Gary Walkers comment immediately put smiles on all of their faces and with that a round of laughter erupted. Momentarily the atmosphere was relaxed and in all honesty most of the men were glad of that fact, Eli at his worse was terrifying and it wasn't a sight they wanted to witness, no matter how much they all disliked

Morris.

"Marcus will be back tomorrow and then we'll wait and see what that cunts next move is once the body is found but I am certain it's goin' to get fuckin' bloody. You all up for it?"

There was a loud unanimous 'Yes!' and Eli just nodded, proud with the men he had handpicked and who were, unlike his own blood, loyal to the core.

# CHAPTER TWENTY

In the early hours of the following Morning, Gus drove a small white Vauxhall van over to the Upminster house to Collect Morris Carter. Chester sat in the passenger seat but conversation was limited, the two men got on well enough but this wasn't exactly a job that either of them were looking forward to doing. Both were desperate to voice their opinions but it was a sad fact of life that neither trusted the other enough to be honest. The van was well equipped, early in the day Gus had stocked the interior with spades, shovels, a pick axe, a hammer and screwdrivers, just in case they had difficulty removing the coffin lid. Pulling up outside the red brick mansion he'd expected Morris to be ready and waiting but when they arrived the house was in total darkness and to say he was pissed off was an understatement. Not wanting to wake the boss as Eli was temperamental at the best of times and lately he'd been even worse than normal, Gus tapped Morris' number into his mobile. The phone seemed to ring for an eternity before it was finally answered.
"Yeah? Whoever you are you can fuck right off, do you know what bastard time it is?!!"

"Yes I do and we're waitin' outside. For fucks sake Morris hurry up will you, we need to get this done before the light breaks."

The only reply was some kind of grunt and Gus knew that the tosser was still in bed. There wasn't anything he could do about it, after all it was the boss's son but by God he wished that wasn't the case. Five minutes later Morris reluctantly came out of the front door and wearily climbed into the passenger seat, he hadn't showered and his breath was rancid as he sighed heavily.

"I really don't fuckin' need this!"

"And neither do we pal but we ain't got much fuckin' choice in the matter so shut your fuckin' trap okay?"

Morris Carter stared at the driver with daggers.

"I tell you somethin' Gus, come the day I'm in charge you won't dare fuckin' speak to me like that."

"Yeah, yeah, that's if you live that long sunshine cause how things are goin' it's a distinct possibility that you won't and in any case by then I'll be long gone."

The words hit Morris like a lead balloon as he suddenly realised that this Del geezer really was out to kill him and if it wasn't for his old man he would probably be toast by now. With that realisation, he would be quiet for the rest of the journey which was totally out of character but welcomed by the others. As soon as they'd arrived at the boss's house Chester had climbed into the back and was now sitting on an old cushion and none too pleased that he would be taking the twenty four mile journey being pushed from one side to the other as Gus manoeuvred the roads. His driving wasn't good at the best of times but just about bearable when you had a seatbelt on. At this ungodly hour Edmonton was relatively quiet, good for traffic but there was also more chance of being pulled over by the Old Bill. Gus knew the area well and slowing down he made sure that he kept to the speed limits. In his younger days, long before joining the Carter firm he'd spent many evenings at Enfield car auction trying to buy something for nothing and turning it into a profit, he hadn't been that successful hence the line of work he was now in. Turning off of Church Street into the cemetery, the van continued through the central arch passing grave after grave and as soon as they reached the right area, Chester had already carried out a search the previous day, Gus immediately turned the headlights off. The silence was eerie to say the least and when Morris switched on his torch and placed it under his chin then shouted 'BOO!' making Gus nearly jump out of his skin it didn't go down too well.

"For Christ sake stop fuckin' about Morris."

They all got out and opening up the rear doors, Gus reached into the darkness until his hand rested on the smooth wooden handles.

"Here grab the shovels."

Chester, now laden down with a pick axe and the holdall containing the extra tools that they hoped they wouldn't need, led the way. The ground was uneven and after Morris was told to turn off his torch, you could hardly see your hand in front of your face. Finally they reached the graveside, which was yet to have a headstone laid and they roughly kicked away the flowers that Jean had so lovingly placed there the previous morning.

"Shush! What was that?"

The three stopped dead in their tracks for a few seconds as they listened to hear what Chester had imagined.

"It wasn't anythin' you Muppet, now get diggin' or we'll still be here when the groundsman arrive and make sure you go a bit further length ways so we have room to lever it up if we need to."

They all began to dig as if their lives depended on it but when they got to about three feet deep two of them had to jump in as the space was restricted.

"Morris, you get in with Chester."

"Oh fuck off! Why me?"

Gus was rapidly losing patience, how in hells name Eli had ended up with such an idiot for a son was beyond him.

"Because I said so and your old man told me I had to make you do the lion's share of the donkey work, considering you caused all of this fuckin' aggro in the first place. Want me to call him sunshine and tell him you ain't playin' ball?"

Reluctantly Morris jumped down into the grave with a thud causing Gus to shake his head in frustration.

"Careful you twat, you could have gone through the fuckin' lid!"

"Alright, alright, keep your knickers on!"

It took another twenty or so minutes and then suddenly Chester's spade hit something that sounded like wood. With the edge of his spade he cleared away the thin layer of soil to reveal the brass plaque. Gus shone his torch down onto it just to make sure they had the right grave. It would have been a nightmare to find out they had wasted all this time and effort only to exhume someone's dearly departed wife.

"Here Chester, get this under the coffin at one end."

Gus threw down a long heavy duty woven strap

like the kind used by lorry drivers to secure their loads. Gus put out his hand and slowly pulled Chester up onto the grass but he didn't offer the same for Morris. When he'd at last managed to climb out, they each took an end of the strap and began to haul the coffin until it was upright but there wasn't enough room to do what they needed.

"Not the best plan I admit so I think we need to get the whole fuckin' thing out of the ground. Chester, climb back down and when me and Morris begin to pull, you push the fuckin' thing upwards. Ready? On three, one, two...."

Kenan Foster's once beautiful polished coffin moved easily and when it was finally placed down onto the grass beside the grave, Gus could see even in the now dim light, that no expense had been spared. Removing a small rechargeable screwdriver from the bag he wiped as much dirt away as he could to find the screw holes.

"What the fuck are you doing?!!"

"How else do you expect me to get the poor cunt out Morris?"

"But I thought the old man meant just the coffin?"

Gus stared at Morris for just a second and then continued with the job in hand. The six plastic fleur screws came up easily and shaking his head, he was surprised that such an expensive looking coffin would have plastic screws. Mind you, his old mum had always told him that undertakers were greedy bastards with no scruples and would bury you in a cardboard box if they could get away with it. There had long since been a rumour that old Archibald Connor over in Bethnal Green actually did just that. It was said he would move the deceased into a box when it reached the furnace at the crematorium and then after a good clean, would resell the coffin to another poor unsuspecting family. Lifting the lid, Gus fell back on his heels as the smell of decomposing flesh filled the early morning air. Feeling the acid pangs of onset nausea in his cheeks, Morris put his palm over his mouth in an attempt to hold back the vomit that was about to explode any second. He wasn't successful and running as far away from the corpse as he could, he retched until there was nothing left inside of him. Gus shone his torch onto the body and grimaced at the sight before him. Somehow the aptly named coffin flies had found their way inside and had laid eggs on Kenan's face. The sight was truly horrific and as Chester and Gus looked at one another, they were both thinking the same thing. This was going to be truly gruesome for the mother and she really didn't deserve it but neither of them could back out without feeling Eli's wrath. As bad as they felt for Jean Foster, they had to see this job out till the end or it could be them being laid to rest, another rumour that had followed Eli Carter for years but that was another story.

"Oi! Get your fuckin' arse back over here, we have work to do!"

Morris grabbed Kenan's legs and Gus held him under the armpits. Together and it was a struggle with the proverbial 'dead weight', they followed Chester through the cemetery towards the archway entrance. Having watched Jean's movements over the last few days Chester knew that she always arrived before anyone else, she was so punctual that you could set your watch by her. It was always eight thirty on the dot to avoid the school traffic, so they knew there was little chance of anyone else stumbling on the corpse and calling for help. Propping Kenan's remains up against the wall in a sitting position, he was slumped over and now resembled a druggie or drunk who was out for the count. On the off chance anyone was here before Jean, they would most definitely take a wide berth.

"Right, let's get the fuck out of here!"

Almost running, the three made their way back to the van, packed in the tools and within a few minutes they were on their way over to the Bull.

It was strange using the place again after all this time but Eli had been insistent that they stay as far away from the office as possible, at least until he told them otherwise.

Jean Foster had just finished her fifth cup of tea and was about to put on her coat and set off when Allison walked into the kitchen. Late the previous night she'd come home, since her brother's death she'd been unable to get a single night of peace in her own flat. Now she couldn't bear to be there alone and even though last night she still wasn't at peace, it had helped her knowing her sister and parents were in the rooms next to her.

"Mornin' mum. Where's the old man?"

Jean shook her head but there was no emotion showing on her face at the mention of her husband, well that wasn't exactly true, all Allison could see was a burning hatred towards her father.

"Mornin' darlin', he ain't here, hasn't been for the last three days. How'd you sleep?"

Allison could only shake her head as her mother touched her lovingly on the arm.

"You two will sort it out won't you mum?"

"I don't know love, I really don't. All I can say is that at this moment in time I can't bear to even look at him. I'm sorry that's not what you want to hear but it's the truth. Whether my feeling will change in the future, well that remains to be seen."

"Would you mind if I came with you today? Only I haven't been since the funeral and I…"

When she saw the tears as they began to well up in the eyes of her normally strong, argumentative and feisty daughter, a woman who no longer resembled her former self, Jean placed the palms of her hands onto Allison's cheeks.

"My darlin' you never need to ask, he was your brother and I would welcome the company. Go and get dressed as we need to get off before the traffic gets heavy. You think Dawn would like to come?"

Jean suddenly realised what she'd said, there was nothing to like in visiting the grave of your only son but the daily ritual did bring her comfort, somehow she felt closer to him there so maybe there was something to like about it after all.

"Probably but when I came down she was snoring her head off and I think at the moment, sleep, when we can get it, is more important for all of us don't you?"

Fifteen minutes later and the Mercedes SLC convertible pulled up in the car park of Edmonton cemetery. Jean was the first to get out and was removing the flowers from the boot so didn't see what Allison did. When she heard her daughter scream Jean ran around to the passenger side of the car.

"Have you hurt yourself?"

Dawn Foster just shook her head vigorously.

"Then whatever's the matter sweetheart?"

Allison could only point her finger in the direction of the archway and looking over Jean suddenly screamed out in horror and then running over, she dropped to her knees. Taking the rotting remains of her son into her arms she began to cradle him back and forth. With shaking hands Allison removed her phone and tapped in her father's number. It only rang a couple of times, since the tragedy Del made sure he was there for his family at all times, night or day.

"Mornin' babe, everythin' alright?"

"Oh Dad you got to get here and fast, we're at the cemetery."

"What's happened? Is it your mum?"

"It's Kenan dad, someone has dug him up. Oh please get here quick, pleeeeease!"

Her voice was almost shrieking with terror. Del snatched up his keys and ran to the door with Levi following close behind. He didn't have a clue what was going on but he hadn't let the boss out of his sight for the past three days and

he wasn't about to start now.  When they reached the car Del threw the keys to his number one and then got into the passenger seat.
"What's goin' on boss?"
"Edmonton cemetery and fast!  I don't give a shit about speed cameras, just get me there!"
That was a first, Del always stipulated that they should never willingly cross the Old Bill so if he was now saying that in this instance it didn't matter, well Levi had to assume it was something really, really bad.  Doing as he was told he tore away from Roach Road so fast that the tyres created smoke on the tarmac.

# CHAPTER TWENTY ONE

In less than ten minutes Del's car came to a screeching halt in the cemetery carpark. Staring in disbelief as his wife cradled the corpse of their dead child, he felt a rage so strong begin to build up inside of him that it was actually painful. Levi couldn't take in what he was witness too, it was like something from a horror movie and a bad one at that.

"Fuckin' hell Guv, whatever's goin' on?"

"You can see what's goin' on and you know who's fuckin' responsible. I'm gonna try and get her away and then you call the old Bill, 'cause this is somethin' they need to deal with. Tell them nothin' other than the fact that you came over to pay your respects and this is how you found him and don't give your name. They can make arrangements to put him back in the ground. When you've made the call get back to Roach Road and wait for me. First go and sort Allison out, put her in my motor, I'll drive it back and you can take Jeans car. When I've got Jean away from him I want you to stand guard."

"What!?"

"Only until we drive off you soppy twat, there's no way she will leave him alone so I need her to think you're his bodyguard."

The order didn't sit well with Levi, Kenan or not, he didn't want to get any closer to a rotting corpse than he had to. Climbing out of the car Del slowly made his way towards his wife and dropping to his knees he tenderly touched her on the cheek.
"I don't know who has done this darlin' but I swear on my life I'm goin' to find out. You need to leave him now babe, come on, come with me." His words made Jean hold on even tighter and thankfully, as she buried her face in his hair she didn't see the two maggots that dropped from his nose onto the ground. Del swept them away with his hand but it made no difference as it still took a good twenty minutes of gentle talking to actually get her away from the body and into the car. At first Jean had refused point blank to leave her boy and had only finally agreed on the promise that Levi wouldn't leave Kenan alone. The three sad figures drove back home in silence, Jean and Allison were in shock and Del wouldn't allow himself to speak as he was so angry that he didn't know what would come out of his mouth. On reaching the house he was surprised to see Dawn standing outside, recently she'd taken up smoking, it was probably the stress and she didn't think her family had noticed. Swiftly dropping the butt onto the ground she stepped on it and smiled in the hope

that she hadn't been seen. As her father got out of the car, the look on his face spoke volumes, something had happened.

"Dawnie get your mum out of the car and then join me in the study. Allison? Come on love, you need to come inside too."

Dawn did what he asked without question and when she'd seated her mother and sister in the kitchen and made them both tea, she gingerly tapped on the study door before walking in. Del proceeded to explain all that had happened and the look on his daughter's face, along with the tears that were now flowing freely, was one of utter disbelief and revulsion.

"I'm goin' to sort this Dawnie but it'll take some time. Your mum and Ally are in a bad way, I think it's shock so I need you to watch them like a hawk."

Walking around the desk he handed his daughter a set of keys.

"Levi has your mum's car and when he returns it I want you to take the keys and these spares as I wouldn't put it past her to go back down to the cemetery. As soon as he hands them to you go straight to my study and put them in the safe, the code is 0798. When I've left, I want you to lock all the doors and windows and take out the keys."

"But Dad, I can't lock them in, it's not....."

"Dawn! This is important. I need to know that you are all safe and no one has gone wanderin'. I don't think your mum is in her right state of mind and I can't stay here and watch her, I need to sort this fuckin' mess out 'cause no one knows what the leery fuckers are gonna do next! Please, will you do this for me babe?"
Dawn bowed her head, she loved her father dearly and knew he wold never do anything to harm them, the complete opposite in fact.
"Good girl, now keep your phone with you at all times and I'll give you a ring in a couple of hours."
With that Del Foster left the family home and as he heard the door lock behind him he nodded to himself. Now it was time to get to work and sort those bastards out once and for all.

Marcus had left Appleby full to bursting after another one of Kezia's hearty breakfasts and arriving back in Essex at just before two he headed straight for the house. His priority should have been going to the Bull but he just couldn't face it and as he let himself inside, he was pleased that his father's car wasn't on the drive. There was obviously a lot of shit going down but for now he just wanted to savour the last few days before he had to put all the love stuff to the back of his mind. Passing Milly

Garrod in the hallway he grinned when he saw her.

"Hello there Milly love and what a beautiful day it is."

Milly laughed out loud and Marcus quizzically moved his head to one side.

"What's so funny?"

"My darlin' I've only ever seen that dopey look you're wearin' a few times before and on each occasion it has involved the fairer sex. Now if I was a gambling woman, which I most certainly am not, I would lay a bundle down on the fact that you've met a woman?"

Marcus could feel his cheeks redden with embarrassment but if the housekeeper could so easily read his emotions then he had no hope when it came to his brother or the old man.

"Is it that obvious Mill's?"

"It most certainly is but a word of advice love, keep it to yourself and don't breathe a word to Morris or your dad. They have a nasty way of ruinin' anythin' that's good and I would hate to see you get hurt through their jealousy."

Marcus smiled, he knew she was right and that his dad and brother would try to spoil things if they found out just for the sheer hell of it.

Milly Garrod had started off at the Upminster house doing just four hours a week cleaning.

She had seen the boys grow up, been there when the lady of the house had passed away and witnessed over the years how utterly cruel Eli could be, especially to his youngest child. It was something she'd never been able to understand because out of the two, Marcus was definitely the nicest. He had a very kind heart and had been his mother's favourite, maybe that was why Eli treated him the way he did. Whatever the reason, she hoped and prayed that Marcus Carter would find happiness and leave this miserable mausoleum of a house. Since Angela's death there was no love in the place and whenever Milly walked in she shuddered at the coldness of it all. There was no laughter, no warm atmosphere and definitely no love, almost as if any happiness the family had previously shared, had gone to the grave with the wife and mother they were still mourning after all of these years.

Taking a shower and after getting his thoughts and emotions in check, Marcus headed back out and drove over to Romford. Entering the Bull he found the men sitting about waiting for orders. Making his way to the rear and his father's office, he tapped on the door and then walked inside.

"You're back then? Alright for some, off on their

jolly's while we've been sloggin' our fuckin' arses of, figuratively speakin' of course."
Morris began to laugh at his own words but was silenced when Eli glared at him.
"Shut it!!!"
Turning to face his youngest, Eli was eager to hear any news that Marcus might have brought back with him.
"What did Duke say on the matter?"
"Just as you'd expect Dad, pick up the blower and he'll have ten of his best with you in no time."
"That's my brother! You two ain't got a fuckin' clue what it's like to be a real Romany, family is all that matters and we all come together in times of crisis and need."
"You really think it's gonna be necessary Dad?"
Marcus was still unaware of what had recently gone down, or he was for all of the next twenty seconds. Before his father had a chance to explain, Morris went in all guns blazing and recapped in great detail just what they had done. Marcus was totally and utterly appalled and directed his next question towards his brother.
"That's sick, what on earth possessed you to do that?"
This time Morris didn't get a chance to speak as Eli replied sharply.
"He hurt my girls and that can't go unpunished

Son."

"Maybe not but ain't you forgettin' one tiny detail? The bloke has lost his only son and deep down, that twat sittin' there getting' excited about diggin' the poor cunt up, is the only one to blame!"

Eli loved his youngest but the man was weak and would never succeed in this world, well not in their line of work at least.

"It is what it is Son and you just have to get used to it. If I hadn't retaliated then I would have been a laughin' stock and my credibility would have been out of the window. At least this way no one livin' got hurt or would you rather I went after the geezer's wife and daughters?"

The look Marcus gave his father and brother was one of total disgust but he didn't add anything further to the conversation. He needed to get out of this hell hole or he was going to explode. There and then he made himself a promise, Rena's dream was really growing on him and when this lot was over he was leaving for good.

At Roach Road, Levi was already there when Del walked in. Gathering the men at the table he began to speak and as he revealed his plan the men couldn't believe what they were hearing.

"I've thought long and hard about this and you all obviously know what went down today?"

Not one of his men could look him in the face, what their boss had just gone through was downright sick in every sense of the word.
"Now we can't get to that cunt as the first pathetic attempt failed and they will now be watching him like a fuckin' hawk, so I've come up with a plan. I know it's goin' to sound off the wall but I need one of you to get hold of a cop car and a couple of uniforms, we won't need them for long, three hours tops, any suggestions as I know it ain't an easy ask?"

Stevie Hunt was the only one to speak but what he said made everyone's jaw drop open.

"You all know I'm queer."

They didn't, well all except Del, who had once again hypocritically chosen not to act on his loathing and hatred of minority groups because Stevie Hunt was a good soldier and they were few and far between nowadays. There was only stunned silence from his fellow firm members but that didn't stop him continuing and he scanned each of their faces in turn as he spoke.

"I never flaunt it and I think what happened to Kenan cut me far deeper than any of you could possibly understand. Gays simply do not fuckin' do that, only sick depraved bastards do but people tend to tar us all with the same brush."

"Where is this going' Stevie?"

"For the last few months I've been havin' a relationship with a married copper called Lance, he works for the Met out of Bow Road station and I have some very naughty fuckin' photos. Leave it with me and I'll make arrangements. When are we looking at?"

"Nice one! Well, unbeknown to all of you, I've been havin' the cunt tailed, that's how I knew all about your bungled hit on him Freddy."

Freddy Wentworth lowered his head in shame, up until this moment no one had mentioned what had gone down and now he felt embarrassed.

Jock McManus was ex force. Having served his twenty years, he had retired just as he was about to be prosecuted for corruption. Since then he had begun to work for anyone willing to pay and as such, now knew all there was to know about Morris Carter and had passed on his findings to Del on a daily basis.

"Jock's been on the books since that cunt got released. He reckons the bastard is always with either his old man or one of the firm."

"So how do we get to him then?"

"I was about to explain Levi, before you fuckin' interrupted me. He has to see his probation officer once a week on a Tuesday in Romford, a stipulation of his release. Next week I want you Stevie and you Gordon, to pull him over and arrest him.  If the old man gets lippy tell him to follow you to Main Road station.  Jock's done a recce and the station carpark is at the rear and only open to staff.  The old man will have to drive on to find a parking spot around the front.  Indicate but don't turn in, when the old man's car is out of sight drive back over the road to the Asda supermarket.  Tony will be waiting with ramps and a removal truck and I want you to drive straight inside.  Get back here, drop the bastard off and then Stevie you can return the car and uniforms.  If your boyfriend starts askin' too many questions tell him to keep his fuckin' nose out or you'll expose him to his Mrs.  Oh, and make sure you put some dodgy plates and roof numbers on so there's no comeback on your friend.  As you are all well aware, this is high risk, so I want you to be a hundred percent, if you ain't then speak up now?"

Not one man voiced an opinion so it was all systems go for five days' time.

"Levi, go and drop Jeans car back at the house and give the keys to Dawn, no one else!  Carl, you can follow him and then bring him back.  Make sure you keep your traps shut, until then we continue to bunk down here I'm afraid."

Now there was a low grumble of complaint but Del ignored it and walked into his office.

Closing the door, he made the call to Dawn that

he wasn't looking forward to but he needed to check on Jean and Ally. Del breathed a sigh of relief when his daughter informed him that all was fine at the house.

"Will you be back later Dad?"

"I'll pop in if I can but things are difficult at the moment babe. Levi is on his way over with your mum's car so keep your eyes peeled for him. If I don't get back, keep on your guard and let me know the second anythin' doesn't feel right or if your mum kicks off again. Okay?"

Dawn didn't reply as she ended the call and Del knew she wasn't happy but what choice did he have? He had to do this, had to see it through to the end for his boy and no one, not even an army of men was going to stop him.

# CHAPTER TWENTY TWO

It felt like a ticking time bomb waiting for something to happen. Eli was convinced there would be further payback and at times not knowing seemed worse than knowing. If it had been about him he would have been able to handle it with no problem, over the years he'd gone through far worse than this, but it wasn't, it was his flesh and blood, the fruit of his loins and that made it almost unbearable. He knew he was suffocating his son but if anything happened to his boy, either of his boys, well he just wouldn't be able to cope. When the four day stage had passed without event, Eli was beginning to think, praying actually, that Del Foster had got the message and had accepted that once and for all this had to end. Still concerned about Morris he watched his eldest son's every move and Morris was beginning to feel like he was back in prison. Finally on the morning of his probation appointment he snapped when over breakfast his father asked him what time they needed to set off.
"For fucks sake Dad! I can't take a shit without you knowin' about it and its doin' my fuckin' head in. I ain't had a night out since I got home and I feel like I might as well be back inside."

Marcus had only just entered the dining room and as soon as he heard raised voices he was about to turn and go out again when he came face to face with Milly.

"There you go sunshine, I've done you some nice scrambled eggs, was always your favourite as a teenager."

"Thanks darlin' you're a real sweetheart."

Marcus didn't have the heart to tell her he'd lost his appetite so reluctantly he turned back and took a seat at the table.

"So what do you think about it all bro?"

"About what?"

"The old man treatin' me like a bleedin' kid? Fancy a night out, we could go down the hut and see who we can pull."

Marcus looked in his father's direction and Eli was staring daggers.

"Nah, I'm good thanks and actually, I agree with Dad. What on earth is the point of takin' unnecessary risks? One way or another it will be over soon and back to business as usual, so for now, well I think you should just do as you're told.."

As Morris stood up in a rage he pushed his chair away so violently that it fell over and then threw his napkin down onto the table as he glared at his father.

"I ain't havin' it Dad, do you hear me, I ain't

fuckin' havin' it. Get out of my way old woman."

Milly Garrod had been about to bring in more fresh toast when Morris barged passed her knocking her arm as he did so, which caused her to drop the tray she was carrying. He only glared at her, as if to say it was her fault and as per usual he wasn't reprimanded by his father. Milly would have left the house long ago if it wasn't for the fact that Eli Carter paid handsomely, so she just had to endure the rudeness that she was shown on a daily basis. Instantly Marcus was on his feet and as he bent down to help her pick up the mess, he smiled and winked.

"Take no notice Mills, he can be a right wanker at times."

An hour later and dressed in a smart suit, Morris descended the elaborate staircase and saw his father sitting on one of the hall chairs waiting for him. Morris shook his head and then walked straight out of the front door. Eli's Jag was already pointing in the direction of the gates and when he climbed into the driving seat, Morris knew he had no option but to join his father. Under his breath he muttered 'This is the last time, the last fuckin' time I swear.'

In Romford, Tony Morgan had been parked up

in Asda for nearly an hour as he'd wanted to make sure he could exit easily and that there were no obstacles stopping him putting the ramps down. Knowing that close circuit television cameras were in operation, where weren't they nowadays? Tony had placed fake magnetic plates over the originals but it still didn't stop him being nervous. He had one tense moment when an old woman with a blue rinse hairdo tried to park her Corsa directly behind him. The rest of the carpark was almost empty but she had to choose right behind the removal lorry. Tony wanted to pull her from the car and throw her in the bushes but he couldn't do anything that might cause suspicion or indeed make the silly old cow call the Old Bill. Instead he jumped from the cab and in the softest, kindest voice he could manage, gently tapped on her window, smiling warmly.
"Mornin' beautiful."
The woman who was at least in her mid-eighties, smiled. Her bright pink lipstick, caked into the deep lines of her cats arse lips, made her appear scary. She must have been a heavy smoker and as she revealed ageing crooked teeth and sighed heavily with old people's breath, Tony wanted to puke.
"I don't mean to be a nuisance my darlin' but I'm expecting a very big load shortly, that's what

these are for."
Tony pointed to the ramps and at the same time he could feel his blood begin to boil.
"If you leave your car there we won't be able to get it onto the back so if I say pretty please, do you think you could move over a few spaces." Again the woman smiled, beautiful and darling in two sentences, could her morning get any better? After telling Tony how nice it was to meet a polite young man for a change, Tony was fifty if he was a day, she noisily crunched the gearbox of the Corsa as she placed it into reverse.
"If more people had your manners young man, then the world would be a much nicer place." When she at last pulled into a parking spot at least six spaces away Tony breathed a sigh of relief and wiped the sweat from his brow. That could have caused major problems for them all and he now willed it to be over with as soon as possible.

Eli and Morris were making good time for a change. Eli took the first left at Gallows Corner roundabout and continued along Main Road until he was level with the turning to Castellan Avenue. Suddenly a patrol car pulled out in front of him and he was flagged down by a policeman who beckoned towards an empty bus stop. Morris instantly became agitated, if he was late it would be a black mark and he couldn't afford that to happen as he'd already had a report put in against him regarding his attitude. Now a second plod got out of the car, Stevie Hunt and Gordon Mayes had scrubbed up well and with the help of the uniforms, both looked the epitome of police officers. Stevie went to Morris's door and Gordon to Eli's. Both men lowered their windows but it was Morris who spoke.

"Officer, what seems to be the problem?"

"Morris Carter?"

"Yes Officer, why what's goin' on?"

"Could you step out of the vehicle for a moment please Sir?"

Morris sighed heavily but did as he was told, at the same time Eli began to fire questions at Gordon but was instantly stopped when Gordon informed him that it was confidential and nothing to do with the driver.

"He's my son!"

"And he's also an adult Sir so if you wouldn't mind refraining from interfering, we will be able to get this matter sorted out as quickly as possible."

Morris shook his head, sighed and rolled his eyes in the direction of Stevie Hunt. Eli and Morris didn't notice that neither of the men had radios or body cams on, a big oversight for them both.

"So what's goin' on then?"

"We've had a call from your probation officer stating that you didn't attend your meeting yesterday. I'm sorry but we have to take you to the station, with any luck we can sort this out swiftly and then you can be on your way."

"But my appointment ain't until today, every week on a Tuesday at ten?"

"Apparently it was changed and they messaged you first thing yesterday morning. That's all the information I have regarding the matter I'm afraid, now I really don't want to cuff you, will it be necessary Sir?"

Morris reluctantly shook his head as he got into the back of the patrol car. Stevie walked back over to the Jag and advised Eli to follow them on to the station.

"Oh and by the way Sir. It's parking for the Force only at the station so you'll have to find somewhere else to leave your vehicle. When you've done that just make your way to the front main entrance."

While the patrol car turned right onto Oakland Avenue and headed towards the gated entrance at the rear of the station, Eli continued on until he could find a parking space. Luckily a car was just pulling out of the library and after locking the Jag he headed back in the direction of the station but Stevie had already turned back onto Main Road. By now Morris knew that something wasn't right.

"What the fuck is goin' on?!!"

His question was met with only silence and about to kick off, he was instantly stopped when he saw the Beretta pistol pointed at him between the two front seats. Gordons face was menacing but he didn't have to speak, the gun said all that was needed. Holding his hands up in submission, Morris could only sit it out and wait to see how bad the punishment was going to be. Turning down Junction Road, the patrol car was now out of sight from the main drag and Stevie Hunt began to relax a little. His heart was racing and the adrenalin was pumping but by God he felt alive! As they neared the rear of Asda's carpark Stevie spotted the removal lorry and honked the car horn so that Tony knew they were approaching. Driving straight up the ramps into the back of the lorry and with the roller shutter now down, everything had gone as sweet as a nut. In less than an hour they would be back at Roach Road and Stevie could get the car and uniforms returned to Lance who hadn't been best pleased with the threat of exposure. For once Stevie was glad that he wouldn't be involved with what was about to happen to the

bastard sitting on the rear seat because it was going to be nasty, of that he was in no doubt.
At the station, Eli Carter entered through the front automated doors and walked up to the counter. His well-tailored suit and crisp tie and shirt made him appear like a city gent and the woman working the front counter, spoke to him accordingly as she smiled warmly.
"Good morning Sir. How can I help you today?"
"My son has just been arrested and they told me to come in here and wait."
"What is his name and I'll go and see what I can find out for you."
"Morris Carter."
Eli then took a seat on one of the fixed, modern and very uncomfortable seats. He waited there for what seemed like an age but finally a uniformed officer walked through the inner doors and over to Eli.
"Mr Carter?"
Eli nodded his head as he got to his feet. The bloody probation service had better apologise for their fuck up or he was going to create merry hell.
"Good morning, I'm Sergeant Parsons and I'm covering the custody suite today. I think you must be confused Sir, as yet there have not been any arrests today and no one has been brought in."

Suddenly Eli's face went ashen as the penny at last dropped regarding what had just happened. How could he have been so trusting, he was a complete fucking idiot!

"Are you alright Sir? Has something happened?"

"Somethin's happened alright but nothin' you can help with."

Eli strode out of the station and when he was once again back in the Jag he called the Bull. By the time he got there everyone was in attendance, Marcus included. Pacing up and down Eli began to rant and rave as he spoke and revealed just what those cunning bastards had masterminded.

"They've got him, those fuckin' cunts have got my boy!"

"Then we need to go and get him Dad."

Eli stared at his youngest as if Marcus was speaking in another language.

"Go and get him?!!! You fuckin' idiot, we ain't got a clue what the setup is and they're probably waiting for us to do just that. Go and find your uncle Duke, explain what's happened and tell him to get some bodies here by tonight, tomorrow at the latest!"

At Roach Road, Del was now patiently waiting for his men to return. He had been on tenter hooks as he'd had no communication for over an hour but as soon as the removal lorry passed Hackney Marshes, Tony had phoned ahead and informed his boss that all had gone to plan. He hadn't wanted to call in earlier and get Del's hopes up, just in case something went wrong but thankfully that hadn't been the case. Spotting an area that wasn't covered by cameras, Tony stopped the lorry and quickly removed the fake plates.

When he heard the lorry pull up outside Del took his seat behind the desk and stared at the metal chair which had been strategically place in front. Attached to the legs, two sets of steel handcuffs had been put in place in readiness for his victim. Tony and Gordon frogmarched Morris inside. He now had a canvas bag over his head and he was disorientated and stumbled several times as he was led along the narrow hallway of the old house. Forcing him down onto the chair, Tony proceeded to remove the bag and at the same time shone a wide angle high watt torch into his eyes so that he wasn't able to see anything. Morris pulled his head back and squinted rapidly. This was the first time he had ever been on the receiving end and he was now scared beyond belief but he wasn't about to show it to anyone.

"Whatever the fuck you're gonna do, just do it

you cunts!"

Del stood up and walking around the desk, nodded for Tony to switch off the light.

"Oh no sunshine, I'm goin' to make you suffer like you wouldn't believe, just like you made my boy suffer and I'm goin' to enjoy it and take my time!"

"Well you'd better fuckin' hurry up 'cause when my old man gets a hold of you you're done for."

Del let out a cackling laugh, this was going to be fun.

"Fuckin' gypo's, always actin' like hard bastards until it comes down to it. You ain't no more a gypsy than I am, you're a dirty fuckin' pikey queer who gets off preying on little boys. Tone, get the acid!"

Morris was squirming, he'd been desperate for a pee since Romford and now when he heard the word acid and knew what damage it could inflict, he felt his bladder release itself.

Whatever his father was doing to set him free and he was in no doubt that the wheels were already in motion, he just payed that it wouldn't take too long.

# CHAPTER TWENTY THREE

Marcus called Kezia from the back kitchen of the Bull and asked where they were camped. When she told him they were on the Isle of Sheppey he breathed a sigh of relief. While not exactly on his doorstep, it would have been a lot worse had she told him somewhere like somerset or West Yorkshire. The Carter camp travelled widely and they could be just about anywhere and usually it made it difficult to locate them without the aid of a mobile, something Duke flatly refused to use. Fortunately for Marcus, his cousin was more technologically minded than his uncle.

"Why? What's wrong Cuz?"

"I'd rather not go into it on the phone Kezia, give me your exact location and I can be there within a couple of hours. Oh and Kezi, I don't suppose Rena's family are travelling with you?"

Kezia Carter couldn't stop herself from laughing out loud, he really was acting like a love struck fool.

"Yes they are Marcus and why might that be?"

Suddenly he became tongue tied and shy, something his father wouldn't have been happy about. In Eli's eyes a man should be a man and never show his emotions.

"Just wondered that's all, see you soon."
With that the line went dead leaving Kezia smiling at the screen of her phone.

Marcus popped his head into the main bar and nodded in his father's direction. Eli didn't speak but lowered his head signalling for his son to carry on. After leaving to fuel up the Audi and purchase a few drinks for the journey, thirty minutes later and he at last set off for Kent. Full of apprehension regarding the situation that was bound to explode further, he was also extremely excited at the thought of seeing Rena again. It was a distance of just over fifty miles and was motorway for most of the way. Even with traffic, if he put his foot down he could be there in not much more than an hour and he couldn't wait. Still, the bad gut feeling that kept coming to the surface was worrying and Marcus used the drive time to run over everything again and again in his mind.

The Isle of Sheppey, only spanning an area of thirty six square miles, is one of the most deprived areas in England, which Marcus found strange as it was a stunning place with fine beaches and he couldn't understand why the Chelsea on sea set from the affluent areas of London hadn't moved in and created overpriced holiday homes. The four lane crossing bridge was busy but Marcus didn't mind too much as the view was amazing and once on the other side he headed in the direction of Leysdown-on-sea. Travellers were never warmly welcomed but Duke always parked up at the far end of Leysdown behind the sea wall and had long since had an unwritten agreement with the parish council that his camp wouldn't stay for any longer than four weeks. It had worked well for several years and the small group always viewed it as a kind of holiday.

Unlike Appleby, this time the camp setup was small with just five vans. Duke's trailer plus his annex van, Paddy Hearn and his wife Nan in their old eighties wagon, Rena's parent's eighteen foot home on wheels and a small van Marcus didn't recognise, were parked up on a small grassed area not much bigger than some of the suburban gardens they often did work on. Manfri Gallagher stood on the steps to his van as Marcus got out of the car and after tipping his hat towards the visitor he stepped back inside and closed the door.

"Who was that da da?"

"Your young man but I don't think he's here to see you Rena. Sometimes men have business to attend to and you just have to wait, if he wants to see you he will come a callin'."

Rena Gallagher couldn't believe that he was

here. She was desperate to see him again and now out of the blue that was going to be possible! Rena had never felt like this about any man but now Marcus Carter was invading her thoughts every waking moment. Knowing her father was right, she sighed deeply, it pained her to admit it but da da was always right!

Knocking on the door to Dukes trailer, Marcus waited to be invited in, it was good manners and he remembered his father's warning that above all else you never entered a travellers van without being invited inside. Kezia opened up but there was no sign of the overly warm welcome at their previous meeting. Duke had divulged some of what had being going on and even though she was all for her family and of the belief that you were there for them no matter what, she also knew that this could mean danger and she really didn't want Duke getting too deeply involved.

Stepping into the pristine interior, Marcus saw his uncle sitting at the table at the far end of the caravan. Two glasses had already been set out with a full bottle of scotch standing beside them.

"Business gettin' out of hand I hear?"

Marcus took a seat and wiped his open palm a crossed his mouth and the action told his uncle that he was nervous. Duke Carter was wise, probably the reason he was Shera Rom and he had the ability to read a situation before a word was spoken, he could also read a person's facial expressions and knew how they were feeling even before they knew themselves.

"It's a lot worse than that Uncle. Earlier this mornin' the bastards snatched Morris and only God knows what they are doin' to him as we speak. The old man is goin' fuckin' insane with worry."

"I can only imagine, any idea where they have him held?"

Marcus took a swig of his whiskey before he spoke, knowing his next sentence would seal the deal and all-out war was about to break out.

"Yes, well we have a good idea but what we don't know is how many are inside or whether they have firearms."

Duke thought for several seconds before he spoke, this could get very nasty but what choice did they have? Family was family and you protected it at all costs. Kezia had been seated at the other end of the van but listening intently to what was being said and when he called her she immediately walked over.

"Contact Vano Young and explain the situation, tell him we need some strong men for a volatile job in London with some gorgers. Tell him I also need him here as soon as possible."

Kezia nodded before disappearing outside and

Duke poured two more drinks as he spoke.
"This could take a couple of hours to sort out Marcus so if you want to see ya girl while you're here I suggest you go find her."
Standing up Marcus smiled in Dukes direction.
"Thank you uncle and I'm truly sorry to bring all of this shit to your door because we both know it ain't goin' to end well for either side."
"No fight is ever without casualty's Son and your shit is my shit, we're family and if any Romany turns their back on family in a time of need, then in my book they are out on their own!"
Stepping out into the sunshine Marcus scanned the vans and when he spied her leaning up against her father's truck, he smiled from ear to ear.
"Hello babe, didn't think I'd see you again so soon."
"Not a social I'm afraid Rena, this is purely business. Wouldn't mind comin' back at the weekend though so we can get better acquainted? I'm in this for the long hall darlin' and I hope you feel the same?"
His words were like music to her ears. Coyly she lowered head and at the same time smiled but she didn't reply, it was best to keep them guessing and to tell him she would go to the ends of the earth so long as he was there, wasn't

yet the right time to let him know.

There are many factions within the Romany community, the old school who just travelled, were mostly honest and just wanted to be left alone to live their lives. Then there were those that offered cheap jobs on people's homes at exorbitant prices and of course there was the new breed, they wanted the glitz and the glamour, were materialistically driven and would rob gorger's without a second thought. Lastly were the hard men, the bareknuckle fighters, who were scared of no one and that included the law. Vano Young, born and bred in Manchester, along with his two sons, Patrin and George, belonged in the latter group. Now permanently sited just outside of Stevenage, Vano would work for anyone for a fee. Lash Cooper and Timbo Holland who during the week, continually travelled the suburban areas around Luton and Watford were also of that ilk. They collected scrap, did tarmacking, anything to make a few quid but on a weekend they could be found in any name of cities earning big money in illegally arranged fights. There was also Ocean Codona ,similar to Duke Carter in his attitude towards Romany customs and culture, he lived for his family, was usually a mild mannered placid man, until it came to fighting and then he was an animal. Lastly there was Billy Buckland, Billy had no ties to any particular camp or site and could only be contacted by mobile phone. He wasn't ever quizzed on this as everyone knew he would never let you down in your hour of need. When the call came through from Kezia, a price, reduced of course, was agreed and Vano then went on to contact the other men who he knew could handle themselves in most situations. By four that afternoon they were all on their way and heading in the direction of Sheppey for a briefing.

Back at Roach Road, the first part of Morris's ordeal was about to come to an end. After Tony had collected the small bottle of sulfuric acid, he handed it to Del and then took his place beside Levi. Slowly removing the screw cap Del carefully filled a glass dropper with the terrifying liquid and then nodded in the direction of his men. Morris was handcuffed so he couldn't get away but Levi and Tony's orders had been to hold his head in position. Then, each of them forced one of Morris's eyes wide open.
"Now timing is absolutely crucial with this procedure gentleman. We need to leave it on long enough to burn through the eyeball but not

so long as it continues to penetrate through to the brain. Tone, you got the water at hand?" Tony Morgan could feel himself getting excited, he loved violence, the more horrific the better and if it was an act that they hadn't carried out before it was like Christmas and birthdays all rolled into one, it was probably the reason why he'd been given the nick name of Mad Tony. As Del allowed the first couple of droplets to fall onto Morris's right eyeball his victim let out the most gut wrenching scream. There was a sickening aroma as the acid burnt deep into the gel-like substance that sits between the lens and retina. Del glanced at his watch, he'd actually timed the assault and a little short of a minute later, he signalled for the water to be applied. Morris was still screaming but the sound was muffled as Levi had placed his huge hand over the victim's mouth.

"Here we go, round two!"

Within a matter of minutes Morris Carter had been permanently blinded but Del wasn't content with that, he wanted to return the bastard to his father in the worst state possible, for a man at least. The last stage of torture couldn't begin until after dark because once it had been administered Morris would need to be returned immediately. Del wasn't trying to murder the beast that had caused his son's death, only to make his life not worth living. After extensively researching the torture he had planned, Del knew that without treatment there was an hour, possibly two, before death would occur. If the old gypsy was fast he could save his son's life, if not, well the blame would be on Eli Carter's shoulders and he would have that fact on his conscience forever.

The mansion in Upminster had been prepared in readiness for guests. Milly Garrod had worked hard all afternoon and now in the kitchen preparing food from the ingredients handed to her by Eli, she knew that travellers were coming to visit. The brace of pheasants along with a selection of root vegetables had been made into a stew and the three rabbits would be fried off later and served with boiled potatoes. Angela had taught Milly basic Romany food shortly after she'd started work at the house. It wasn't the kind of cuisine the family usually ate but on special occasions Angela had liked to cook dishes that her husband loved.

At just before eight the gates were opened and a range rover and two pickup trucks screeched to a halt in front of the house forcing shingle to spray up and hit the windows. Marcus was following closely behind and he really wasn't looking forward regarding what was to come. At Sheppey he had allowed his uncle to explain to the men what was going on or at least as much as Duke knew, as for the rest, Marcus had decided to leave that to his father.  Eli greeted the guests warmly and his use of the word 'welcome' but spoken in Romani, an Indo-Aryan language, still widely used today, was much appreciated by Vano Young.

"T'aves baxtalo"

"Thank you brother."

Vano then glared at those with him, as much as to say 'make sure you behave yourselves'. After being shown to their rooms to freshen up, not something they would have usually bothered with before eating, they were then served up a feast by Milly who didn't mind admitting that she was a little scared, especially of the one who had tattoos on his neck but in all honesty she couldn't complain.  While she thought their table manners left a lot to be desired, thankfully they treated her with the utmost respect.  When the meal was over and the dishes cleared away, the door was firmly closed and Eli then went into great detail regarding what had occurred.  Duke had only been able to tell them so much and the finer details of what they could expect, were gratefully received.  Eli had to force himself to

continue when it came down to explaining what Morris had actually done to Kenan Foster but he knew he had to be open and honest.
Homosexuality and the Romany community do not mix, it's a man's world and being gay is seen as something dirty, so Vano's response somewhat surprised Eli but in a good way.
"I have no interest in what your son chooses to do between the sheets or with whom Eli. Whether what he did was right or wrong, he is still your son and we will help bring him home to you."
A few more beers were consumed before everyone turned in for the night, they were in for a busy day and having a hangover wouldn't bode well in a violent situation.

# CHAPTER TWENTY FOUR

At precisely eleven thirty that night, a bucket of water was thrown over Morris Carter to wake him up. Coughing and spluttering, it took him a few seconds to get his bearings and remember where he was. The pain he felt was excruciating and there was nothing before his eyes but blackness. As he remembered what they had done to him, tears streamed down his face. Call it luck but at least he couldn't see the table that had been set up in the middle of the room, on top of which sat some kind of clamp and a knife, that even from a distance anyone would have been able to tell was razor sharp. Del had been taking a nap, he was exhausted but the pain he had inflicted had at least brought him some kind of peace of mind. It wouldn't bring his boy back and Del's heart ached at the very thought of Kenan but what he was about to do, would at least stop that monster from ever doing it to someone else. Staring out of the bare window at the moonlight, he wondered if life would ever feel normal again. His girls were heartbroken and the only woman he had ever loved was cold and distant towards him in a way he'd never experienced before. Well it was time to bring this nightmare to a close, so hauling himself from one of the single beds he'd installed for his men, he made his way downstairs. Levi and Tony, having heard him moving around above them, went into action and began to get things ready for the next onslaught. Silently entering the room, Del stood and watched as they lifted his prey from the chair, hauled him across the floor and then forced him down onto the table. Once again Morris's wrists were secured with handcuffs and he began to fiercely twist and contort his body in an effort to gain his freedom but it was futile. The blackness was all consuming and he was terrified. Walking over Del smiled and at the same time slowly stroked the sweat drenched hair of his victim.

"Dear, dear me Morris, was raping my boy really worth all of this?"

"Please let me go Mr Foster, I'm so sorry about Kenan but I never knew he would…………"

Morris was instantly silenced when Levi roughly rammed a filthy rag into his mouth. With his hands tied and now totally blind, he was as helpless as a new born. There and then he realised that if by some miracle he was to survive, in all honesty what would be the point of living? He felt his urine soaked trousers being pulled down, he also now had an inkling of what was about to happen but he didn't resist further. Resigned to his fate, Morris just prayed it would be over as quickly as possible. Someone, he guessed Del Foster, grabbed hold of his penis and then Morris could feel some kind of clamp as it was painfully tightened at the base of his penis. It must have been the tightness that stopped any feeling of pain because he was actually unaware when they sliced off his manhood.

"Right boys! Time is of the essence so let's get this piece of scum back to his daddy shall we?" The question was rhetorical and neither Levi nor Tony replied. Lifting Morris's limp body from the table they carried him out to the van where Freddy Wentworth was waiting. Spayed and sign written to read 'Motorway Maintenance', even the flashing light on the roof was switched on. If it looked authentic then there was little chance of them being stopped if it appeared as if they were on their way to an emergency call out. The side door had been opened in readiness and laying Morris down, Levi and Tony got in beside him. Del was actually taking part in the delivery and climbing into the passenger's seat he gave Freddy a silent nod indicating that it was time to set off.

"Keep to the speed limit, the last thing we need is a pull from the Old Bill 'cause explainin' this little lot would be fuckin' near on impossible." The eighteen mile drive was taken in silence as each man thought of their guvnor and what he must be going through. There were no words any of them could offer that could even come close to easing his pain so in times like this it was best to say nothing at all.

The main gates to the Upminster house had strangely been left open which instantly put Del on his guard. Unaware of the people inside, for a fleeting moment he had the insane notion that they were on to him. In reality Eli hadn't bothered locking up as who in their right minds would try to enter a house that contained some of the hardest men in the Romany community, not that anyone would be aware of that fact but all the same, he would like to see them try. Freddy took the approach slowly so as not to wake the occupants and when they pulled up outside the massive oak front door, they were like ninja's from a B rate Japanese movie. The side door had been well greased so it slid open without so much as a squeak and they were all careful not to scuff up the shingle. Morris had been gagged to stop him calling out and once he had been propped up in the doorway and when all but one of the men were back inside the van, Stevie Hunt removed the clamp from Morris's groin, snatched the scarf away from his mouth and then hot footed it in through the side door of the van. Pulling slowly away, when they reached the gates Freddy gave four or five loud blasts on the horn before driving off. Marcus was the only one to be woken by the sound and peering out of the bedroom window, he saw only the taillights of the van as it disappeared into the distance. Shrugging his shoulders and about to climb back into bed, something stopped him and to this day he couldn't explain what it was but he had an overwhelming feeling of fear. Grabbing his dressing gown he took the stairs two at a time. The hallway was brightly illuminated from the gigantic chandelier that his mother had chosen years earlier and which Eli had left burning for the entire night ever since she has passed. As he placed his hand onto the doorknob he momentarily froze in fear. There was something bad waiting to greet him on the other side, he just knew it but he couldn't stop himself. Slowly turning the key he opened the door and stepped back in shock as Morris's body fell backwards. Marcus screamed out for help and in less than a minute he was surrounded by the house guests who just stared at the broken, bloody body before them. By now Eli was halfway down the staircase and when he saw his son lying in a heap he ran as fast as he was able down the remainder of the stairs.

"Is he dead?"

"No Dad but this is bad, really, really bad."
Kneeling down Eli took his son's head onto his lap and gently stroked his hair.

"Can you hear me Son, Morris? Can you hear me?"

At the same time as Morris Carter opened his blackened hollow eyes Eli saw the blood as it seeped from the front of his trousers. He knew what they had done, knew this was the end for his boy. It had to be, no longer a man and with the added torturous fact that they had blinded him, what life could he possibly have.

"Dad? Dad? I can't see you Dad!"

"Lift him through to the dining room and place him onto the table, be careful with him."

Vano and his sons did as they were asked without a word. This was horrific even by Gypsy standards of justice and as they carried the battered body of Morris along the hall, Vano looked at both of his own sons. How Eli must be feeling was beyond words, had it have been one of his then Vano would have literally ripped out the hearts of the aggressors with his bare hands. Back in the hallway Eli just stood staring out into the night and it took Marcus pulling on the sleeve of his silk gown to bring him back to reality.

"Dad! Dad!!! We need to get him to a hospital and fast."

"Why?"

"Fuckin' hell, have you lost your mind! To save his life that's why."

Eli glared at his youngest and in that split second of a moment Marcus could see all of the hurt, all of the pain and all of the rage that had festered deep inside his father for years.

"Tell me, what sort of a fuckin' life would he have?! The cunts have blinded him and cut off his cock! Would you want to live like that?"

Marcus held his forehead in his hand. This was a nightmare, one caused by his brother without a doubt but a living nightmare all the same.

"So we just let him die, there on the dining room table?"

Eli didn't reply and strode off to where his first born would take, in the next hour, his final breath. Entering the room he saw Vano, Gorge, Patrin, Ocean, Timbo, Billy and Lash standing in a straight line beside the table and they all had their heads bowed.

"Dad! Dad are you there?"

Eli walked over and taking Morris's hand in his, gripped it tightly.

"I'm here Son and were gettin' you to the hospital as soon as the ambulance arrives, just hold on for a bit longer."

Glancing at the men Eli saw that Vano had lifted up his gaze and was staring intently at his host.

Eli could only shake his head in the man's direction.

"You're goin' to be fine Son."

"But I can't see, I can't see anythin' Dad."

"I know but you will boy, they have hurt you but you'll heal in time."

Walking over to the sideboard, Eli poured a large measure of brandy. As he tenderly held the back of his son's head he gently lowered the glass to Morris's mouth.

"Drink this boy it will help with the pain. Vano, I can handle things from here."

Without a word Vano Young, his sons and the men he had invited along to help, left the room.

"Is that helping boy?"

"Mmmm but I ain't in any pain Dad, I just feel really tired and so cold."

"Then sleep Son and get well."

As Eli lay his sons head back down he could see how pale Morris had become. The table was now swimming in blood and he knew Morris couldn't last for much longer. Marcus came through the door just as his brother took his last breath. Eli bent over and clutching his boys chest let out one continuous howl. There was no comfort Marcus could offer and even if there was he knew his father would never accept it, so making his way along the back hall to the kitchen, he joined Vano and the others. The men

stood drinking coffee but there was no conversation, they were simply killing time waiting for further instruction. Fifteen minutes later Eli appeared and handed Vano a scrap of paper.
"This is where the cunts will be. Make sure your main target is the one with the scar running down his face!"
"You want then brought back here?"
"No, I want you to kill them, kill them all!!!!"

At Roach Road the mood was sombre. No one had any regrets about what had been done but would things really change? Gordon, Sammy, Carl and Steve Lennon were all still upstairs asleep, Del hadn't wanted them involved, they weren't needed and the less people that knew the details, the safer it would be. They were all aware of Morris Carters abduction but not his final fate. In hindsight Del now realised he'd been incredibly stupid bringing Morris back here but why hadn't they come looking for him? Surely by now Eli Carter knew where their base was? He could have stormed in and slaughtered them all before they had chance to harm his son, Del just couldn't work it out.

It was just after three that morning and Vano Young's Toyota Hi-lux slowly came to a stop at the end of Roach Road. The men climbed out and then removed the arms that had been supplied by Eli. Vano and Timbo had sawn off shotguns, Billy, Lash and Patrin had handguns pushed down into their belts and George and Ocean carried razor sharp machetes. Walking up to the door and front window, Vano and Timbo simultaneously fired two shots each. The glass shattered inwards and the door flew open revealing a long hallway. As Del's men scattered in search of weapons, he legged it through the back door. At times like these it was every man for himself and running as fast as he could he made it to one of the shed's on the edge of the canal just as the next onslaught of firing began. The outboard didn't start on the first pull but luckily for him the second was a success. As the inflatable sped down the canal, he could only pray that his men had been able to fight back. That wasn't the case, while Vano and Timbo reloaded, Billy, Lash and Patrin ran into the old front room firing rapidly. Levi was the first to fall but luckily the bullet had only grazed him badly. He knew to stay down and play dead, they were outnumbered and to try and fight back would only end up in certain death. More bullets quickly followed but Freddy and Stevie, hit directly in their heads, were no as lucky as Levi and both died almost instantly. George and

Ocean ran up the stairs only to come face to face with Gordon Mayes wielding a baseball bat. It was no match for a machete and he was swiftly beheaded as soon as Ocean reached the top step. Sammy, Carl and Steve Lennon each received similar fates though the blow aimed towards Sammy's head had initially missed. He fought hard but with two men on one, he never stood a chance.

Del made it to the Hertford Union Lock and then abandoned the inflatable. On the chance that what happened would happen, he had parked a van close to Jodrell newsagents. Suddenly his mobile rang and staring at the screen he couldn't believe the name that was showing.

"Levi?!!!"

"Hi Boss, I managed to play dead and got out seconds after they left. The boat wouldn't start so I had to swim across the Cut but at least I'm in one piece. I don't think any of the others made it though."

For a few seconds there was silence, neither man could believe that almost the whole firm had been wiped out.

"Nothin' we can do about that now but at least you're safe. I'm goin' to disappear for a while Levi and I suggest you do the same. I'll keep in contact, salvage what you can of the business and as soon as it's safe for me to come back I'll

let you know."
With that Del ended the call. It would take him twenty five minutes to get home and in that time he phoned Dawn and told her to pack and get her sister and mother ready to leave by the time he got back.
"But where are we goin' Dad?"
"We just need to get away for a while until the dust settles. I've paid back that cunt for what he did to your brother but I'm under no illusion that they won't come after me and if they can't get me then you are all targets. I think I've lost all my men Dawnie, well except for Levi. All gone darlin' and for that I'm heartfelt sorry but until I can regroup we need to lay low."
Pulling into the drive he saw Jean and Allison in Ally's car and Dawn was standing outside waiting for him. Dashing into the house Del opened the safe and grabbed the large bundle of cash that he always kept for emergencies. It would keep them going for a while, at least until he could get to a bank but he hoped to be back in London long before that situation arose.

# CHAPTER TWENTY FIVE

By lunch time that day the Upminster house was full of people. Duke and Kezia had arrived along with several heads of other Romany families. Rena had accompanied Duke at his request, he thought her presence might help Marcus and it had, as soon as he saw her face his pain slightly eased. Women were now congregated in the luxurious kitchen and were making a mountain of food and the men, in true style had all gathered in the front room. Bottles of whiskey were being passed round while memories of Morris and the escapades he had gotten up to, especially when he was a child, were being relayed by Eli. Every single story resulted in tears streaming down his face and it was the first and last time he would ever allow anyone, even his own community, to see his vulnerability. When exhaustion set in he took a walk to his study, the stress was causing his COPD to be bad today and he was starting to feel like he couldn't breathe. A few moments alone to calm down and gather his thoughts were needed but his alone time didn't last for more than a few minutes. Duke knocked on the door, came in and then closed it firmly behind him. Taking a seat opposite his brother he could see the lines of pain etched on the man's face, lines that hadn't been there the last time they had met which was not that long ago.

"So what's your plan Eli? What justice are you going to seek?"

Eli stared at his brother for a few seconds without speaking. Duke was looking old and he realised that neither of them probably had much longer left on this mortal coil. They had both been happy once, back when they had their wives but since Angela's death, Eli knew he had only been surviving and the same could probably be said for Duke. Now he wanted to be with her more than he'd ever done. It would soon be time and he welcomed that fact but first there was one last thing he needed to do.

"Nothin' for now. I have to lay my boy to rest and until that is done, there will be no reprisal."

"Do you want one of us to contact the undertakers for you?"

"No! No one is to know, not the undertakers, the law or any of the departments that are supposed to be contacted. No one do you hear me?!"

Duke only nodded his head as he allowed his brother to continue.

"Morris will have a traditional send-off, like the one I wanted for his mother but couldn't have. After Angela died I purchased an old barrel roofed wagon.  Unbeknown to the boys I slept in it for six months so that it truly had been the home of Romany, though I always thought it would be burnt after my own funeral, never for one of my boys.  I want you to find me somewhere we can camp up Duke without interference from the law or complaining gorgers.  When the men get back and have finished makin' the coffin I want my boy placed inside and then taken down to the trailer.  He is not to be left alone until his final journey so we will all take turns having a sit up."

No Romany should be left alone from the time of death until the time of burial and the sit up was a term used that meant people took turns sitting with the deceased and Eli was determined to make sure that would stand for his own son.

"Where will Morris be buried?"

"He won't.  I did that with Angie and it tore me up to put her into the ground.  She had a traditional Romany funeral but when it came to her remains, the ending was not what I wanted.  I tend that grave every Sunday but who will do it after I'm gone?  I don't want him in some cold unfeeling cemetery.  Those cunts will extract further vengeance and desecratin' his grave would be unbearable.  I know that's hypocritical but I can't help it.  I have decided to see him on his way like they did many years ago, that's why

I don't want any gorger authority to be informed. Do you understand why I'm doing this brother?"

Again Duke knowingly nodded his head. He was pleased that after all these years of being away from the community Eli was still upholding their traditions, even if this one had long since disappeared.

"I have a spot in mind Eli, leave it with me." With that Duke Carter left his brother alone to grieve, at times like these a man needed a little solitude to gather his thought and come to terms with all that he had lost.

Marcus sat alone in the dining room, his hand holding that of his brothers but the flesh felt strange and so cold. Tears streamed down his face and he wasn't able to contain them when Rena walked in. Morris's body had been temporarily covered with a sheet and Marcus was grateful that she wouldn't have to see the state he was in. Taking a seat beside him she leaned over and tenderly kissed his cheek.

"You okay sweetheart?"

Sighing heavily Marcus smiled and gently shook his head. Dressed in dark clothing and with her hair scraped back revealing large gold hoop earrings, he silently thought how beautiful she was, not just on the outside but on the inside as well.

"This is a nightmare Rena, one I want out of as quickly as possible."

"I know you do and it will be over but its early days yet. When are they going to move him?"

"Billy and Ocean Codona have driven into Romford to buy timber and when they get back they will make his coffin. I loved my brother Rena but the Lord above knows he wasn't an easy person to love or get on with. That said, to do this to him? It was gruesome and I just can't get my head around it."

"Are you going to make them pay?"

"We already have, well to a degree but we didn't get the main man. I suppose the old man will insist on hunting him down but in honestly, what purpose will it serve? The only thing to happen will be more bloodshed and hasn't there been enough of that already?"

Staring at him longingly Rena Gallagher knew in that moment why it had taken her so long to find her true love. She'd never been interested in the hot headed travellers who would kick off without a seconds notice. Her dream had been to find a kind man, a man that thought things through and in Marcus that's exactly what she had.

"I love you Marcus."

He instantly stared at her, unable to believe what he'd just heard. It wasn't that he didn't feel the same way because he did, it had just come so out of the blue and at such a terrible time that it had shocked him. Rena took his look of surprise and the silence as a signal that he didn't feel the same and her eyes filled with pool of tears.

"Whoa hold on there a minute, whatever's the matter and what's with the tears babe?"

"You obviously don't feel the same way, it's evident by your expression."

Marcus laid down Morris's hand and covered it with the edge of the sheet. Taking her right hand in his, with his left he awkwardly rummaged in his pocket for a tissue and then tenderly dabbed at the tears on her cheek.

"Don't be so silly, of course I do! It just came as a bit of a shock that's all, well not really a shock 'cause it was what I've been dreamin' of hearin' but I just didn't expect it today of all days."

Giving her a lingering kiss on the lips made Rena smile.

"I'm so pleased Marcus, for a second there I though my heart was actually goin' to break. When this is all over can we be together, I mean all of the time? I think Morris's death has taught us both that neither of us knows how much time we have left."

"Definitely, I just need to get the next few days over with and then make sure that the old man is okay first."

Billy and Ocean Codona returned and set about making a basic oblong box and lid. When they had finished and the coffin had been inspected by Eli, Morris was placed inside and the lid was sealed.

Each man at the house took a turn at sitting with the corpse of Morris Carter, even Eli dutifully did his turn. A fire had been set in front of the wagon and whoever was taking a turn would just silently sit until they were relieved by the next in line. Marcus chose to actually go into the van and stay beside his brother's remains, he was there longer than anyone else and his sobbing could be heard by many. There was almost a five years age difference between the brothers but they were so close that they might as well have been twins and Marcus just didn't know how he was going to live his life without his older sibling. Even Rena's declaration of love hadn't changed that and with no comfort shown to him by his father, Marcus was distraught.

Morris's send-off had been set for two days' time but none of the firms men had been invited, this was Romany business and gorgers had no place in that.. Duke had contacted his old friend Django Gray who owned land, eight acres to be exact, over at Writtle, just outside of Chelmsford.

It had been in his family for years and apart from setting up camp for the odd week a couple of times a year, it wasn't used. The land was surrounded by woodland on all sides and Duke knew it would be a perfect location to hold the funeral. Django had instantly agreed to the request, so many of the younger travellers no longer adhered to the old customs and he felt it was an honour to be asked. It pained him to learn that when some of his old friends had passed, their trailers hadn't been burnt but sold on by sons, daughters or even grandchildren. Years ago it would have been severely frowned upon by most Romany's but today no one really seemed to care and it was becoming another true tradition that would soon be lost.

The wake was held on the eve of the funeral and the house was bursting at the seams with so many people that they had been forced to spill out into the garden. Milly Garrod was running around like a headless chicken, trying to hand out trays of sandwiches. She smiled when Rena stepped in to help, this girl was a good fit for Marcus and Milly was glad that he had chosen her. The drinking continued into the early hours but not until the last of the extended guests had left, at around three am, did they all manage to finally get some sleep.

By eleven on the morning of the funeral, the house was again filled to capacity. True blue blood Romany travellers who had been childhood pals of Eli, had come from all over the country to congregate and pay their last respects. The men and women were all dressed in expensive clothing and their finest gold jewellery had been brought out of safe keeping. Lavish oversized floral tributes filled the driveway and a large pickup truck was parked at the front of the house, on top of which sat the old wagon with Morris's remains inside. It was tradition for the wagon to be pulled by a horse but logistically due to the distance that wasn't feasible but Vano Young had gone ahead and arranged for one to be at Writtle ready and waiting to take the wagon for the last few hundred yards onto the hidden field. The service was due to take place at dusk and the eighteen mile journey shouldn't have taken much more than half an hour but the funeral procession was so large, that everyone knew you could expect to at least double that time scale. With the old barrel top leading from the back of the pickup, everyone departed at six thirty and the gigantic row of cars and vans seemed to go on forever. Eli, Duke and several of the older generation wore red rosettes and ribbons, again another tradition that was fast dying out.

Travelling in a custom build Mercedes V-class, Marcus sat opposite his father and as they travelled in silence he studied the face of his dad, the dad that had made him feel like he was never quite good enough and would never come close to his brother. The last few days had taken its toll on Eli Carter and though Marcus wasn't privy to the COPD diagnosis, he knew that something was very wrong.

Reaching Django's land the cortege slowly came to a halt, everyone got out of the vehicles and stood quietly while Vano and Billy allowed the barrel wagon to slowly roll down the ramps. The massive Clydesdale shire was hitched up and as the wagon gradually pulled away, the line of well over a hundred people silently walked forward. The spot Duke had chosen was truly beautiful and apart from the noises made by the wagons movement, the only sounds that could be heard were the soft rustle of the long grass from a gentle breeze and the last of the day's bird song. When they reached the spot, well away from any prying eyes, several of the men moved forward and took hold of hay and wood, which Vano had unloaded earlier that day and after placing the tinder under the wagon, everyone took a step back. There was no priest or a religious service of any kind. Everyone took a moment to think of the deceased, some recalled memories of meeting Morris Carter and those that never knew him said silent prayers. Eli was handed a long wooden torch, its end was tightly wrapped with cloth and had been dipped in Paraffin. Stepping close to the wagon he addressed his son.

"My boy, my beautiful boy, what they did to you was sickenin' and undeserved. You lived your life on your terms and some of the choices you made were not the best. You hurt people Son and for that you paid dearly but your punishment was unjust and did not fit your crime. Justice for what they did to you must be served and if it takes the last breath in my body I will avenge your death. Sleep well my boy, safely back in your mother's arms."

Marcus stepped forward and with a lighter ignited the torch. Eli lowered the flaming wood down onto the tinder and then gently taking his father's arm, Marcus led him away to a safe distance. Together they silently stood and watched the wagon burn. It took less than an hour and by now it was dark so many other torches had been lit to guide the people back to their vehicles. In turn each attendee shook Eli and Marcus's hands and offered words of support and it was well over two hours later when they were finally ready to set off for the return trip to Upminster. Handing Vano Young a large envelope of cash, the man was thanked for all that he had done but Eli's was now dismissing his services, something Marcus found strange.

When they eventually returned to the Upminster house the place was sparkling clean and Milly had worked so hard that you never would have known that only a few hours earlier every room had been filled with guests. After joining his father for one final drink, Marcus made his way up to bed. The house felt eerie, it had always been quiet with just the three of them but now it was down to two it felt as though every word spoken echoed off of the walls. Luckily he was so tired that sleep was instantaneous but the same couldn't be said for Eli. Alone in his study he downed several more shots as he toasted his son and swore vengeance. This time he planned to carry out the reprisal himself and it was going to be so personal that the Foster family would have nowhere left to hide.

# CHAPTER TWENTY SIX

For the three weeks that Del Foster and his family had been in hiding, he had kept in constant contact with Levi Puck. Business was slowly getting back to normal as Levi had hired a whole new bunch of men, far harder and fearless that the old crew but as yet their loyalty hadn't been put to the test. There was also the added fact that Del would have to vet them on his return so they could still see themselves out the door if he wasn't satisfied. With Levi now in charge there didn't seem to be anything out of the ordinary happening, which at least put Del's mind at rest. Had Levi wanted, it would probably have been a good time to attempt a takeover of the Foster firm. The new firm members liked and respected the man but it would never happen. Levi adored and was loyal to the core when it came to his boss and while Del still drew a breath, Levi would stand beside him, faithful to the last.

Every morning after breakfast, Del would walk outside of the hotel and call his number one for an update.
"So there's been no contact from the Carter's then?"

"Not a word Guv and I haven't heard a whisper about any kind of funeral either but then the gypo's are slippery fuckers so that's nothin' unusual. So when are you comin' back?"

"Probably at the weekend, Sunday maybe. Jean seems to be pickin' up a bit so another couple of days won't do her any harm. Can you drive over to the house Friday mornin' and check everythin's okay?"

"Sure thing Boss, let me know when you get back will you?"

With that the line went dead and Del walked back inside. The family had been staying at the Carbis Bay Hotel in Saint Ives. Awarded five star gold by the quality and tourism board, it was far from cheap and the two rooms had, for their stay to date, set Del back over twenty grand and that was without food, save for breakfast. The girls were sharing a double while Del had booked a junior suite for himself and Jean. It was luxurious and had its own private terrace with sea views, a place Jean had been spending most of her time since their arrival. With the decision now made to return to Edmonton in a couple of days, Del made his wife a hot drink and took it out to the terrace. The sun was bright but it was now early September and the temperature was cooling. For a second he stopped and studied his wife who was seated on a lounger but wrapped tightly in a faux fur blanket. Initially she had been cold and distant to him but over the last week and he didn't know if it was this place or just the fact that she was at last coming to terms with Kenan's death, but she had slowly begun to talk to him, not much but it was a start and Del was grateful for any show of improvement.

"Here you go darlin' a nice hot cuppa. Can we have a chat Jean, only I think it's time we returned to Edmonton."

The look she gave was one of fear as if the very thought of going back to the house, a house she had loved since the day they had moved in, now scared her terribly.

"It's okay sweetheart, there's nothin' to be frightened of. I know you have bad memories, we all do but there were also a lot of happy times spent in that house. Remember, we raised our family there, we had fabulous times at Christmas and the kids loved the place. What say you at least give it a try if I promise not to hold you to anythin'?"

With her eyes full of tears Jean slowly nodded her head and as he touched her arm she placed her hand over his. It was the first sign that she could possibly forgive him and for Del it was the sign he'd been waiting for since the day they had lost Kenan, a day not so long ago but which now

felt like years. So much had happened and the events had almost torn his beautiful family apart but luckily it hadn't, they were Fosters and being a Foster meant being a fighter in life.
"Let's enjoy the rest of our time here babe. I was thinkin' we could drive back Sunday night?" The question was rhetorical and knowing that was exactly what would happen and that he wasn't actually asking for her agreement, Jean thinly smiled.

Eli Carter, unbeknown to anyone, had hired the services of Weasel. Andy Mason, referred to as Weasel on account of his small sharp features and tiny teeth, liked to call himself a private investigator but in reality it was a slur on any real PI's. Weasel was around the age of fifty but no one knew exactly how old he was and he was disliked for his sneaky, arse kissing ways that made most people's skin crawl. Raised in Pimlico, at a time when the place was beginning and still is, to experience rising violent crime rates, you only had a couple of options in life, become a villain or as close to that profession as you could get, or live in fear of those that were. Weasel had chosen crime though it was plain to see from the offset that he was useless at it. Where he did excel was finding out people's business, a skill he'd honed well over the years and love him or hate him, he was very good at what he did. His services had been used many times through the years by Eli even though Weasel resided in London. He would travel anywhere if the price was high enough and had worked as far down as Cornwall and right up as far as Glasgow. Things on the work front had been quiet of late so when he got a call early one Friday morning and was asked to pay a visit to the Bull over in Romford, he knew it could mean only one thing. Andy travelled everywhere on his trusty Norton ES2 500 motorcycle, that he had fondly named Louisa. It was a nineteen sixty one model but had been completely rebuilt in seventy four. Running like a dream Louisa allowed him to get anywhere in the capital fast. The bike was his passion and he had even moved to a ground floor flat so that he could accommodate her and keep her safe. When not in use she now took pride of place propped up against the sideboard in his front room. The chrome work gleamed, the leather seat was highly polished and when Andy straddled her he felt like he was the King of the road. Arriving in Romford, he parked Louisa on the pavement and surveyed the surrounding square. Andy was always fearful that someone would try and take Louisa but apart from the stallholders, who were still setting up, nothing looked out of the ordinary and besides, no one would dare rob Eli Carter or anyone he was associated with. Stepping inside the pub he was beginning to feel a little apprehensive and when he spied Eli sitting alone Andy was surprised to say the least, the man was normally guarded by at least one tooled up heavy.

"Morning Mr Carter, see you've returned to your old haunt then?"

Hoping that the man would reveal why he was using the pub again, Andy was disappointed when all he received was a glare.

"Weasel. Take a seat."

Doing as he was told Andy pulled out a chair but didn't speak further. Usually he was nosey asking question after question but he had been in the game long enough to know that when you were in the company of a hardened villain and he gave you the look, you kept schtum until spoken to you.

"I need some surveillance work done and it may or may not be a lengthy job."

"Not a problem Mr Carter."

Andy Mason nodded and after being given Del's address, a burner phone so there was no chance of a trace or for conversations to be recorded, he had strict instructions to report back each day even if there was nothing to report. Walking outside, he mounted Louisa and was back in the

East End in less than thirty five minutes. Obviously he couldn't watch the place twenty four seven, even he had to sleep, so returning to his flat he grabbed the old military sleeping bag that he kept ready rolled and then headed over to Edmonton. Bringing Louisa to a stop between two large conifer trees on a small patch of grass a couple of roads away from his target destination, he disconnected the sparkplugs and placed them safely into his pocket. The waste land, though it was well manicured and mown, was triangular in shape and separated the two properties that sat at the end of a circular shaped road. It was an affluent area, he could tell that by the size of the houses and the amount of Jags and Mercs that were parked up in the drives, so if anyone did have the audacity to try and steal her they would have to push Louisa and she was a heavy old girl. Making his way to Streamside Close, Andy purposefully walked straight by the Foster house but glancing out of the corner of his eye, took in as much information as he could. Unlike many of the other properties in the vicinity, there was no milk bottle crate on the doorstep, a strange thing nowadays but he supposed the rich still liked the luxury of a personal delivery. Reaching the end of the close he crossed over and walked back down the other side. The house opposite Del's had a For Sale sign outside and walking up the short drive as if he was interested Andy peered through the window. What a touch, it was empty and would be perfect for surveillance. Walking around to the back he could see that the old wooden conservatory would be his best point of entry and removing a small packet of screwdrivers from his chest pocket, he was able to gain access in less than a minute. For all of the money in the area, these people obviously hadn't invested in too much security, the windows were still the old timber kind and there was no sign of an alarm. Slowly moving through the house Andy made his way upstairs to the empty front bedroom. Luckily there were still net curtains at the window so he could observe openly without being seen. He opened the window slightly, not enough for anyone out on the street to notice but enough so that he would be able to hear any voices or cars that went to the property. Deciding to investigate the house a bit further, he soon found a stool in the bathroom, the kind used by disabled people when they wanted to sit in the bath or shower. Carrying it into the bedroom and positioning it in front of the window he took a seat and prayed that the agents hadn't arranged any viewing which would scupper his plans completely. Andy didn't usually take photographs and today was no different, it was a real ball ache carrying expensive camera equipment around but he did always have his trusty notebook and pen to hand which he placed onto the window sill.

At just before noon and when he had begun to nod off through boredom, Andy heard a car door slam and it sounded as if it had come from across the road. On his feet in seconds he peered through the glass and saw Levi Puck get out of his car carrying a Tesco's shopping bag. Levi then walked over to the front door, tried the handle and then checked that all of the windows were secure. He then disappeared around to the back of the property and Andy wondered what on earth he was up to. He obviously wasn't a burglar, he wouldn't be so blatant but then again, anything went today and he supposed the more brazen a person was the less anyone would take notice. A few seconds later and Levi emerged through the side gate, he was talking on his mobile and then ending the call he got into his car and drove off. Scribbling in his note book Andy described Levi, his car and exactly what had happened. After dark he would investigate the property himself but for now at least he had something to report back to Eli Carter.

A little after ten Andy Mason let himself out of

the house and after walking to the end of the road he crossed over and made his way back down to Del's house. The front porch lights were on and he imagined they must be on some kind of timer, it made sense with so many break-ins but Andy was sure that no one was at home. Walking purposefully so it looked as though he was just a visitor calling at the house, Weasel let himself in through the side gate and walked around to the back. Switching on his small hand torch he shone it into the lounge windows but there was nothing out of the ordinary so moving to the kitchen he immediately noticed provisions had been left on the worktop. Bread, a carton of juice and there was probably fresh milk in the fridge. They must have been left by that guy he had seen earlier. The bloke had obviously been getting things ready for someone's arrival. Returning to the house opposite, Andy made sure he wasn't being watched and when he thought the coast was clear, he slipped around to the rear and let himself in through the conservatory. Back in position, he scribbled away in his notebook being careful not to exaggerate anything, he'd done that in the past and it had gotten him into a shed load of bother. Just before eleven that night Andy decided to call in all that he had found out, which wasn't much. Taking out the burner phone he dialled

Eli Carters number and he could actually feel himself getting nervous. Marcus was in the den watching a movie and Eli, having decided to turn in for the night, was half way up the stairs when his mobile rang. Fishing it out of his pocket he stared at the screen and raised his eyebrows as he pressed accept.

"Yeah?"

Weasel had been in the game long enough and knew better than to mention any names.

"Reportin' in Sir. Not a lot happened, the place is still deserted but a big black bloke came to the house earlier. He was carrying a Tesco bag when he arrived but didn't have it when he left. I've done a recce and he was obviously dropping off supplies. There was fresh stuff, you know bread and the likes so I reckon there will be people there in the next couple of days or so."

"Good work, things are happenin' sooner than I thought they would. I won't need you anymore so come by the Bull tomorrow. Make it early, let's say eight and I'll settle up with you."

With that Eli ended the call and Andy Mason was left holding the phone and feeling well and truly pissed off. He had hoped for at least a few days' work but as it was he hadn't even managed one.

# CHAPTER TWENTY SEVEN

The next day and parking Louisa up just as he'd been told, Andy Mason walked into the Bull at eight on the dot. Once again Eli was sitting alone at one of the tables and he glanced up when he saw Andy enter but there was no warm greeting. The man looked troubled, scared almost and that realisation frightened Andy. If a face like Eli Carter was scared, what an earth was going down?

"Take a seat Weasel. Tell me again everything you said last night and leave nothing out."

Andy Mason did as he was asked and Eli listened but his interest was heightened even more when Weasel explained about the empty house opposite.

"Is the place as you left it, the entry point I mean?"

"Well yes Mr Carter, I didn't bother callin' out a locksmith to secure the house!"

His sarcasm didn't go unnoticed but one look from Eli and Andy Mason knew he had overstepped the mark big time so he had no option but to suck up to the man.

"So, so sorry Mr Carter, that was rude of me. I really do apologise."

Eli didn't respond and placing an envelope onto

the table he pushed it towards the creep, a man he couldn't stand but one who always got results.

"There's a grand for your trouble. Make sure you keep your fuckin' trap shut 'cause if anyone gets wind of this I'll know where it's come from."

"That goes without sayin' Mr Carter. In my line of work keepin' quiet is paramount or no fucker would use me again."

Eli waved his hand signalling that it was time for Weasel to leave and he didn't need to be told twice. Outside in the fresh morning air, he breathed a sigh of relief. He was happy to work for the villain community as they always paid extremely well but dealing with them always brought an element of danger and deep down he was glad that this little job was over. He hadn't expected to be paid so handsomely and with the envelope burning a hole in his pocket he decided to venture into the market and treat himself to some breakfast.

Eli didn't move for quite a while as mentally he was planning his attack. It had to be fine-tuned and as he would be acting alone, there would be no back up if things went tits up. Removing his phone he tapped in the number of Arty Pullman. A local taxi driver, for years Arty had ferried around most of the Essex villains at short notice.

He was trustworthy and never revealed to anyone who his passengers were or where he had taken them. The conversation was short and after instructing Arty to collect him from his home at five that day, Eli hung up. Returning to the Upminster house he was pleased to see that Marcus was home and after letting himself in Eli called out for his son. Marcus had enjoyed a lie in and had only just got dressed. Running down the stairs thinking something was wrong as his father voice sounded urgent, he was just in time to see Eli slip into the study.

"What's up Dad?"

"I've got a bit of business to sort out and I don't want you in the area when it goes down. Find Duke and go and spend some time with that young woman of yours."

"So who's helpin' you?"

"No one, this is somethin' I need to do alone."

"I'm not leaving you Dad, no way!"

Eli stood up from the deep buttoned leather office chair and as he stared intently at his son he placed both of his palms flat onto the desk.

"It wasn't a request! Now for once, do as I fuckin' ask! When it's safe to return I'll get word to you."

Suddenly Eli did something he'd never done before. Walking over to his youngest son he placed both hands tenderly onto Marcus's shoulders.

"I've lost one boy, I ain't riskin' another, now please will you do as I ask Son?"

Marcus smiled, this was the first show of affection his father had shown to him in years.

"Of course I will Dad but please be careful."

Within the hour Marcus Carter had packed a holdall and was on his way to join Duke, Kezia and of course Rena. Alone in the house, Eli was just about to start gathering all he needed when he heard the front door open and Milly call out, just as she did every day.

"Anyone in? It's only me!!"

Eli cursed under his breath, he'd forgotten all about the woman who had looked after his family every day apart from Sundays, since Angela's death. Opening the safe he removed a wad of cash and peeled off five twenty pound notes. Walking into the kitchen Eli was just in time to stop her removing her coat.

"Mornin' Mills. I won't be needin' you today darlin' so here you go, have a day off on me and treat yourself."

When he handed her the cash Milly Garrod was momentarily struck dumb. He was a good boss when it came to wages but he'd never given her more than she'd earnt not to mention the fact that most days she was lucky if he even grunted in her direction. Today he was upbeat and friendly and as far as Milly was concerned it could only mean one thing, he was up to something. Eli could read her like a book and he needed to stop her suspicion or she would be like a dog with a bone until she got to the bottom of his business.

"I have a visitor comin' today and to be honest I would rather that no one else was here."

As he spoke Eli winked which made her smile.

"Well if you don't mind me saying, it's about time. Thank you for the money Mr Carter but you really don't need to…."

Eli cut her off mid-sentence, why the fuck wouldn't she just go! Walking towards her he picked up her wicker shopping basket and then gently taking hold of Milly's elbow, guided her towards the front door.

"You look after us all and with never a complaint, so it's about time I rewarded that loyalty. Now off you go and I'll see you on Monday."

Almost forcing his housekeeper out of the door, he could see the frown on her brow but it didn't stop him and as Milly walked towards her cycle that was propped up under the lounge window, she heard the front door being locked. Shaking her head, Milly hung her basket on to the handlebars and slowly pushed her bike along the gravel driveway. Leaning up against the wooden door, Eli let out a loud sigh. He could feel that his breathing was becoming difficult and he had to calm himself down if he was ever to complete his plan. A few seconds later he slowly walked in the direction of the kitchen confident that he could now get on with his tasks. Removing a small key from one of the many hooks that hung next to the wall phone, Eli Carter made his way outside and headed down to the end of the large manicured lawn. The small brick shed which was almost covered in ivy and virtually hidden from view had been locked for several years. No one was allowed entry and as Eli placed his key into the padlock, he wasn't sure whether it would be seized shut. After wiggling the key for a few moments the lock at last gave way but he wasn't so fortunate when it came to opening the wooden door. Years of neglect had seen it swell and distort and he had to put all of his effort in to lift and pry it open. The musty smell instantly invaded his nostrils and Eli leaned heavily on the old workbench. The physical exertion had tired him and his breathing was now laboured again. Years earlier there had been a couple of occasions when fire had been needed and looking around Eli could see three or four boxes piled up against the far wall. Opening up the first he found exactly what he was looking for, it was three quarters full with rolls of copper pipe lagging. Felt like, it would conduct accelerant perfectly. Placing the box near the door he then opened another. This one was full of litre bottles of odourless fire lighter fuel. Eli wasn't sure if it would still be any good so grabbing one of the bottles he went outside and tipped a little onto the grass. Removing a box of matches from his pocket he struck one against the sandpaper side and dropped it onto the liquid. When it instantly flamed he almost let out a cheer. Slowly carrying the boxes up to the garage he removed the old tin bath from the wall and smiled as he did so. Back in the day when money had been in short supply Angela had used it to bath Morris when he was small and even though they had eventually moved to a mansion, she would never part with it. Looking upwards he said a silent prayer that he would at least be allowed to complete this last task, after that if God wanted to take him he was more than ready. Placing all the opened rolls of lagging into the bath he liberally cover them with the lighter fuel and grabbing the wooden handled end of a rake, he stirred until he was confident that it was all covered. Eli hadn't planned to leave until late afternoon so closing the garage door he made his way into the house. The exertion had completely knackered him and a nap was called for if he was ever to get the job done.

By four thirty that afternoon and now dressed from head to toe in black he removed a large holdall from the wardrobe. Packing was kept to a minimum, in all honesty where he was going there would be no need for fancy clothes. Glancing around the bedroom he spied a small silver frame that contained a picture of him and Angela and although he had sworn to take no personal possessions, he couldn't leave this one. Returning to the garage Eli then put the lagging, which had now soaked up all of the liquid, into a second large holdall. Picking up a plastic can of petrol that was always kept full to top up the lawnmower, he carefully placed it into a carrier bag along with a container of sandwiches, a bottle of drink, his inhalers and a balaclava. Walking outside, he didn't have to wait more than a few minutes when Arty Pullman, punctual as always, arrived on the dot of four fifty five. Taking a moment to glance all around and take in the beauty of his home, Eli sighed deeply knowing this would probably be the last time he saw the house. Opening the boot he put the bag containing his clothes inside but the other bags went into the back of the car with him.

"Afternoon Mr Carter. Where are we off to today?"
Eli gave directions and then sitting back on the seat, closed his eyes. Arty dropped his fare off at the end of Streamside Close and he was instructed to leave the bag in the boot and to collect Eli as soon as he received a call. Handing the man an envelope of cash for his trouble and also so he didn't take any more fares that weekend, Eli removed his bags and then strolled off down the road. Reaching the property where only a few hours earlier Weasel had been holed up, he made his way to the rear and let himself inside. Now all he had to do was wait until nightfall and pray that the family didn't return at least until tomorrow. Taking a seat on the bedroom floor he thought about all that had happened in the last couple of months. True Morris had been totally out of order but he hadn't killed the kid and as far as Eli was concerned, that Del bastard had gone way too far. Payback was in order for his boy and by God it would be payback like never before. Wiping away a lone tear as it dropped onto his cheek he suddenly smiled as he looked upwards. "This is for you Son!"

Eli must have drifted off to sleep because when he woke it was dark outside. Cursing under his breath he tapped his phone and was surprised to see that it was just after ten thirty. Peering out of the window he looked for any signs of life at the house opposite but thankfully, save for the two porch lights being on, which were obviously on a timer, there was none. Making his way downstairs, Eli lifted the holdall and pulling the balaclava over his head, quietly made his way across the road, all the time looking around to see if anyone was watching but the road was like a graveyard and for that he was thankful. Lighting his way with a small torch, Eli ran the lengths of lagging along the back of the house and then down each side. Luckily Jean Foster was a keen gardener and there were so many bushes and shrubs that after Eli had pushed the material to the back they were almost invisible. When he reached the front door, he tucked the excess lagging behind the two large potted bays that stood each side of the entrance. His breathing was becoming laboured but he was done for now so slowly walking back across the road he took refuge once again in the empty house. Thankfully the water in the property was still connected, he felt dirty and the liquid soaked lagging may well have been odourless but his hands were still covered in the oily residue. Eli had been careful to wipe each surface after he'd touched it and after he'd washed himself, the tap and basin received the same treatment. It was highly unlikely that this house would ever be checked but he wasn't about to take any chances. Now it was just a waiting game, for how long he didn't have a clue but one thing was for sure, his timing had to be perfect if his plan was to succeed.

# CHAPTER TWENTY EIGHT

Del was up with the larks and after breakfast was eager to set off, they had a long drive ahead but Jean seemed to be dragging her heels. He knew better than to complain, they were only just getting back on an even keel, so instead he asked Dawn to intervene. She had a real knack of getting her mother to do as she asked and after checking that Allison was okay to drive they were on the road less than half an hour later. After four and a half hours Del finally gave in and allowed them to stop for a toilet break at Buck Services. They were now only seventy nine miles from home but after stretching her legs, Allison announced that she couldn't possibly drive any further. Del sighed, this was typical of her but then he smiled, if she was starting to play up again it meant she was at least starting to get back to normal. Dawn swapped places with her sister and agreed to drive Jean back while Ally got in beside her father who really wasn't looking forward to the rest of the journey. He loved his eldest child but her continuous bitching and moaning wore him down at the best of times, without the added pressure of what might go down after they got home.

"So, have you enjoyed your time away Dad? Feel a bit more relaxed?"
"Yes thank you Ally and you?"
"Okay I suppose but the hotel left a lot to be desired. I mean the staff were surly at times and the food……"
By now Del had switched off, Ally was back to normal alright!

Finally at just before five that afternoon both cars at last turned into the drive and Eli Foster was watching every move from the house across the street. He noticed how tenderly Del helped his wife out of the car and how pretty both of the young women were but not one single thing made him have second thoughts about what he was going to do later that night. Del opened the front door and one by one they slowly entered. Unlike before, the place seemed eerie and quiet and for a second Del wondered if he had done the right thing in bringing his family home, was it a home anymore or just a box full of bad memories? Jean, who had been quietly standing and observing her husband, instantly knew what he was thinking. Walking over she placed her arms around his neck, stared up into his eyes and tenderly fingered the scar on his face
"Don't worry its goin' to be fine, we're goin' to be fine."

Nodding his head she could see the tears in her husband's eyes, something she'd never seen not even when Kenan……She didn't want to think about that at the moment, so standing up straight she turned and looked at her daughters who both seemed to be just loitering in the hallway.

"Right! Come on you two let's get these cases unpacked and then see what we have in the fridge."

Suddenly the space was filled with chatter as the girls made their way upstairs and Jean walked through to the kitchen. Spying the supplies Levi had left she smiled, people could be so kind and that kindness often came from people you least expected it from.

By eight, the house was shipshape, Jean had cooked them a meal from the reserves she had in the freezer and they were now all seated in the front room. The TV was on but no one was really watching it. Allison and Dawn were riveted to their mobiles and Del and Jean were just sitting quietly on the sofa, both engrossed in their own private thoughts. Suddenly Del's mobile rang out to the sound of Johnny Kidd and the Pirates singing 'Shakin' all over' and for a second the noise startled him. He didn't recognise the number so was cautious when he answered.

"Yeah?"

"Is this Del Foster?"

"Who wants to know?"

Del was always very careful who he gave his number to and most people, especially if it was business related, had to go through Levi first. This was strange but then again it could be just a random nuisance call from one of the Indian call centres that even though he had call blocking, somehow managed to occasionally slip through the net.

"This is Eli Carter."

Immediately getting to his feet, Del walked from the room and tried his best not to raise any suspicions with his wife. How dare that bastard ring him at home and whatever the cunt was about to say, he definitely didn't want his family to hear the conversation. Closing the study door behind him he made his way over to the window and with the phone still glued to his ear, peered through the blinds totally unaware that he was being watched from the first floor window of the house opposite.

"You're a cheeky cunt phonin' me!"

"Look, if this war is to stop then we need to meet."

"For what?"

"Don't you think this needs to be talked over

once and for all?  Or are you happy for us to end up killin' each other and our men, until there's no one left.  We've both lost enough don't you think?"

Something didn't feel right but Del knew to refuse would only result in more bloodshed.

"When and where?"

"Tonight and the location is up to you but make sure you come alone, this is between you and me only."

They agreed on ten o'clock and Del chose the carpark at the King George hospital in Ilford.  It was roughly half way for both men and being a busy public area covered by close circuit cameras, Del was confident that the bastard wouldn't try anything.  Returning to the front room Del again took a seat next to his wife.

"Who was that?"

"Just a bit of business I need to take care of babe.  I'm goin' out in a bit so lock up when I leave.  I shouldn't be too long."

"Okay darlin', I think I'll have an early night and the girls look done in anyway."

They continued to sit in silence until twenty past nine when Del stood up and announced he was going out.  Jean followed him into the hall and after he kissed her lovingly on the lips he set off but not before he had heard her lock the door behind him.

Across the road Eli watched until Del's car as it pulled out of the drive and when he saw the lights downstairs go off and the ones upstairs go on he smiled. Glancing at his watch he reasoned that fifteen minutes would be long enough before he would strike and Del wouldn't even have arrived at the agreed destination yet. Calling Arty Pullman, he instructed the man to collect him at the same destination as he'd dropped him off at in twenty five minutes time. Eli also told Arty to park the car in such a way so that it was ready to go at a moment's notice and to switch off the headlights until he was safely inside. Now intently staring at his watch, as soon as the minute hand hit the mark he made his way down stairs, grabbing the petrol can as he went and pulled down his balaclava to cover his face. Just like before, the road was deathly quiet as he slipped across to the other side. For a man of his age and considering his illness, Eli Carter was surprisingly swift and light on his feet. At the front door he careful lifted the hidden excess webbing from both sides and quietly pushed them through the letterbox. With a torch he looked through the gap and when he was happy that they were far enough in and lying on the carpet, he undid the petrol can and gently began to pout the liquid through the letterbox. He had to take his time so that there were no loud glugs as the last thing he wanted was to wake anyone. When the can was empty he placed it into the bushes beside the front door. When the place went up there would be little left of the evidence and that included the accelerant. He knew there was a slight chance of it remaining after the fire but to walk along the street carrying it could have raised suspicions should he have been seen. Pulling off his balaclava he also threw that into the shrubs before removing a lighter from his pocket. It was an old Zippo that Angela had given him many years ago. It had never let him down and for this job it seemed very appropriate. Staring up at the sky Eli whispered again 'This is for you Son' before he rotated the wheel and a small flame appeared. Eli had used so much fuel that he knew as soon as it ignited he had to get away and touching the small flickering light to the lagging he stepped back, turned and swiftly walked away. The fire quickly took hold and in less than a minute had spread rapidly across the front of the property and down both sides. Being timber clad, the house went up like a tinderbox and when the petrol inside had ignited there was a flash of light as the inner hall began to burn out of control. Arty was waiting just as he'd been told and although he never asked his fares any questions, it wasn't rocket science to guess what had just gone down. The smell of burning fire hit his nostrils as soon as Eli climbed into the back of the car but still no words passed between the two men.

Allison was the first to be alerted when the smoke detectors began to rapidly beep. Jumping out of bed she ran onto the landing towards her parent's room. The smoke was thick and black and as she turned the handle and went inside she found Jean cowering under the window.
"It's okay mum. Come on darlin' we need to get out of here now!"
"Where's Dawn?"
Allison looked out of the bedroom door and could now see the flames lashing the floor and ceiling at the top of the stairs, there was no way they would be able to make an escape let alone help her sister. Grabbing her mother's mobile she tapped in nine nine nine. Dawn had also heard the alarm but after opening her door and seeing the flames as they engulfed her only means of escape, she slammed the door shut and running into her bathroom soaked as many towels as she could. Ramming two under her bedroom door she then went into the bathroom, closed the door and then did the same with the remainder of the towels. Small wisps of smoke began to seep through the gaps in the frame and

curl up towards the ceiling so Dawn grabbed her dressing gown from the hook and as quickly as she could, soaked it in the basin. With difficulty she somehow managed to pull on the sopping wet fabric and then getting on her hands and knees, she moved over to the corner of the room and lay down. The training given by the bank had served her well and unlike her sister, she knew better than to open the window. Venting the fire would only draw it into the bedroom and lying as low as she could would reduce the risk of smoke inhalation. Like most domestic houses, the doors were not fire retardant and seconds after Allison opened the window in the room next door, the fire fought through and engulfed the bedroom. The two women moved closer and closer towards the open window until there was nowhere left to go. Jeans nightdress was the first thing to catch on fire and in seconds her entire body was alight. The screams were horrific and as Allison began to burn as well Dawn could hear their tormented cries for help.

Glancing at his watch every couple of minutes, Del waited for almost half an hour before it finally dawned on him that he'd been set up. Driving at break neck speed, he didn't care if he was caught speeding. The only thing on his mind was his family and if that bastard had hurt them he would be out for blood and this time he wouldn't stop until they were all dead. The journey was taken in half the usual time and he turned into Streamside close eleven minutes later. Straight away he could see the flashing blue lights of the fire engine, ambulance and police cars. Most of the neighbours were standing in the road and screeching to a halt Del stared up at the burnt out remains of his home. As paramedics pushed a stretcher from the house Del ran over, only to see his youngest daughter with an oxygen mask covering her blackened face and struggling to breath. Del stared into the paramedics face as he pleaded "my wife?" Barry Parker had worked for the ambulance service for over fifteen years but had still never got used to scenes like this. Slowly shaking his head he looked to the left of the front door and as Del followed the man's gaze he saw the two body bags lying on the ground. Dropping to his knees Del began to wail as he moved his body back and forth. Two uniformed officers immediately came over and helped him up from the driveway.

"Dad! Dad! Where are you?!!!"

Dawn's cries brought him back to reality and realising that he couldn't help his wife and Allison, he ran over to the back of the ambulance. Climbing inside he took Dawn's

hand in his as tears streamed from his eyes.
"I tried to help them Dad but the fire! I just couldn't…."
"I know baby, I know."
With that the doors slammed shut and the ambulance sped off to the hospital with blue lights flashing. She was alive, at least she was alive was all Del kept telling himself, over and over again.

# CHAPTER TWENTY NINE

Eli didn't go home, he'd planned everything down to the last detail. Instead Arty Pullman drove the ten mile journey to the Courtyard by Marriott Hotel close to London City Airport. After removing his bag from the boot, Eli thanked the driver but stared hard at the man for a few seconds which slightly unnerved Arty and made him feel as if he had to reassure his passenger.
"Where my cab goes is my business Mr Carter and no one else's."
Eli nodded before closing the door and disappearing into the seven story building. His flight to Dublin didn't leave until quarter to two the following afternoon, so after checking in Eli made his way up to his room and the first thing he did was to take a shower and get rid of the smell of fire. He fell asleep as soon as his head hit the pillow and didn't wake again until eight the next morning. A full English was then enjoyed in the restaurant but although he had several hours to kill until his flight, Eli knew better than to go wandering around East London. He may have been from Essex but he was still a known face and word could easily get back to Del Foster, who Eli imagined must have

been going out of his mind with grief. Alone in his room he started to think about all of the recent events and something about the crime he'd committed the previous night had given him a new lease of life and it wasn't only that he had avenged Morris's death. For years Eli had taken a back seat when it came to actually participating in jobs, oh he was brilliant at planning but there was nothing to match the adrenalin rush that you got when you were in the throes of a job that was going down. Knowing that he would never be able to operate as he had before and with his illness it would have been out of the question anyway, Eli just hoped that his new life would be more interesting than the one he'd left behind and he had a gut feeling that it would be.

At North Middlesex hospital Del silently sat beside his daughter's bedside. In the accident and emergency department Dawn had been sedated and was on oxygen to help her breath. Thankfully, apart from the smoke inhalation, there was only scorching and no deep burns to her skin. For both of them their lives would never be the same again but for now his girl was sleeping and for that he was at least grateful. When the curtain surrounding the bed was slid away he looked up but he wasn't pleased to see a uniformed officer accompanied by a plain clothed detective.

"Mr Foster, Mr Del Foster?"

"Yeah, why?"

"Mr Foster, might it be possible to have a few words in private."

Del nodded then followed the two men out into the corridor.

"What's all this about?"

"I think it would be more prudent to speak in here."

The detective opened the door to a small side room that he'd been given permission to use. Taking a seat at the table he invited Del to do the same. This was obviously routine after a death by fire, or at least Del hoped it was. The last thing he needed was the Old Bill poking their noses in. When the time was right he would sort this once and for all but for now he had to look after Dawn, not to mention two funerals to arrange, the thought of which actually made him feel physically sick.

"I'm sorry for your loss and I realise that this is a difficult time for you but there are a few questions we need to ask you. One of your neighbours reported the fire at around ten fifteen this evening and we would like to know your exact whereabouts at that time?"

For a second Del couldn't believe what he was

hearing and when it finally dawned on him his brow furrowed and he was instantly on his feet. As he spoke his words came out loudly and with venom.

"You think I had somethin' to do with this?!!!!"

"No Mr Carter I didn't say that but as you are the only member of your family to be unscathed, then the question needs to be asked."

"I was in the carpark of the King George Hospital in Ilford you muppet and if you don't believe me then view the fuckin' CCTV. So this wasn't an accident then?"

He needed to try and find out what they had, anything that might hinder his own future plans.

"I'm afraid not Sir. The fire Chief found the remains of some kind of fabric accelerant, tests will be carried out but at the moment that's as much as we know. It's not a lot to go on but believe me when I say, we will leave no stone unturned in bringing the culprit to justice. Can I ask if you have any enemies? Anyone who would wish to harm you or your family?!

Del took a moment to think or at least make it appear that he was thinking.

"No one comes to mind."

"Well if anyone does please contact me. For now, the footage you have mentioned will be viewed and I hope for your sake you are on it. Where will you be staying?"

Del hadn't even thought about that and he immediately said '

"The Premier Inn to begin with but once Dawn is released then we'll move to somewhere better, at least until we can go back to the house."

"I'm afraid that won't be for some time Mr Foster. I will be back in touch in the next few days and once again I'm sorry for your loss."

The detective and his sidekick walked from the room leaving Del just sitting in stunned silence. His, their, home was totally gone leaving just a burned out shell but he hadn't given it any thought at all. Memories of his family had all gone up in flames, pictures, keepsakes, there was nothing left! Wearily making his way back to A & E, he only just reached the bedside when Dawn's doctor entered and his face gave away his concerns.

"I'm sorry Mr Foster but we need to move your daughter. I'm afraid her lungs are not clearing as quickly as we would like."

"What are you sayin'? Is she goin' to die?!!!"

"No, no, nothing like that but we do have concerns so it's best if she stays here so that we can monitor her. We will shortly be moving your daughter up to the ward so if you would like to take a break and come back later?"

Del nodded his head and once he was out of the hospital he called Levi Puck and arranged to meet the following lunchtime at the Crown and Anchor on Fore Street. Levi was still oblivious to what had happened and Del wasn't looking forward to going over it all again so soon but he was hoping for the man's help so he had to be upfront.

Historically listed, the Crown and Anchor had been home to an array of landlords over the years. Situated on the corner of Fore Street and Fairfield Road, it had long been frequented by Del and his firm when they were enjoying a night out. A traditional pub renowned for its good Guinness, it was homely and the kind of place that the Old Bill never went into without good reason.

As Levi entered he spotted his boss sitting at a table at the far end of the bar. He could also see that his pint was ready and waiting which made him smile.

"Fuck I'm glad you're back Boss. It's been terrible since the boys….."

Levi stopped midsentence when he saw the look on his boss's face. The horrific deaths of his fellow crew members was still raw and due to the ongoing police investigation, not one of them had yet been laid to rest and now he could tell that something else had happened.

"I have more bad news. Jean and Ally are

dead."

Levi was completely speechless and as he looked into his boss's eyes he could see the pool of tears, something Levi had never witnessed in all the years he'd been in Del's employ. Deciding not to comment, he waited for Del to compose himself and listen to what had happened.

"The cunts weren't content with killin' my boy or my firm, they wanted revenge for that nonce and Jean and Ally were the cost. Innocent, two beautiful innocent women! What kind of fuckin' animals are these Gypo's? I can't let this go Levi but after all you've been through of late I understand if you want no part in it."

"Don't be fuckin' stupid Del, your kids have always felt like my own family and Jean was always so kind to me, especially when Glenda fucked off with that paki. What you got planned?"

"I haven't, I just need to find the bastard and I think he's holed up in that fuckin' mansion he calls a home. First thing in the mornin', after I've checked on Dawn, I'm goin' to take a drive over to Essex. You up for a little trip?"

Levi Puck grinned from ear to ear. He was always up for a scrap and if it involved payback then the more the better.

Even with all that had happened, Marcus, for the

first time in years, felt alive. He was spending every free moment with Rena and shortly after arriving at the camp had realised that he never wanted to be apart from her again. He spoke to his father the next day but was completely oblivious to what had happened twenty four hours earlier in Edmonton. Eli had kept him in the dark to keep him safe and when he'd spoken to his dad earlier that day Eli had informed him that he'd gone to live with the travellers in Ireland and that he probably wouldn't be going back to Upminster again. To say it had come as a shock was an understatement but his father sounded happy and that was all that mattered.
"Are you sure about this Dad?"
"Never been more sure about anythin' Son. I've also signed the house over to you."
"What?!"
Eli knew that he wasn't long for this world and it made complete sense to get his affairs in order before he died.
"You heard me. I've handed the firm over to Dennis Shannon but I expect there to be a power struggle in the not too distant future. That's up to them to fight it out amongst themselves. I'm getting too old for this game Marcus and I know your heart has never really been in it."
"Are you really okay Dad?"
"I'm fine boy but after losing your brother, I've

had enough.  When I'm settled I'll let you know where I am.  My cousin Patrick has a camp and so does Fergus McKenna so I ain't sure where I'm goin' to be for a while.  Take care Son and look after that little girl."
With that the line went dead but something in his father's words made Marcus feel incredibly sad.  Maybe it was losing Morris, maybe it was just that everything had now changed but his heart felt heavy.

Milly Garrod rode along the country lane and all felt good in her world.  The sun was shining and it was nice to have some time to herself, even if she was missing Mr Carter and Marcus.  Her friend Faith had invited Milly to a BBQ and about to set off for Faiths house, Milly remembered that she'd left her Kagool at the mansion.  It was only a short detour and you always had to second guess the British weather.  Today they had forecast rain so collecting her jacket was a must.  Parking her bicycle at the front of the house she let herself inside and made her way to the rear kitchen.  The place was so big that she didn't hear Del Fosters Mercedes pull up outside the front door.  With Levi by his side he tried the door and was surprised to find it open.  Slowly walking through the house they suddenly came face to face with Milly clutching her Kagool.

"Who the hell are you and what are you doing in Mr Carters house?!"

Levi stepped forward and his sheer size saw Milly shrink back against the wall. Levi grabbed a handful of her hair and for a fleeting second she thought how he was ruining her shampoo and set that she'd had done this morning especially for the BBQ.

"Shut your trap old woman!"

Del walked towards her and though nowhere near as big as the coloured man, his face was mean and it frightened her.

"Where is he?"

"Where's who?"

Patience had never been Del's strong point but since losing the majority of his family he had absolutely none. Raising his hand he punched Milly straight in the mouth and she instantly felt the iron taste of blood. Running her tongue over her bottom teeth she knew that a couple of them were now loose, seventy one years of meticulously looking after them and now she would have to have dentures!

"Don't fuck me about lady 'cause I ain't in the mood! Now tell me where that cunt Eli is or things are goin' to get very fuckin' nasty!"

Milly felt the blood as it ran down her bottom lip and as she shook her head Levi again grabbed her by the hair and dragged her back into the kitchen. Literally throwing her down onto one of the chairs he snatched the old lead that still hung on the hook ten years after Ruddy the Labrador, had passed over the rainbow bridge. Bending down Levi roughly tied her ankles together so she couldn't run off and then out of nowhere Del punched her again, only this time it was straight in her left eye. Milly's head flew backwards with the force and in seconds her eyelid had begun to swell and close.

"That bastard killed my son, burnt my wife and daughter alive and my only living child is in the hospital. Now I'm goin' to give you one more chance, where is he?"

Milly didn't reply fast enough and grabbing her wrist with both hands, he used all of his might and Milly screamed out when she felt the bone snap. With laboured breath she appeared to pant as she struggled to speak.

"I, I, I'm just the cleaner! I came to get my Kagool that's all."

As Del raised his fist to lash out he was suddenly stopped by Levi.

"She don't know anythin' Boss. The silly old cow would have talked by now!"

Del just stared at the bloodied beaten woman in front of him but he felt no remorse.

"When you see the cunt! Tell him he's on

borrowed time, a dead man walkin' and that goes for his boy as well! Come on let's get out of this shit hole."

Milly didn't attempt to move for what seemed like an age but in reality it was only a few minutes. Now sure that they had gone she tentatively used her good hand to undo the lead. It was a struggle and she cursed under her breath a few times but finally she managed to free herself. The phone on the wall began to ring and Milly thought for a moment before she answered.

"H, h, h, hello?"

"Hi Mills, I rang your house and when there was no answer I hoped you would be at ours. I've had the strangest call from the old man, he......"

When she began to sob uncontrollably and then dropped the handset, Marcus ended the call and ran from the caravan.

Duke and the other vans were still parked up at Leysdown on the Isle of Sheppey and jumping into his car Marcus didn't even stop to tell Rena what was going on. The fifty mile journey was covered in forty five minutes as he travelled at just above the speed limit but not so excessive as to warrant a pull from the Old Bill. At the best of times most of the local Plod preferred to park up somewhere quiet and not challenge, there were some hard bastards in this neck of the woods and no pay packet was worth road rage by some villain, possibly holding a gun.

# CHAPTER THIRTY

Shingle flew in all directions as Marcus screeched to a halt outside the house. Adrenalin had taken over as he blindly ran inside not even thinking who or what he could be greeted by. That's where he differed so much from Morris and his father, neither of them would ever have ventured in without being tooled up and ready, no matter who was hurt inside. Calling out as he ran through the hallway and into the lounge, there was no reply and he started to panic. Running up the stairs he raced from bedroom to bedroom but suddenly it dawned on him, Mill's almost lived in their kitchen, that's where she'd be! Taking the stairs two at a time he ran into the kitchen and found Milly passed out on the tiled floor. She had tried to hold on until he got there but the pain had become so unbearable. Marcus quickly filled a tumbler with water and kneeling on the floor, tenderly lifted her head in his hand. As softly as he could and without trying to alarm her he spoke to her over and again.

"Come on Milly sweetheart, its Marcus. Come on my sweet friend I need you to wake up Mill's."

Slowly she opened her eyes and even though she

winced in pain she also managed a week smile for the man that she'd always looked upon as a son.

"My arm, my arm!!!!"

Marcus looked down and could visibly see the break.

"Here darlin', drink some of this."

Milly took a sip and turned up her nose when she realised it was water. In a husky voice she looked into his eyes.

"You could at least have given me some brandy."

Marcus laughed but his face showed the concern he was feeling and Milly could see it.

"Come on sweetheart, let's get you up off of that cold floor."

Slowly he helped her to her feet, led her over to the table and when she was seated on one of the farmhouse chairs and he was sure she wouldn't pass out again, he filled the kettle and put it on to boil. Removing one of the best china cups from the cupboard he placed a teabag in to it but as he spoke he didn't turn to face her as he didn't want her to see the tears in his eyes.

"Mum always said people need a hot drink for the shock. When you're feelin' a bit better we'll get you down the hospital, no arguments."

Milly softly coughed and then sighed deeply, he was such a good boy.

"Don't forget the brandy this time!"
Again Marcus laughed and slowly shook his head from side to side as he reached up to grab a packet of pain relief tablets that were kept, along with a host of other medications, in an old biscuit tin..
"No Mills I won't I promise."
Carrying the drink over he joined her at the table and pushed a cup and saucer in her direction, making sure to turn the handle so that it was easy for her to hold with her one good arm.
"Here, take these paracetamol, they'll help with the pain, well at least a bit. So, what happened my darlin', who did this to you?"
Milly Garrod studied his face, he really was a handsome young man and kind with it, unlike his father and brother. Fear filled her heart when she recalled what her attacker had said to her. What if they kept to their word and hurt him? She wouldn't be able to bear it, so in this instance honesty really was the best policy and she knew she had no choice but to warn him about the message she'd been told to pass on.
"It was strange, I came in on Saturday as usual but Eli gave me some money, he said it was a bonus and told me to take the day off, well I wasn't about to refuse. Anyway, my best pal Faith had invited me to a BBQ on Sunday and I realised I'd left my kagool here and….."

Marcus wanted to shake her and tell her to get to the important stuff but he didn't, he loved her too much for that and besides she was in shock and to get it all out would be good for her.

"I parked up my bike and had only just got to the kitchen and grabbed my jacket when they walked in, as bold as brass would you believe. I don't know their names and I've never seen them before but there were two of them, one was a great big black man but the one who really hurt me, he was white with a big scar on his cheek. I could tell he was in charge as the other one, the darky, did everything he said. He wanted to know where your dad was, told me Eli had killed his son and burnt his wife and daughter alive? He said his other daughter was still in the hospital but Mr Carter wouldn't do such an evil thing would he Marcus?"

Marcus had his mouth wide open in shock, what the hell had been going on while he'd been away? Obviously he was aware of Kenan but he couldn't share that with her but as for the others?

"I really don't know Mill's but I need to find out and fast. Drink your tea and then we have to get you sorted out."

With her good hand Milly suddenly grab his arm and for someone in such poor condition her grip was tight.

"There's more, he said Mr Carter was a dead man walking and you as well. Oh Marcus, please be careful my love."

Helping her to her feet he led her towards the hallway and she was still clutching the Kagool as she went. Suddenly Milly stopped, grabbed his arm again and looked deep into his eyes, she was desperate, desperate for him to tell her all would be well.

"Don't you worry about me Mill's, I can take care of myself. It's you I'm concerned about and the sooner we get you looked at the better." Marcus was sure none of her injuries were life threatening so he took the drive slowly as Milly winced in pain with every bump in the road. It was probably the first time in her life that she'd been hurt in any real sense of the word and it bothered him that on the one occasion she had been hurt, it was because of his family and the way they chose to live their lives. Dropping her off at Queens Hospital in Romford and after giving her a twenty for the cab fare home, Marcus said she needed to rest but he promised to call in and see her the next day. Milly had no intention of going home, when they had patched her up she was off to the BBQ, what had happened to her was far too interesting not to share.

Sitting in the hospital carpark Marcus desperately tried to contact Eli several times but there was no answer and now he feared for his dad's safety. Whatever was going on was a complete mystery to him but one he couldn't ignore, not if what Mill's had told him was correct and he had absolutely no reason to doubt her. Marcus was angry, angry that they had hurt the woman who'd been like a mother to him since the day his own had died and angry that the choice of revenge his father had chosen could possibly now be the cause of both of their deaths. Why did there always have to be revenge and heartbreak, if he was honest with himself, Morris had deserved what he got. That poor innocent kid had taken his life because of the vile act that Morris had carried out, so why did his father feel it was okay to kill almost all of Del Foster's family? Driving back to Upminster he continued to call and finally, just as he pulled into the drive, Eli answered.
"Hello Son I see you've been tryin' to reach me?"
"Thank fuck! Tryin' to reach you!!!! What the fucks been goin' on Dad?!!"
There was a few seconds silence and for a moment Marcus didn't know if his father had hung up. Finally he spoke but what Eli said, Marcus didn't want to hear.
"So you know then?"

"It's true?!!! Why? Why did you do that Dad, ain't we all been through enough?"

"They killed your brother or has that somehow slipped your fuckin' mind?"

"Of course it ain't but has it slipped your fuckin' mind what Morris did to that boy and what the outcome of that was? When's it goin' to stop Dad?"

"It has I ..."

"Oh no it hasn't! They came lookin' for you and stumbled upon Milly, beat her bad, broke her arm and I've just left her at the hospital. They're comin' after you and me now."

Normally Eli planned everything in minute detail and covered any eventuality but this time it had been very personal and he really hadn't given much thought to his actions. Suddenly he was worried for his boy.

"No! Is she okay? Where are you Son?"

"On my way back to the house why?"

"Don't, get out of the area, go and be with that little girlie of yours, you have to lie low until I can figure somethin' out."

"What like you've done in the last couple of days? I don't think so! I'm goin' to sort this once and for all. I'll call you if and when it's all over."

Marcus hung up, he was raging, what an earth had his old man done. He knew where this was all going, knew how it had to end and what he had to do but it went against the grain so badly. Having Hobson's choice in the matter didn't make him feel any better but if he was to live his life without continually having to look over his shoulder, there was only one thing he could do. Eli could only stare at his phone in disbelief, if this went wrong he could end up losing both of his sons. There was no time to stop his boy, by the time he got back to England it would probably all be over and all he could do was pray for his boy to stay safe. As a child and now as a man he had never given Marcus the love and attention he'd deserved and instead had focused totally on Morris. As worried as he now was, Eli was also immensely proud that his boy had finally stepped up to the plate but it wasn't fair that his hand had been forced and now he was risking his life to save them both. One certain fact that Eli now realised, was that if anything happened to his baby he would never forgive himself.

When Marcus arrived at the house he pulled the car around to the back just in case they came to see if anyone was at home. Running upstairs he packed the majority of his clothes and personal possessions and placed them into the boot of his car. He knew he wouldn't be returning and that thought saddened him as the place was full of memories of his mother. Entering his father's study he pulled back the carpet and lifted the two long loose floorboards. Eli always kept a stash of firearms there in case of emergencies and glancing down Marcus studied the selection of neatly wrapped hardware. Two rifles, a sawn-off shotgun and several handguns were crammed into the small space and picking out a GLOCK 17 pistol, he placed it, along with a silencer and some ammunition, into a small backpack. Next he chose a set of fake magnetic vehicle plates that his father kept handy on the off chance they might be needed and running outside he secured them to the front and rear of his car. Taking a moment to run over everything and make sure nothing had been missed he finally climbed into the Audi. Milly had said that Del's daughter was in the hospital so tapping into Google maps on his phone he searched for the nearest one to Del's address. North Middlesex had to be the best bet so after making sure everywhere was locked up he set off for what might turn out to be the last drive of his life.

Parking up as far away from the main entrance

as he could, Marcus reached over to the back seat and retrieved his baseball cap. With his collar pulled up he was pretty much unnoticeable as he walked the entire perimeter of the large building. He was looking for anywhere that wasn't covered by close circuit television but after covering three sides he wasn't hopeful until a single door on the corner of the building opened and two cleaners emerged chatting away in some eastern European language. Gossiping, they had been too engrossed to check that the door had closed behind them and Marcus managed to grab the side before it slammed shut. After walking down a long corridor he came to the cleaners' cloakroom. Spying a couple of lockers with keys hanging from the locks and with no names written on the front, he opened one, checked that it was empty and then locking it, placed the key into his pocket. Continuing on he entered through two double doors into the main hub of the hospital. For a moment he stopped and studied just where he was and then approaching the reception area, he asked for directions to the burns unit. Luckily it was on the same floor and only a short distance from where he'd entered. Things so far were going well but he had to make certain that the Foster girl was even at this hospital. Nearing the ward, he noticed a figure walking towards him so lowering his head he continued to walk in such a way that told anyone he knew exactly where he was headed. As the two men passed each other Marcus glanced sideways and instantly saw the scar but he also thought Del had looked at his face for a few seconds longer than usual and he was praying that he hadn't been recognised. He'd scored a jackpot but his heart was racing as he continued on, thinking that any moment he would be called out. That didn't happen and he realised it was just nerves, a feeling he didn't like but one that he knew would keep him on his toes. Now he had to put his plan into action but as his target was leaving he knew it would probably be a few hours until he returned. It didn't matter, Marcus was happy to wait so long as he was successful.

Back at the carpark he rummaged through his bags in the boot and pulled out a bright red t-shirt with the word 'Ibiza Forever' emblazed across the front in canary yellow font. Next he pulled out a matching bright yellow cap, both had been joke gifts from Morris on his last holiday. His choice wasn't anything to do with his preferred dress sense but purely down to the fact that anyone looking at him would take far more notice of his garish clothing than they would his face. Marcus removed his jacket and placed the t-shirt over the top of the blue one he was already wearing. Pulling on his jacket again he then stuffed the yellow cap into a carrier bag along with the loaded handgun and silencer. Now he moved the car and placed it as close as he could to the carpark entrance. Reclining the seat he thought it would be a good time to try and get forty winks, the next few hours would be hectic and he didn't want to make any slip ups.

# CHAPTER THIRTY ONE

Within a day of the fire, Del had rented a small lock up on Stour Road. The police were still investigating the murders at Roach Road but only two streets away, the new place was close enough to allow him to keep an eye on the old house. Initially the killings had made headline news and it was over a week before the media had stopped coming to the site. Del was waiting until he could get back into Roach Road, he had stuff stashed all over the place in lead lined boxes but there was no way he could check on the drugs and cash while the Old Bill were sniffing about. The best he could hope for was that they didn't snoop about too much and find it. The property was registered to Del so he had received a call from the law but as he was down in Cornwall they had stupidly ruled him out regarding any involvement but if they had bothered to delve further they would have realised that the time scales didn't match. Luckily Levi Puck also hadn't been drawn in and now the two men were engrossed in the process of putting together a new firm. Del was introduced to the crew Levi had taken on but more bodies would be needed. It would take time and patience, not to mention a long hard slog before they could trust anyone else but life had to go on and Del was going to make sure that Dawn would be well protected, it was the least he owed her. After calling in three blokes who had come highly recommended, he ran through what would be expected of them. He did touch on the subject regarding what had happened at Roach Road and studied their expressions for any sign that they were not a hundred percent willing to get involved but there was nothing so he hired them on the spot. Del left Levi to go over the finer details and then he set off for his evening visit to the hospital.

In the hospital carpark Marcus had managed a couple of short naps but as time moved on the adrenalin was now beginning to surge. Getting out of the car he zipped up his jacket, pulled the collar up and placing his old cap onto his head he grabbed the carrier bag. A short walk would clear his mind and hopefully calm him down, not to mention the fact that it would help to stretch his legs as he could feel the onset of cramp in his right calf. He got close to the pavement when he suddenly saw Del's Mercedes enter the carpark. Running as fast as he could, Marcus entered the hospital through the rotund entrance foyer. Stopping to glance at a notice board to give himself time to calm down, he then continued on to the cleaners' locker room. Removing his jacket he placed it into the locker and swapped his black cap for the canary yellow one. He also put on a pair of dark rimmed reading spectacles that he'd found in the glove compartment of his car, Lord only knew who they had originally belonged to. Taking a moment to study himself in the mirror, he smiled when he realised that he looked a complete dick! The bag now only held the gun with the silencer attached and pushing his wrist through the handles, he walked back out into the hub of the hospital. When it came to visiting, evenings were always the busiest with family and friends calling in to see their loved ones on the way home after work. This allowed Marcus to fall in with the hordes of people walking in all direction. Approaching the burns unit he stopped suddenly when he saw Del walk through the doors. He'd missed his opportunity and would now have to hang around until his target emerged again. It wasn't too problematic but it did raise his risk of being studied too closely by people. Taking a seat in one of the small relaxation areas, he grabbed a magazine and lifted it close to his face. His heart was beating rapidly and every few seconds he would glance in the direction of the ward but it would be over an hour before he would get another chance.

As Del approached his daughter's bed he could instantly see how drawn and tired she looked. He accepted that it was partly due to the smoke inhalation but also the fact that his poor baby had just lost her mother and sister and he felt totally and utterly helpless.

"Hi babe, how you doin' sweetheart?"

Dawn smiled when she saw her father, he was all she had left now and she didn't want him to know just how lost and lonely she was really feeling.

"No so bad Dad and you?"

"So, so."

She knew he was lying and holding it together just for her but she wished he wouldn't. He had to allow himself to grieve or he would eventually crack.

"Has there been any news?"

"No babes, the Old Bill are still investigatin' and we both know that will result in them finding out fuck all. The Insurance people are comin' out on Friday but it will take months to rebuild the house, actually I don't think I want to live there again. Maybe it's time for a fresh start honey, just you and me?"

For a moment they just stared at one another, both taking in the enormity of what he had actually said, from now on it was only the two of them, in just a few short weeks, their beautiful family of five had been reduced to the two sad figures here in this hospital ward with neither of them really able to comfort each other emotionally.

"The Old Bill did say that they will release your mum and Ally by tomorrow, so at least I can start plannin' the funerals."

Del fell silent again as his mind wandered back to the last time he saw Jean, God it felt like a lifetime ago now and he missed her more than he could ever express.

"Can we have a joint one Dad?"

"A joint what?"

Dawn's brow furrowed, she couldn't believe he didn't know what she was talking about.

"The funerals!"

"Okay, okay calm down. Of course we can darlin', I hadn't given it any thought but I think it would be perfect and what your mum would have wanted. I'm goin' to get off now and let you get some rest. I'll be back to see you in the mornin' babe."

Del lent over the bed and kissed her tenderly on the forehead. She was now so precious, not that she hadn't always been but now she was all he had in the world and he was going to wrap her up in cotton wool and never let anyone hurt her again.

When the ward doors opened, Marcus raised his eyes and as soon as he saw it was his target he was on his feet. As the two men got closer and with his hands now starting to sweat, Marcus pulled the handgun from the carrier bag and aimed it directly at Del's head.
"What the fuck!!!!"
Del instantly raised both palms upwards, he didn't have a clue what was going on or who this man was. For a second Marcus was hesitant, he'd never killed anyone before and much to Eli's displeasure, had always shied away from violence.
"What? What do you want from me?!"
"I'm truly sorry for what my old man has done to your family but beating up a defenceless old woman and tellin' her me and my dad are next can't be left alone."
"Look pal, let's just call it a day shall we? Ain't we all been through enough?"
For a split second Marcus lowered the gun but when Del moved forwards Marcus knew he had no choice so he quickly raised his arm and pulled the trigger. The silencer dulled the sound of the bullet but not enough for the nurse who had just turned the corner not to hear it. She let out a terrifying scream and Marcus turned and ran. Struggling to place the gun into the carrier bag he moved at lightning speed. When he

reached the corridor that led to the cleaners' room he slowed down as he didn't want to draw too much attention to himself. His hands were shaking as he tried to put the key in the locker door and it took two attempts before he was successful. Quickly pulling the garish t-shirt over his head and stuffing it along with the yellow cap and glasses into the bag, he then pulled on his coat and black cap and let himself out through the back door. Walking at a steady pace and trying to appear as normal as possible, he at last made it back to the carpark. His hands were again shaking as he pressed the release lock button on his key fob and he could feel the stirrings of nausea in his jaw. Driving slowly towards the exit Marcus could hear the sirens of several police cars and he knew he wasn't in the clear just yet. As he turned left onto the main road, Levi turned right and for a split second the two men made eye contact. Neither knew the other but the idea crossed Marcus' mind that maybe he was the big Blackman that Milly had told him about. Shaking his head at the thought, London was a huge place and filled with all colour and creeds of people and the chances of the man being the same person must have been a million to one. It was a further ten minutes before he turned into a side road and stopped the car. As Marcus removed the magnetic plates he suddenly and without warning projectile vomited into the gutter. Tears streamed down his face but they were not from being sick, the enormity of what he had just done was starting to sink in. He had taken a life and what right had he had to do that but from somewhere deep in his mind came the words 'it was kill or be killed'. He knew it was true, knew he had done the only thing he could but it didn't make him feel any better.

At the hospital there was chaos as medics from several wards close by attended Del who was still lying on the floor. The bullet had hit his forehead off centre and somehow he was still alive! Dawn had heard the commotion from her ward but she was in no state to go and see what was happening. She had a sinking feeling in the pit of her stomach even though there was no way she could have known what had just happened.
"Nurse! Nurse!!!!"
Janet Henson, who had been looking after Dawn since she had been brought in came running from the nurses' station.
"What Dawn? What's the matter?"
"What's goin' on, what's happened?"
"Someone has been attacked in the corridor but that's all I know. Now don't worry yourself you

are quite safe here in the hospital."
"Really? Well however got attacked wasn't!"
Nurse Henson just gave Dawn a look that said 'don't make such a fuss' and then she walked back to her station.

Levi approached the final corridor that led to the ward but was stopped by a makeshift barrier and unbeknown to him, the doctors were pushing a covered stretcher that held Del, out of the area towards the ICU. Suddenly the heart monitor he was linked up to began to beep loudly and quickly bringing the stretcher to a halt, one of the doctors began CPR but stopped a few seconds later when his colleague touched him on the arm and slowly shook his head. Derek Foster was pronounced dead at 19.27 and now instead of being taken to the intensive care unit, his body was being wheeled towards the morgue. The police were talking to all those who were in the vicinity at the time but no one could shed any light, they all said that the shooter was wearing a bright red shirt and yellow cap but nothing more than that was added. A few minutes later and the cleaners were brought in and instantly began to wash and mop the blood from the floor. The police had decided that it would be impossible to collect any DNA evidence as thousands of people passed through this area daily. Levi had little interest regarding what had happened, he was more bothered by the fact that he couldn't get through, so he waved his hand to get the attention of the security guard.

"Excuse me Guvnor but I need to get to the burns ward."

Ben Sutton was as big as Levi but quite a bit wider so he never had any problems with Joe public.

"Sorry pal but this route is temporarily out of bounds. Take a right down that way then left and left again and you'll end up at the rear of the ward. Everyone is aware of what's happened so they should have opened the doors by now."

Sighing heavily, Levi did as he'd been instructed and after walking through a series of long corridors he finally arrived at the back entrance to the burns unit. As he pushed through the doors he passed two nurses walking in the opposite direction and he couldn't be off hearing one of them say that a visitor had been shot. For a moment Levi stopped dead in his tracks and the hairs on the back of his neck weirdly stood up on end or at least that's how it felt. Something wasn't right and his step quickened as he entered Dawn's ward. She smiled when she saw who her visitor was, Levi had always been so loving towards her and her brother and sister and it was kind of him to visit.

"Hi Uncle Levi, what a nice surprise."
"Hello sweetheart."
Levi bent over the bed and kissed her forehead.
"You seen your dad today?"
"Yeah, you must have just missed him. I can go home tomorrow Levi, well not home but you know what I mean. I think I'm going to the hotel with Dad…."
Levi had stopped listening after her last sentence and as he stood up she couldn't be off noticing the look of panic in his eyes.
"What is it Levi, what's wrong?"
"Just give me a minute sweetheart, I need to check somethin' out. I won't be long."
With that he swiftly walked from the ward and once out in the corridor he approached one of the many uniformed officers who were milling about in the area.
"Excuse me Sir but you cannot enter this area."
"I think I might know who the victim was."
The officer immediately called to his superior and Levi explained about Del visiting just a few minutes before he had arrived and that their paths hadn't crossed. He also explained that Del had a few enemies and elaborated on the trouble that had happened at Roach Road, which had been hot news at most of the London nicks. He was taken to a side room and shortly after was joined by detective Andy Munroe. Detective

Munroe tried to take a statement but Levi wasn't able to tell them anything nor would he even if he'd known something. The only option left was to escort him to the morgue and see if he could identify the victim. As Levi entered the sterile room the stretcher was straight in front of him. There had been no time to place the deceased into a viewing room and as Levi saw a spot of blood drop onto the tiled floor, he could feel himself begin to shake.

"Are you alright Sir?"

Detective Monroe had real concern on his face, the man had gone ashen if that was possible considering his race.

"Can we just get this over with?"

Andy Monroe slowly pulled the cover back from Del's head and Levi let out a gasp. At the same time and as tears rolled down his cheeks he slowly nodded his head.

"Now what happens?"

"We will need to interview you further Sir but I understand you are shaken by these events so we will be in contact with you tomorrow morning. Please give the constable your details."

"What about his daughter? Who's goin' to tell Dawn?"

"Normally in these circumstances we find that it's best coming from a family member or friend.

Do you think Dawn will have any information that could assist us?"

"Definitely not, she's been in the burns unit since yesterday. Her family have been wiped out so please leave the poor little cow alone. I'm now gonna go and see her and tell her what's happened."

With that Levi Puck walked out of the morgue to break the worst news he had ever had to give anyone.

# CHAPTER THIRTY TWO

Levi took his time going to the ward and as he walked he tried to imagine in his mind breaking the news of her father's death to Dawn. Nothing would enter his head, no words of comfort, no promises of revenge, nothing that he could say that would offer any kind of comfort at all. As he poked his head around the semi drawn curtain she looked up and could instantly tell that something was wrong. Dawn tried to speak but no words were forthcoming, something inside told her that whatever Levi was about to say would be terrible and she didn't think she could handle any more pain. Taking in a deep breath, she at last eased his path by speaking first.

"It was my dad wasn't it?"

All Levi could do was nod his head as the tears flowed freely down his cheeks.

"Why Levi, why would someone hurt him, what did he do?"

Taking a seat on the bed, Levi gently took both of her hands in his. The size difference was massive and her lily white palms seemed to sink and almost disappear beneath his large brown fingers.

"Do you know what happened to Kenan?"

"Of course I do."

"No, I mean what really happened?"

"You mean that he was raped by that monster and that's why he took his own life?"

Levi just stared wide eyed, he really didn't think she would know but it was more than that, her voice now sounded so cold and unattached but who could blame her, in just a few short weeks her entire family had been wiped out.

"Well, when Del found out he went crazy, swearing vengeance on Eli Carter and his sons. We kidnapped the one that hurt Kenan and did him some real damage and I mean real. He probably died as a result but no one's certain of that. Anyway, seems that Eli then wanted revenge, he wiped out the entire firm apart from me and your dad and we're pretty sure it was him who torched the house. Oh honey it just goes on and on, are you really sure you need to hear this?"

"Definitely Levi, that's if I'm ever going to have any peace and understanding. Please tell me the rest."

Levi sighed deeply. He hated having to do this and Del would have a fit if he was here but Del wasn't here and Levi had been left to try and pick up the pieces.

"After losing your mum and sister I saw a rage in Del like never before and he just wouldn't leave it alone. We went over to the Carter's home but they were out. There was just the cleaner inside, an old bird that'd done no harm to anyone."

Dawn put the palm of her hand over her mouth, she knew what was coming and felt utter disgust but still she needed to know.

"The old girl didn't know anythin' but your dad still beat her, broker her arm and told her to tell Carter that him and his son were next. I suppose she passed on the message and that's why what happened today happened."

"Are we safe Levi, me and you?"

"I think so sweetheart."

"Then I want this to stop now! You can have Roach Road as well as the rest of my dad's businesses, I want no part of it. When the insurance is finally sorted I'm going to move away and start again. Will you do one more thing for me?"

"Anythin' babe."

"Help me plan the funerals, I just don't think I can handle it on my own."

Unbeknown to anyone and at his own expense, Levi had put feelers out all over the city and had even engaged the services of Andy Mason, aka Weasel. When informed who the target was Andy had been more than a little reluctant but Levi assured him that all he wanted was a location and for that information he would pay handsomely. He didn't have a vast amount of cash but what little he did have he was more than happy to hand it over if it meant finding Del's killers. The pound signs saw Weasel instantly agree and within the hour he had his nose to the ground. Four days later he finally decided to give up, for the first time in years he wasn't able to find anything out and having to go back to Levi with absolutely nothing really stuck in his craw.

"What do you mean you can't find out fuck all?"
"Like I said Mr Puck, it's as if they've disappeared. Gypo's are a slippery lot at the best of times and if they don't want to be found then there's really nothin' anyone can do. Now you know how good I am at my job and if I haven't been able to locate them then no one else will, I can guarantee it."

Reluctantly Levi handed over the agreed amount but it really went against the grain having to pay out for absolutely nothing.

Marcus drove to the camp on the Isle of Sheppey. Duke hadn't yet moved on from Leysdown-on-Sea and Marcus knew he would be safe there. He wasn't worried about the Old Bill because villains, no matter what had happened, would never reveal anything to the

law.  He was however concerned with any repercussions from Del Foster's men even though he had it on good authority that apart from one, they had been completely wiped out but one was enough and he didn't want to get caught out by being too complacent that all the shit was finally over.  Rena saw him arrive but just as she was about to walk over, he disappeared into Dukes Caravan.  She was a traveller and knew fine well that something was wrong, that said, she had also been raised not to poke her nose into men's business.  Marcus would tell her when he was good and ready, on that she had no doubt.  As usual his uncle was seated at the table at the far end of the van and as he raised his head from his newspaper, Duke frowned.
"Marcus?  You look like you've lost a quid and found a penny, what's up?"
"You're never goin' to believe what's happened, what's been goin' on while I've been here with you."
"If it involves my brother then nothin' will surprise me."
Marcus took a seat and wearily explained all that had happened.  He told his uncle what his father had done, about Milly and the threat that had been made.  When it came to Del Foster he left nothing out but not once did Duke's expression

change.

"Well, how I see it you didn't have a choice so why is it playin' on your mind so?"

"Because I took a life Uncle and it felt wrong!"

"I understand that boy but better his life than your own. Now go and see that girlie of yours and tell her to let Manfri know we're packin' up and on the move."

"When shall I say we're going Uncle?"

"Now!"

Marcus walked up to Rena who was now standing with her father. He relayed what Duke had said but there was no comment from the man or his daughter, instead they both set about their chores with military precision. Marcus just stood mesmerised as Manfri hitched up the van to his Toyota pickup and Rena swiftly packed away anything that had been on the outside. Returning to Dukes van, he and Kezia were doing exactly the same, it was as if they were on auto pilot, like they'd been programmed from birth. Maybe all of the abuse they had suffered over the years had instilled an urgency in them whenever it was time to move on and as Marcus scanned the small camp, the inhabitants of the four other vans were doing exactly the same. Within the hour the group of caravans were once again on the road with Marcus following closely behind in his own car. Duke loved the sea and

normally after his stay at Leysdown the group would move on to Whitstable but not this time, this time they needed not to be seen. The group travelled for just over three and a half hours and when they were near to Birmingham, Duke pulled into a layby and they all followed suit. Climbing from the cab of his pickup he walked over to Marcus and tapped on the window.
"Sorry Son but you have to ditch the car now."
"Ditch it! Uncle Duke, its worth over fifteen grand!"
"And your life is worth a whole lot more. I'll have someone burn it out tonight, for now you travel with me and Kezia until I can sort you out some new wheels."
Reluctantly Marcus did as he was told and got out of his prized possession. Taking one last lingering look at the Audi he then jumped in beside his cousin and smiled meekly.
Continuing on, the troupe didn't stop for another two hours until they reached Bootle, Merseyside. As Shera Rom and spokesman for the whole Romany community in the United Kingdom, Duke knew nearly all of the travellers in the country, or at least the heads of the families and as such, he and his own extended family would be able to disappear without trace, something he now felt was necessary after what his brother had been up to. Eli would have a lot

of answering to do if and when they ever met up again but somewhere deep inside Duke had a funny feeling that was never going to happen. He loved his younger brother dearly but Eli seemed to have a burning anger inside of him and that was never a good thing.

Three weeks to the day of the murder, Dawn Foster held a triple funeral for her father, mother and sister at All Saints church in Edmonton, the same one that just a short while ago she had said farewell to her baby brother. There were many known faces in attendance and after the service they all shook hands with the sole remaining member of the Foster family but it meant nothing to Dawn. The way her father had chosen to live his life was the cause of all of this heartbreak and even though she had forgiven him, she would never be able to forget. Unlike her brother, the rest of her family were cremated and Dawn planned to inter their ashes in Kenan's grave, just in case the Carters tried to repeat what they had done to the remains of poor innocent Kenan. There was also no lavish after event but that wasn't a surprise to anyone under the circumstances. Instead, Dawn just asked Levi to simply take her back to the hotel.

A week later, Dawn received word from the

police, they had completed their investigations and access could now be gained to Roach Road. She didn't bother to go there and instead passed the message over to Levi and reiterated that everything was his. That same day he stepped over the threshold carrying a large holdall but it was difficult, as images of that fateful night flashed before his eyes. There were still the remnants of blood on the floor and walls and the sight made him feel sick inside. Pulling himself together he made his way upstairs to the small back bedroom and removed a panel of boarding that covered the front of the old cast iron fireplace. Reaching up he wriggled one of three bars that spanned the flue and pulled out the first oblong lead box that his hand touched, it was heavy and he smiled knowingly. Repeating the act twice more, he then replaced the board and carrying the boxes through to the middle bedroom he laid them onto one of the beds that Del had installed. This room had a cupboard which held the hot water tank but there had never been any hot water in the property as it wasn't even connected. Twisting the top pipe, it soon came lose and he was able, with a bit of might, to turn the tank around so that the rear was now facing him. A large opening had been cut into the copper and reaching inside Levi retrieved a further five boxes. In total he had eight but he was sure there were at least a couple more, so moving into the front room he scanned the space looking for somewhere Del had used as a hiding place but had chosen not to tell his number one. There was nothing and about to walk out, content with his lot, he suddenly looked at the old wooden shutters that ran down each side of the sash window. Typically one was painted shut but the other definitely had a gap all around it. Running down to the kitchen he was able to find a flat headed screwdriver that had long since been sitting under the sink. It was rusty but would do the job and as he ran back up the stairs his heart was racing. Moving the screwdriver down each side of the surround and then positioning the flat side into one of the corners he was surprised when the wood gave up its hold easily. Levi gasped as he removed the shutter, stacked from top to bottom were ten more boxes. Admittedly they were a lot smaller than the others but all the same he couldn't wait to find out their contents. Placing them on to the bed along with the others, Levi took a seat and with the aid of the screwdriver he slowly began to prise them open. The three from the chimney place each held a kilo of cocaine. With a street value of 40K per kilo that was 120 grand. The five boxes from the copper tank held another 2 kilos along with gold jewellery, loose diamonds and old medals. There was even one which was full to the brim with sovereigns. Levi had to take a moment to absorb all of this, he was rich and he hadn't even opened the ten smaller boxes yet. With shaking hands he slowly opened the first and it was cram packed full with twenty pound notes. Levis eyes were on stalks and he rapidly opened the next and then the next until the last one. Each was exactly the same and he couldn't help but raise his hands it the air and mouth the word 'Yes!' Packing everything into the holdall it was now considerably heavier and leaving the led boxes on the bed he walked from the property with a spring in his step. Driving back to his flat Levi carried his precious cargo inside and flopped down onto the sofa. Now he had some decisions to make. He could stay, build the firm up but possibly risk the wrath of the Carters, or even another firm feeling that they had a chance at a take-over, or he could head for pastures new. Levi Puck chose the latter. In nineteen seventy one and on the tail end of the Windrush immigration he had come to the United Kingdom when he was five years old and he'd always had a hankering to visit Barbados and find out why his mother had chosen to bring them to England over the golden beaches and glorious sunshine of his home land. He supposed it was because she had been dirt poor but that wouldn't be the case for Levi Puck, he was going to travel like a king and live like a king, for the rest of his days. He did momentarily think of Dawn and whether he should share the haul but she had made her feelings towards her father's business perfectly clear and besides, Levi reasoned that Del would have taken good care of her. Pressing his answer phone to check for any messages, he listened to two that had been left by one of the new firm members. Shrugging his shoulders he deleted the messages. A few minutes later Levi had packed a bag and after one last glance around the place he had called home, locked up his flat and headed into town. Making his way up West to Old Burlington Street, Levi entered Lombard Odier, one of the oldest private banks in the city. Within an hour he had opened an account, acquired a safety deposit box and stashed the gold, diamonds, medals and coke. Certain that all would be safe, he then headed for the hotel to say a final farewell to Dawn Foster.

# CHAPTER THIRTY THREE

Two hours before Levi arrived at Roach Road, Dawn had entered the offices of Morgan, Morgan and Hayes on Philpot Street in the City. Knowing that parking would be a real problem, Dawn had taken the train from Edmonton Green to Bethnal Green. According to Google map it was then a fifteen minute walk but she didn't mind, there was little left in her life to be in a hurry for. It wasn't a firm of solicitor's she was familiar with as her dad had always employed Marty Shulman. Marty was an old time Jewish lawyer who would fight until the last for his clients which were mostly from the criminal fraternity, so why her father had chosen an upmarket firm to deal with his estate she really couldn't fathom. The highly polished doors looked daunting as she entered and an array of even shinier polished plaques stating the names of all the solicitors in the building, filled a large area of wall in the entrance foyer and did even less to quell her nerves. Greeted by a stunning red head who would have looked more at home on a catwalk, Dawn suddenly felt intimidated and very inferior when the woman looked her up and down.
"Can I help you?"
"Yes please. I'm here to see Michael Stubbs."

"Name?"

"Dawn, Dawn Foster."

Michelle Smithson had been pre warned that this client would be arriving and her tone instantly changed. This probate case was a high earner for the firm and if it was noted that she had been rude in any way, she could find herself out of a job. Standing up from her chair she quickly walked around the counter and politely offered her hand.

"Very pleased to meet you Miss Foster. Please, do take a seat and I will inform Mr Stubbs that you are here. Might I offer my condolences as well, it must be a very distressing time for you."

Dawn didn't reply, the stroppy bitch knew nothing of her family or what she was going through so why she was coming over all friendly now was beyond Dawn. Only just sitting down, she was about to reach for one of the glossy magazines on offer when a door opened further along the corridor and a tall dark haired and extremely good looking man emerged. Heading directly towards her he smiled warmly at Dawn as he offered her his hand.

"Miss Foster, so pleased to meet you. It's unfortunate that our meeting isn't under happier circumstances. Please come this way."

Dawn followed Michael Stubbs into a bright, airy and very modern office. Taking a seat

opposite his desk she waited for him to begin.
"Did you bring along your birth certificate and passport?"
"Yes but the certificate is a copy and my passport had to be renewed, everythin' was lost in the fire."
Suddenly she had a flash back to that fateful night and was momentarily silent. He could see her upset, in his line of the law it was an emotion he witnessed on an almost daily basis from clients but this young woman, with dark circles under her eyes, looked as if she had the weight of the world on her shoulders.
"Of course and I am truly sorry for your loss. I only ever met your father once but he certainly made an impression and came across as a very interesting character."
Dawn couldn't help but softly laugh at the man's choice of words.
"You can say that again. I've heard my father described many times Mr Stubbs but never as interesting."
Michael Stubbs smiled though he didn't quite understand what she meant but it was irrelevant, he was here to do a job and he planned to carry that out to the best of his ability.
"Right. Your father's affairs were in order, in fact he only updated his Will a month before his

death. Now as the sole beneficiary you will inherit, after probate fees, inheritance tax and funeral costs, his entire estate."

Dawn still didn't understand why Marty Shulman hadn't been called upon, well she didn't until Michael revealed the sum total of the estate.

"After all of the fees have been deducted, the balance will be in the region of three point five million, give or take. It seems your father invested well over the years and the insurance company dealing with the house fire have paid out directly to this firm as you requested. Now obviously probate can take several months to complete, so in the interim there has been a sum of one hundred thousand pounds set aside for you to have immediate access to."

Dawn left the office in complete shock, now she understood why her father had chosen this firm. Marty Shulman was a good criminal lawyer but could he be trusted with such a vast amount of money? probably not.

Returning to the hotel she was surprised to see Levi sitting in the foyer and looking very sharp in a suit and tie.

"Hi Levi, you okay?"

"I'm fine babe. I'm getting' off in a bit and just wanted to make sure you were alright?"

"I've just come from the solicitors and my dad

has left me very well provided for. Levi? I meant what I said about the business and Roach Road you know? I actually asked the solicitor to transfer the title deeds into you name but it will take a while to get it sorted."

"Thanks babe but I've decided not to stay around, this has all been a big fuckin' wakeup call for me."

Suddenly Levi felt guilty, like he was robbing Dawn of what rightly belonged to her. He could keep his mouth shut and just walk away with all the goodies he'd found but would he ever truly be at peace or sleep well at night knowing he had robbed this sweet innocent young woman?

"When I went over to the office, I found cash and a whole load of other valuable stuff that rightly belongs to you sweetheart."

Dawn smiled affectionately and taking his hand she pressed Michael Stubbs business card into his palm.

"I told you before Levi, I want nothin' to do with that side of things. What you found belongs to you now. This is the name of the solicitor, give him a ring and let him know how to contact you, sell Roach Road if you want. I'm leaving in the mornin' and I don't really know where I'm headed, a bit of an adventure I suppose."

About to walk away, she stopped dead in her tracks at his next sentence.

"I've been tryin' to find them for you Dawn, the Carters I mean but it seems like they've dropped off the face of the earth?"

"Levi, stop please. No good will come of it and we've both lost far too much already so why stir the pot. Live your life in peace just as I'm plannin' to do. I think we both deserve that don't you?"

Standing on tip toes Dawn tenderly kissed his cheek and then walked away.

## 6 Months later

The Upminster house had now been sold and Marcus was pleasantly surprised at the amount it achieved. Just as Eli had told him, all proceeds were paid directly into his account and the bank manager nearly had a heart attack when he saw his clients account rise by two million, seven hundred thousand pounds overnight. Rena and Marcus said their vows in a small ceremony at St George's Hall in Liverpool. The only people in attendance were the occupants of the six caravans in his uncles group. Marcus had asked his uncle Duke to contact his father and let him know about the wedding but a few days after the request Duke informed him that Eli couldn't be located. He had stretched the truth massively as the King of the Gypsies, Danior O'Brien, sent word from Ballyhaunis that Eli had passed away in his sleep three days earlier. Duke decided there was nothing to be gained from telling Marcus, the lad was about to marry and that should be a time filled only with joy and happiness.

With the ceremony over, Marcus swiftly took hold of Rena's hand and led his bride towards the main entrance.

"Whatever are you doin' Marcus, we have guests?"

"It's a surprise darlin', my wedding gift to you."

Stepping through the large double doors of St George's Hall, Rena saw the most beautiful motorhome she had ever laid eyes on and her mouth fell open. It stood 12 meters long, the biggest size allowed on UK roads and as she climbed the steps Rena began to cry tears of happiness. The lavish interior with a separate bedroom and bathroom was totally stunning.

"Is, is this really for me?"

"For us babe, we leave tonight. The world is our oyster, no more violence or snide remarks from Gorgio's. From now on we're just a normal couple travellin' the county, the world come to that. Wherever you want to go I will take you."

Dawn Foster finally settled in Dorset. She purchased a picture perfect cottage with roses around the door and along with her three newly acquired dogs, would sadly live her life alone. While the money left to her by Del had allowed

Dawn to never want for anything, it was also a curse as she didn't know who, apart from her dogs, she could trust. From time to time she thought about the killers of her family but it was only ever fleeting. Life was too short for vengeance, there were never any winners, history was proof of that.

Levi Puck remained in Barbados and just as he'd planned, would live out his life in the style of a King. He often recalled his old firm buddies and the escapades that they had all gotten up to but that was all it ever was, just a memory of a past life. He had taken Dawn's advice and given up the search for the Carter's, there was nothing to be gained from opening up old wounds except more pain and heartache.

Within a year of Rena and Marcus hitting the road, a new member of the Carter family had arrived and the decision was made to settle down somewhere permanent. Marcus started his own second hand car business and to anyone who took the time to look, they appeared like any other young couple with a baby but once a year the motorhome was brought out of storage and the family headed off to Appleby. After all, you should never forget your roots!

## The End

Printed in Great Britain
by Amazon